Promise of Darkness

Book 1

by

Clifford M. Scovell

www.scovellbooks.com

*

A RED MOONS PRESS PUBLICATION

First Printing

A RED MOONS PRESS PUBLICATION

ISBN-13: 978-0984732449
ISBN-10: 0984732446

Printed in the United States of America

Cover artwork by Kari Angle

Other books by Clifford M. Scovell

Prison Earth - Not Guilty as Charged
Prison Earth - A Loss of Face
Prison Earth - The Resurrection and the Lie

For more information about the Prison Earth series, go to
www.prisonearth.com

For information on *Promise of Darkness*, go to
www.scovellbooks.com

Dedication

To Jessica Maxwell. Without her support and guidance, I would never have accomplished so much, and whose perceptive insight into my own past sowed the seeds for this great adventure.

Many Thanks

To Kari Angle for the best cover art.

Chapter 1

Devonshire, England, Fall of 1896

I am going to die!

The world around her blurred as she struggled with her assailant on the narrow, poorly-lit stairs: painful blows striking her face; knees slamming hard steps; her long, brown hair being torn out by the roots. His foul breath came in gasps as her attacker hauled her up the last step. She grunted a scream and hammered fists against his arm as it squeezed the wind out of her.

"Phillip! Please!" she pleaded. "Stop!"

"Shaddup, bish!" he growled, his alcohol-slurred words barely understandable. "I'll teash you…na to defy me."

Afraid to look, but more afraid not to, she watched the stiff, gloved fingers of his right hand make two attempts at flipping up the latch before he finally pushed through to haul her onto the flat roof of their sprawling two-story manor house. Stumbling along beside him, she sobbed at the realization that his violence was now invading her rooftop sanctuary: the only place in the house her acrophobic husband feared to go.

Her overwhelming despair quickly turned to anger.

"No!" she screamed before spinning around to push with all of her remaining strength.

The move caught him off guard and allowed her to twist free, but she managed only two steps before he lunged forward to grab her hair and bellow a torrent of slurred obscenities.

As he pulled her across the roof, she struggled to regain her footing, but instead stepped on the hem of her long dress, and pitched forward. Grabbing wildly, she managed to wrap her fingers around his upper arm, but he reflexively stiffened and jerked back, releasing her so quickly she started to spin. The sudden rotation tore her grip from his arm, and though she grabbed desperately with her other hand, it found only empty air. After two off-balanced steps, she felt something solid hit the back of her legs. Unable to stop her momentum she screamed a terrified "Noooo", and toppled off the roof.

Streaked images filled her vision as she somersaulted, but in that stretched-out instant, she caught a glimpse of his head silhouetted against the gray sky.

I hate you!

Chapter 2

Salem, Oregon, Fall of 2011

I hate you!

A slap to the head shocked me awake.

"Huh?" I gasped while sitting up in the small cluttered bedroom I share with my younger brother, Matthew. "What?"

"Will ya *shut up*?" Matthew protested sleepily from his bed against the opposite wall.

Stunned by his statement, and the strange thought that flashed into my head just before my rude awakening, I rubbed the spot of impact, my fingers snagging pillow-matted hair as I looked around the dimly lit room, first at the shoe on my pillow, and then at him. Light from the street illuminated his face enough to see his eyes were already closed, but what surprised me even more than his assault was my own hard breathing, and a tingling in my face and knees. The sensation disappeared when I sat up, but I'd obviously had another nightmare, and like the others, I remembered nothing about it.

"Again? What'd I say this time?"

Pressing his face into a pillow, Matt's response was muffled. "I so don't give a rat's ass if you hate me. Just stop shouting it. OK?"

"Hate you?" I protested. "I don't..."

The bedroom door burst open, Dad almost falling as he charged in, his broad shoulders filling the doorway, his eyes wide, jaw clenched.

"What the hell is it now?" he demanded as blinding light filled the room.

When he moved further in, I squinted to see my diminutive mother, her shoulder-length, blond hair flying, blue eyes wide with alarm as she appeared from behind him, her bathrobe billowing out before she abruptly stopped and wrapped it around her thin body, but not before I caught a flash of gold from the cross permanently chained to her neck.

I'm not sure why, but at that instant I was struck by how our parent's physical differences were reflected in my brother and me: Matt, a year younger, was chunky and dark-haired like Dad, but I inherited Mom's fair hair, light complexion, and thin frame.

"Oh gawd," Matt moaned. "I just wanna sleep!"

"Don't swear," Mom protested as automatically as most of us breathe.

"Aaawww," he whined before rolling onto his back and again yanking a pillow over his face so only his short-cropped hair showed.

"What is it this time?" Dad asked testily as his hand massaged his equally short hair. "Another nightmare?"

Feeling my own head shake, I probed the dark vapors of my subconscious for some clue as to why my hands were trembling.

"I don't remember anything before..." I held up a tan Adidas Star Wars. "...Matt, like, threw his shoe at me."

A look passed between my parents that made Mother cringe and turn away.

Sighing loudly, Dad faced me. "Any problems with people at school?"

I winced at the repeat of a question he had already asked after each of the previous two nightmares. This was my first year at community college, and the nightmares started a month after classes began. Naturally, my parents were convinced there was a connection.

"Aw, come on, Dad," I whined. "We've been over this…"

"Well, not enough if you're still having nightmares," he interrupted angrily. "You don't have 'em for no reason."

"But I…" His intense stare stopped my argument, and I shook my head. "None that I know of."

"Teachers?"

"I'm getting straight A's, Dad," I answered defensively. "Teachers totally love me."

"Other kids?"

As my head shook, I felt lightheaded and leaned back into my pillow. The nightmares were an enigma, a dark void in my memory, which by itself was totally scary, but if they had nothing to do with what was going on in my life, why were they happening?

"Seriously, Dad," I finally said while holding up the Adidas. "The only thing I…"

"Oh God," Mom interrupted. Her outburst defying her own admonition against using the Lord's name in vain. "Remmy? Is she...?"

The question was new. My attention jerked from the offending shoe to my mother holding both hands over her stomach. Dad saw it too.

"Damn," he whispered while shifting his attention back to me.

I rolled my eyes and protested, "I'd *never* do anything like that to her."

Remmy Reed transferred to my high school class last fall, and I was surprised by the immediate magic between us. I was also a bit frustrated because something I couldn't explain kept us from the kind of intimacy my parents were worrying about. Maybe it was because I'm only a college freshman, and though I wanted sex as much as the next guy, the thought of asking a girl for it terrified me. Of course, even if Remmy and I had actually done it, there's no way I'd ever tell my parents.

One hand scratching the back of his neck, Dad held up the other and waggled it. "You know, you two been dating over a year. It's only natural for a guy to wanna..."

"Alvin!" Mom cried as she slammed a fist into his arm, her small frame unable to generate enough force to make him do more than flinch. "Not our Gerry!"

Surprised by her assault, he faced her, looking confused. "But you just said…" Her angry glare made him bite off the sentence and shrug. "Well...anyway..."

I was also struck by the duplicity of her statements and that made me angry.

"Remmy's totally not pregnant. I have no clue as to what's going on."

"So shut up and go to sleep," Matt whined. "I've got a test tomorrow."

I quickly faced him, mostly because I was afraid of saying something I'd later regret. When Dad sighed loudly, I turned back to my parents, but the blackness of my mood kept me quiet. After a long moment, Dad shrugged and gave Mom a questioning glance, but her attention was already on me, her expression a mixture of frustration and confusion. When Dad put a hand on her shoulder, she jerked a nod and quickly moved over to kiss my forehead.

"Trust in Jesus," she whispered while patting my cheek. "He's watching over you."

Her statement adding to my irritation, I made a face, but she was already moving toward the door. I slipped back under the covers and stifled a scream as my parents shook their collective heads, flipped off the light, and exited.

"Maybe I should sleep in the barn," Matt muttered from under his pillow.

"We don't have a barn, you dork!"

My eyes quickly adjusting again to the dim street light, I saw Matt lift the pillow off his face and stuff it behind his head. "Well if we did, I'd totally get more sleep there than here."

"You gonna have cows too?"

He snorted derisively. "I ain't livin' with any damned cows."

"You're going out with Loretta Hasmere. Cows can't be much worse." I grumbled, not because there was anything wrong with his girlfriend, but my sour mood made me want to piss on someone else's happiness.

Anticipating his response, I rolled over just before his other shoe bounced off my shoulder.

Chapter 3

Death and hope are a curious mix,
Yet together shall they play
A perplexing role in our torn lives
Over which we have no say.

Elizabeth's diaphragm spasmed, pulling in a gasp of fresh air as her heavy eyelids fluttered opened. It took her a long moment to realize she was in her bedroom, and another moment before a sound pulled her attention to the left. Her maid, Tilley had settled her rotund body into a stiff-backed Victorian chair beside Elizabeth's canopied bed. The girl was dressed in her usual black-and-white outfit, her mousey-brown hair pulled into a tight bun, her starched white maid's cap rumpled and off-kilter, a scowl on her ruddy face as she hummed the vulgar popular tune *Throw him down, McCloskey* and picked at the starched white lace at the edge of her apron.

Realizing the maid had not heard her gasp, Elizabeth let her eyes drift around a room densely packed with stylish dressers and tables, overstuffed chairs, and lavish paintings. She struggled to contain a sob when her eyes stopped on a lamp, its ornate design reminiscent of an Egyptian lotus flower. Not something she would have chosen, it was a gift, of sorts, from her husband after a temper flare-up in which he gave her a black eye.

After briefly closing her eyes to collect herself, she continued her search of the room, and finding no one, decided to let the girl fuss a moment longer. However, when she tried to move her head slightly to see if someone might be sitting at the dressing table on her right, a sharp pain produced an involuntary groan and the flighty creature jumped to her feet, nearly knocking the chair over.

"Saints preserve us, yer goin' ta..." The maid's wide-eyed attention jerked toward the door then back to her. "Yer goin' ta live, Mistress Elizabeth."

Feeling a surprising sense of disappointment, Elizabeth tried to look away, only to be stopped by a painful stabbing in her neck.

"The master's been nearly out of 'is 'ead all the night long, Mistress," the maid announced while her eyes again flicked to the door and back. "'e paces, 'round and 'round the library, all the while askin' why ya done it."

The side of Elizabeth's face throbbed, but when she lifted an aching arm to touch it, bandages on her hand met bandages on her face. Even though the touch was painful, the sudden recollection of what had happened was even more so.

At least she thought she knew what had happened. She had fallen off the roof, that was certain, but the details were jumbled with the fuzzy whirlwind of memories, some too horrible to believe, some less so. The pain in her body told her she had been badly hurt, so the doctor had undoubtedly given her something, which would explain why she felt so sleepy.

"Don' know why I did wha, Tilley?" she asked through swollen lips and in such a low whisper she wondered if the maid would even hear her.

"Don' ya remember, Miss?" Tilley sobbed, her cheeks wet with tears. "The Master says ya jumped clear off the roof. If it weren't fer the lilac, you'd a been a gonner, surely."

Her eyelids closed involuntarily as she focused what little energy she had on remembering, but it was like trying to look across a mist-shrouded field. Bits and pieces of what happened were there: some details fuzzy, others sharp and inflamed with violence. Just the same, her maid's explanation sounded wrong.

I *jumped from the roof?*

She started to ask the question out loud, but stopped when she remembered that Phillip had been with her. He had been drunk and angry, but had he shoved her off, or was he trying to stop her? Years of experience with his violent moods gave her the answer, but even if he had pushed her, one simply did not confide such things to a servant.

The effort to think of a response brought confusion to her already tumultuous mind, and to regain focus, Elizabeth opened her eyes to stare at the poor creature bouncing from one foot to the other. The constant movement made Elizabeth dizzy and she closed her eyes again to quell her churning stomach.

In the two years Tilley had been in her service, Elizabeth had tried to calm the wretched girl's anxious nature. Unfortunately, there was only so much she could do for a servant because her husband demanded a strict separation between staff and gentry. The mistress of the house did not go to servant's quarters and treat them as though they were her own children. It simply wasn't…

Her mind went suddenly blank, and she fought against overwhelming fatigue to stay in the moment. Opening her eyes once more, she saw Tilley staring at her as if expecting a response.

"The lilac," was all she could think to say as her throbbing head settled back onto the pillow. "I hope it wathn't ruined." When the maid continued to gape at her, she lifted a hand only slightly and pointed at the door. "Pleath inform my huthband that I am awake."

Closing her eyes, Elizabeth tried to take a deep breath, only to be stopped by pain in her ribs. Despite her condition, she reveled in the peacefulness of it, but after a long moment realized she could still hear her maid's labored breathing.

"Tilley?" she asked while struggling against aching muscles, and the incessant pull of gravity to lift her head and look at the girl at the foot of her bed.

The maid's hands flew to her mouth, and she started the vibrating dance again.

"We knows what he done, Miss."

At first, Elizabeth's mind refused to process the statement. Even if she couldn't remember the actual chain of events, she had a good idea of what had happened as well, but there was nothing she or her beloved servants could do about it.

"Wipe your fathe, girl," she nearly whispered, "and tell your mathter I am awake."

"Mistress!"

"Do it now," she said slowly, but firmly before lowering her voice again. "It will all come right in the end. I promith."

A white handkerchief suddenly appeared in Tilley's hand, and in a few whisks the tears were smeared across her flushed cheeks.

"Yes, Mistress," she said before tucking the cloth into a pocket of her apron and hurrying off.

As the door closed, fatigue overwhelmed her, and once again, that feeling of disappointment.

Again?

And then it came to her. As she was falling off the roof, she had felt a brief moment of comfort in the thought that she would finally find peace in the darkness of death: the one place he could not follow her.

She recalled the stanza from the poem that filled her head just as she awoke, but had no recollection of ever hearing it before. Even so, it hit so close to her current feelings she wanted to cry out in frustration. She had been safely cradled in Death's arms, welcoming her release from this hellish existence with Phillip, but her hopes had been dashed. What came after death she did not know, but the indescribable frustration of waking in her own bed made her want to find a window without a large lilac under it and throw herself out.

Taking another painful breath, she sighed, but the effort to keep her laudanum-weighted eyelids up was too much for her. Letting them close, she started to relax, but tensed again when excited voices filtered through the wall. Feet pounded stairs as she tried to complete the breath, but the pain forced out another groan. Before she could collect herself, her husband exploded into the room with Tilley and the butler, Jason close behind.

At the sight of her, Phillip stopped so abruptly the two following nearly ran into him. Her thinking distorted by the opiates, she suddenly saw the scene as uncommonly comedic: her servants scrambling back to avoid contact with her unsteady husband who hesitated briefly before stumbling over to lean heavily on the back of a nearby chair. She tried to keep from giggling when Tilley and Jason's heads turned in perfect synchronization to follow their master's path.

Too obviously inebriated to be aware of what was going on around him, Phillip gasped desperately and used his good arm to push his stocky body to its full six-foot height. Even with the chair's support, he swayed from side to side, his forest-green smoking jacket askew, waistcoat unbuttoned. She flinched involuntarily when she saw his face was flushed from the effort and alcohol, making the scars on its right side stand out even more than usual.

Her drug-induced giddiness vanished when his good eye turned toward her, staring uncertainly, and even the shriveled remains of the right one seemed to throw off its blindness to focus on her. As she continued to stare mutely at him, he looked away, leaning even more heavily against the chair as though trying, and pitifully failing to steady himself. When he turned to face her again, a small trickle of drool ran from the right corner of his scarred lips, but now his expression was so unfathomable, even after ten-years of marriage, she had no idea what was going on inside his damaged brain.

Fear-generated adrenaline mingled with the opiates in her blood to make her giddy again. As the death poem echoed in her mind, Phillip waved his claw-like right hand at the servants.

"Leaf ush!" he demanded.

At the edge of her vision she saw Jason and Tilley turn questioning faces toward her, but kept her eyes on her husband. Knowing what his reaction would be if he knew they were more loyal to her than him brought on a sudden sobriety, and she hesitated only briefly before giving the slightest of nods to send the servants away.

Handkerchief again pressed to her face, Tilley rushed out. Jason hesitated a moment more, his short, stocky body tense as his eyes jerked from her to her husband and back several times before he backed out and slowly closed the door. Phillip's attention was entirely on her, and he remained anxiously silent until they were gone.

He jerked noticeably when the latch rattled into place, a confused expression on his face as he started to speak, but stopped long enough to drag a sleeve across his mouth, the action opening his smoking jacket enough to reveal blood on his white shirt.

Did he help rescue me from the lilac?

"Look here, old girl," he said haltingly, the fingers of his good hand raking through his mop of graying brown hair. "I don't know...how I can possibly apologize...you must understand...Good

God! I didn't intend for you to... I swear to God in Heaven it will never happen again."

The disjointed lie revived memories of hundreds made in the years since his return from the Boer War. The sweet, tender man she married was no longer in this room, having been transformed by the horror of that experience into a violent, unpredictable creature, scarred as much on the inside as out.

The sadness she felt made her incredibly tired, her eyelids drooping again as a whirlwind of snappy remarks she could never voice swirled in her mind.

"Yeth, Dear," she finally lisped. "I am thure it won't."

The lie slipped from her with such automated ease she was not sure if she had said or just thought it. Her eyes closed before she could see his reaction, but a caricature of his angry face played against the golden background of her eyelids. She longed for the man she married, but knew he had been taken from her and replaced by this wretched, angry shell.

What does it matter? echoed in the encroaching darkness of her mind. *You are my husband. There is nothing to be done.*

Chapter 4

The tinkling sound brought Elizabeth to the very edge of her laudanum-induced slumber. Without opening her eyes, she listened for a long moment before hearing it again: two keystrokes. C and then E.

Not middle C, but an octave lower, as though the person at the piano was only playing with his left hand. Yes, she knew it was Phillip, and the tune he was trying to play was one they used to do together.

Her mind fogged by the drugs flooding her body, she listened as he played the left-hand part of Beethoven's *Für Elise*. In the first months after Phillip was finally released from the military hospital, they often played the piano together. He, being unable to use his right hand, played with his left, and she, her right. It was a definite restorative for him: a respite from the pain and frustration his injuries forced upon him. When the happiness of those precious moments flooded back, she started humming the tune.

She had barely begun when someone on her left gasped.

Tilley

"Are you awake, Miss?" the young girl asked hesitantly. "The Master is ever so eager to speak with ya."

Without opening her eyes, she ran her tongue over dry lips, pleased to realize the swelling had gone down.

"Speak with *you*, Tilley," she corrected the girl. "We do not say, 'ya' in this house."

"Yes, Mistress," Tilley responded dejectedly. "Sorry, Mistress."

"Did Master Phillip say why he wished to speak with me?"

The sound of Tilley flattening out her starched apron told Elizabeth the girl was frowning. "No, Ma'am, but he looked ever so nervous 'bout somethin'."

Elizabeth opened her mouth to again correct the girl's diction, but released a sigh instead. After a moment of hoped-for silence, ruined by Tilley's congested breathing, Elizabeth slowly turned her head to look at her maid's pale, round face which was so contorted she struggled to keep from laughing, all the while unsure if her mirth was because of the maid's expression or the irony of her own situation.

"Tell Master Phillip I am awake and will see him now," she nearly whispered.

Tilley hesitated briefly before jerking a curtsey and rushing from the room.

"Does that girl ever do anything by half?" she muttered while gingerly working her body into a sitting position and straightening the blankets.

Though it had been three days since the "accident", most of her wounds still ached, her left eye would not completely open, and the throbbing in her head, though less than it was a day earlier, still made it hard to concentrate. Many times since she had tried to recall what happened, but could only manage vague recollections of shins painfully crashing on stairs, and the heart-stopping sensation of falling to land in...

What was it? The lilac?

Tears leaked from her eyes as she slowly shook her head and wondered what brought on his outbursts. By this point in their marriage, she should have stopped trying, however...

The opening door interrupted her thoughts.

"How are you today, my darling?" Phillip asked with a forced sweetness that made her want to snap back a nasty response, but she coughed it away and smiled.

At least he is not drunk.

"Better," she said even though the sight of his gloved right hand made her face ache briefly.

She could not remember how many times he struck her, but by her reckoning, once was too many.

"I'm off to London, and wondered if I might bring back something pretty to brighten your recovery."

Still caught up in her recollection, his request took her by surprise. Her mind now blank, she gaped at him for a long moment before looking around a room cluttered with many of the useless trinkets Phillip had purchased after each of his previous assaults.

Why would I wish for yet another permanent reminder of your brutality?

"That is most kind," she heard herself lying, "but there is nothing I need."

Phillip froze for a moment before briefly turning his attention to Tilley then jerking back with an enigmatic expression that gave Elizabeth a chill.

"Are you certain?" he asked, the tension in his voice subtle, but enough to make her blink.

The stress of the moment kept her mind blank, lips closed. For his part, Phillip did not move, his eye squinting at her, his demeanor demanding an answer she did not have.

The anxious impasse dragged out for what seemed like minutes before her wide-eyed maid blurted, "Remember, Mistress, how you were ever so taken with that bonnet at Barnstroms?"

Suddenly realizing she was holding her breath, Elizabeth sucked in air, the action allowing her to think, though she had no idea what hat the maid was referring to.

"Thank you, Tilley," she said as casually as she could while looking from the girl to her husband. "It completely slipped my mind." She waved a hand at the maid. "I shall give Tilley a note for you to take to Barnstroms. They will have it boxed and ready in a wink."

Phillip seemed to relax as a smile brightened his face. "Excellent! I will pop in and collect it straight away."

Though he turned quickly and marched from the room, Elizabeth could see Tilley blanch and jerk her head down when he faced her. After the door closed, the maid slapped her hands together so hard her whole body shook.

"He's a bloody..."

"Tilley!" Elizabeth snapped before the girl could complete the sentence. "We do not use such vulgar terms in this house."

The red-faced maid turned toward her mistress, her eyes mere slits, lips pinched together, but the angry expression on Elizabeth's face made her look down and curtsy.

"Sorry, Mistress," she grunted angrily. "It won't happen again."

Elizabeth wanted to laugh at the absurdity of chastising her servant for having the same thought as she did. On the other hand, she knew that being too permissive with the staff always led to trouble.

When Tilley continued to look at her feet, Elizabeth stifled a sigh and nodded. "Bring tea, and my writing tablet, and then you can tell me what hat it is I am so fond of."

Her face relaxing slightly, Tilley looked up and hesitated for a long moment before bobbing a curtsey. "Yes, Mistress."

As the door latch clicked into place, Elizabeth closed her eyes and let out a long sigh. The strain of the moment now gone, an immense weariness flooded her body while she slipped under the covers and sank into her pillow.

"So this is what Hell is like."

Chapter 5

"...just that I, like, don't know what to do about it."

I blinked reflexively when the space in front of me filled with people, and I found myself in the middle of a busy Taco Brothers restaurant. The shock made my gut cramp so suddenly it pushed air from my lungs, and forced out a loud "Hunh!"

Across a small, yellow-topped table, my girlfriend, Remmy Reed glared at me open mouthed.

"What?" I blurted as the loud lunch-crowd noise filled my ears. "How did I get..."

"Are you serious?" she protested. "Like, right in the middle of our conversation?"

"What? I...huh?"

"I'm talking to you and you just, like, space out like I'm not even here. You on drugs or something?"

I looked around the eatery again before dropping my gaze to the untouched meal in front of me.

I was in a room full of old stuff. How did I get here?

Feeling the sudden urge to be alone, I tried to jump up, but something blocked my chair and almost made me fall. Untangling my legs from the chair, I looked down to see a huge, black-and-white dog lying behind me, a flapping tongue hanging out one side of his open mouth as the creature lolled his massive head to one side and looked as though he expected a treat.

"Holy shit!" I squawked before taking a quick step back from the chair. "Where did that come from?"

"Where did *what* come from?"

Eyes on my confused girlfriend, I pointed at the floor.

"That dog," I answered indignantly.

Jumping up, my short, thin girlfriend stepped around the table and peered at where I was pointing. "Dog? Are you, like, nuts?"

I looked again to see my backpack lying where the dog had been. Reflexively grabbing the bag, I scanned the room, but saw only people and tables.

"Where'd he go?"

My attention returned to Remmy: her fisted hands on narrow hips, green eyes hidden behind slitted eyelids, mouth a tight frown.

"You're shitting me, right? You can't have a dog in here, unless you're, like, totally blind or something."

"No, I swear, there was this..."

Her annoyed expression stopped me for a moment, but I was preparing to insist I wasn't imagining it when Jamie Curtman appeared from the crowd.

"Hey man, you gonna make basketball tryouts today? Word is, Miss Framshorn will be the freshman assistant coach this year."

"A woman coaching the men's basketball team?" Remmy asked excitedly. "Awesome!"

At six-foot-six, and over a foot taller than Remmy, Jamie bent down to grin at her. "It would be even more awesome if we got to, like, take showers with her."

Remmy turned so quickly her auburn pigtail nearly slapped Curtman's eye. "You're a pig!"

Straightening, Jamie grabbed his crotch and lifted. "A totally horny pig, truth be known."

Normally, his irreverent statements made me laugh, but at that moment I felt serious panic. "I gotta go."

Hefting my backpack over a shoulder, I rushed through the crowded dining area and out the main door.

"Wait up, jerk."

I heard Remmy call, but my mind was so full of confusing thoughts, and an unhealthy dose of terror, it didn't register.

How did I make it all the way here, order my food, and sit at a table without realizing it?

She grabbed my arm, forcing me to stop and face her. Though I outweighed her by a good eighty pounds, this lovely redhead was not intimidated.

"Where are you going?"

I opened my mouth to answer, but the truth was I had no idea. Clamping it shut, I shook my head.

"So, what was that thing about a dog?"

I shrugged. "I saw him behind my chair. He was there one instant, and gone the next."

Her look turned cautious. "You ever, like, see a dog in your nightmares?"

"How would I know? I never remember them."

"So, where were you just now?"

My attention jerked to a group of noisy kids shuffling past on their way inside. To my relief, they ignored me. When I continued to watch them, Remmy yanked on my arm, pulling me away from the entrance.

We stopped next to a window made mirror-like by bright sunlight, and I was drawn to my reflection in the glass. I could see my mom's unruly blond hair; narrow face; and a thin body, not hunky enough to play football at Marion County Community College, but tall enough to possibly start on the freshman basketball team.

What surprised me was the shorter, ghostly image superimposed over me: a woman, barely five feet tall, broad shouldered, and holding up a delicate hand with slender fingers. Her head seemed small for her body, but the face was indistinct, and I squinted in the hope of seeing more detail.

"So?"

Remmy's question pulled my attention to her.

"You think I've totally lost it?"

She shrugged. "Tell me what you saw and I'll let you know."

"No shit?"

Looking perturbed, she faced the parking lot, and in that instant I was struck with how beautiful she was with her diminutive body stuffed into that red-and-green pleated miniskirt over black leggings, with skin-tight, double-layered green-over-pink tank tops. I was also painfully aware of how utterly strange it was that as close as we were, I hadn't yet tried to get naked with her. I desperately wanted to, but something held me back.

Shit! I'm probably gay.

Before I could pursue that illogical source of angst, she turned back and locked eyes with me.

"You ever known me to hold punches?"

Had I not been so confused, the question would have made me laugh. I knew no one as plain spoken as this girl.

I shook my head.

"Spill it."

Sucking in a deep breath in the vain hope it would calm my twitching stomach, I tried to regain my composure, but felt outside myself as I looked back at the window to find the lady gone.

"It was totally weird. I was in this room, in a bed, I think."

"With someone?"

I felt my head shake though I honestly didn't know why.

"Not in the bed. I'd been in some kind of accident and was really hurting. There was this dude standing beside the bed. Half his face was messed up -- burned, I think."

"Were you burned as well?"

Shaking my head again, I closed my eyes to see him staring at me. Though the sight sent chills up my spine, I wasn't repulsed by his injuries. It was like I was used to them.

Forcing my eyes open, I looked at Remmy. "His scars were old."

"Was there just the two of you?"

"Nah. I also saw this chubby girl dressed up in some kind of maid's outfit."

"Rich people?"

I shrugged. "I kinda thought so. The room was full of all sorts of old-fashioned furniture, paintings, and stuff, but it wasn't old, if you know what I mean."

"Yeah," she responded before turning to face the parking lot again. "So what happened?"

"Nothin' much, except I was scared," I looked down at my trembling hands. "*Seriously* scared."

When I turned my attention to Remmy again, she seemed really upset, and it was reflected in the tone of her questions. "Why? Was he, like, threatening you? Did he have a weapon?"

Taken aback by her aggressiveness, I continued to shake my head while looking at the window again, thankful to find the woman gone. "I'm totally losing it."

Grabbing my arm, Remmy pulled me around to face her. To my surprise, the very sight of her calmed me. There was magic between us, which at times was scary, unbelievable, horrifying, incredible, and totally outside my understanding, but right now it made me feel...safe.

"There might be another explanation."

"Huh?"

She started to speak, but her response was cut off when a cluster of people burst from the restaurant, talking loud and laughing at someone's punch line.

"Meet me after your last class," Remmy insisted

"Basketball trials are this afternoon. I gotta be there."

"Then text me, like, before you shower and we can meet outside the gym. There's someone you need to talk to."

"Who?"

Smiling, she patted my cheek. "Text me. OK?"

A shudder ran through me. Cute though she was, my feet were suddenly agitating to move away from her. Thankfully, my legs wouldn't cooperate.

"Sure."

"Super," she chirped and started to walk away, but after two steps she turned abruptly and gave me a concerned look. "You gonna be OK?"

When I jerked a nod, she smiled and continued on to her car. I watched her go: hips swaying, skirt flapping, head bobbing, and to my surprise, the sight produced a strange mixture of lust and revulsion.

What in the hell is wrong with me?

As her car moved through the parking lot, I slumped against the wall, feeling confused and angry.

She's the best thing that had ever happened to me. Where's the evil in that?

Lost in thought, I nearly dropped my backpack when Jamie Curtman slammed his way out of the restaurant.

"If you want to ride with me, you'd better move it, Patterson" he shouted without stopping his jog into the parking lot. "Math class is in twenty minutes."

Stunned by all that had happened, I tried to follow, but my legs wouldn't cooperate until I saw his right hand waving for me to follow.

"Let's go, idiot," he insisted. "We don't get good grades, we don't play basketball."

Pushing off the wall, I broke into a trot and caught up with him as he reached his car.

Jamie slipped into the driver's side, but I stopped to look back at the restaurant, my mind awash with unsettling confusion.

"Dude! Get your butt in the car!"

After taking one last look at where I'd seen the woman's reflection over my own, I jumped in, and settled my backpack onto the floor between my knees. Jamie was nattering on about something when Remmy's invitation to meet flashed in my head.

I will, my friend, I thought as the car accelerated. *If I'm not locked in a padded cell by then.*

Chapter 6

"Jason has informed me that the master has returned, Mistress," Tilley announced, her expression confused. "I am to tell you he is bringin' somethin' special for you."

Though woozy from a recent dose of laudanum, Elizabeth felt anxious as her eyes jerked to her bedroom's elaborately carved double doors. When Phillip did not immediately appear, she took a deep breath and felt her attention drift.

"A nice hat, I presume?" she asked, knowing that it was, but feeling she had to say something to keep her panicking brain occupied.

"No, Mistress. I mean, yes," the girl stammered, "but somethin' else as well."

"Flowers?"

"No, Miss. He wouldn't say what is was, but…"

The bedroom doors flew open and Phillip burst in gripping the strings of a hat box with one hand while struggling to hold onto a leather strap attached to a black and white blur at his side.

Elizabeth's hands flew to her mouth as she gasped, "My word!"

Phillip shoved the hatbox at Tilley and turned his attention to keeping a nearly-pony-sized dog from bounding around the room.

"He is a Great Dane" he announced breathlessly, "and presently lacking in discipline."

Barely hearing Tilley's nervous giggling, Elizabeth blinked twice before asking, "Is he fully grown?"

Her husband pulled back, seeming surprised when the dog rose up on his hind legs to lick his face. "Only a puppy, I'm afraid. The kennel owner assured me that they are all the rage."

Elizabeth held up a wobbly finger and was about to point out the unsuitability of such a large animal in a proper household when she saw her husband eagerly scratch the dog's ears and make a sound that surprised her.

My God. He's laughing.

Even in her drug-fogged state she knew that to reject his offering would bring an immediate reversal of mood.

After briefly closing her eyes to collect herself, she leaned over, but did not have to look down to see the wiggling hound.

"He is gorgeous," she finally said with an exaggerated wave of her hand.

Phillip jerked around, his face awash with joyful astonishment. "Do you really mean it?"

Ignoring Tilley's expression of utter horror, she pulled her chin down in a half-nod. "It is what I have always wanted."

"I am so very glad," he gushed as the huge dog lunged away from him, nearly pulling Phillip over when the leash snapped taught. "He will fit right in, I promise you."

Her eyes still on the dog, Elizabeth felt her neck muscles strain as she transformed a head shake into another nod. "I am certain he shall...with proper training, that is."

Her husband nodded eagerly. "William will keep him in the stables until he learns his manners. I shall take him there straight away."

Phillip started for the door, but the excited puppy lunged in the opposite direction, jerking the leash from his master's hand. In a single leap, he was on the bed, staring face-to-face with his horrified mistress.

Everyone froze when the dog let out a nervous yip, shaking his body along with the bed before unceremoniously plopping his butt beside her legs. Elizabeth sat transfixed for a long, tense moment until she finally got the nerve to reach out a shaking hand and pat his nose. To her surprise, he whined and lay next to her, his large eager eyes only on her.

"Good Lord," Phillip cried as he rushed to her bedside and prepared to wrap his good arm around the dog.

In that instant, Elizabeth's attention was drawn to the dog's pleading eyes and she felt a powerful, almost telepathic connection.

Don't let him take me! screamed in her head.

"No," she heard herself protest as she threw up a hand, palm out. "Leave him be. Please."

Still over the dog, Phillip looked at her. "You can't be serious, surely."

Her mind in turmoil, Elizabeth watched the dog lower his head to the bed while keeping his eyes on her, and though she was not sure why, she nodded.

"If…he is to be…mine," she said hesitantly, "then it is I who should train him."

"Mistress?" Tilley protested.

Phillip's good eye squinted angrily as he turned toward the maid.

"If that is what your mistress wishes, that is what she shall have."

Tilley's mouth dropped open for a moment, before she bowed her head. "Yes, Sir. Very sorry, Sir."

Turning back to his wife, Phillip's expression brightened. "Then I shall leave you to get acquainted."

Before she could protest, he straightened, rushed to the door and closed it behind him.

Wide eyed, she glanced at her stunned maid before turning her attention to her new companion.

"And what are we to call…" She was stopped by the sudden mental image of a castle her parents had once taken her to; a place she had instantly fallen in love with. Chuckling to herself, she added, "You shall be Master Beauregard, after Castle Beauregard in France." She giggled while timidly patting the dog's head. "What do you think, Tilley?"

The girl sucked in a deep breath. "That's a real monster, that is, Mistress."

Elizabeth shrugged. "Monster or not, he is now ours. Aren't you, Master Beauregard?"

As if in response to her question, the dog let out an excited woof, and drooled on her comforter.

Chapter 7

"Where are we going?" I asked as we hurried down the sidewalk of a narrow, winding street about five blocks from Remmy's home.

While plodding along beside her, I was at a loss as to how anyone could help me. It had been my experience that people who claim to have connected with past lives are crazies and con men. I'd never known anyone to actually do it, as if there was any way to prove you had.

"You'll see," she answered with a smile, as though she had heard my last thought. "It happens more often than you think."

"But why didn't we just, like, drive there?"

"This has all been quite a shock to you," she said, her head shaking as she looked at me. "I thought you needed to walk a bit to clear your head."

I was about to ask another question when the sidewalk rose sharply and my focus shifted to the effort of keeping pace with her. By the time we reached the top, I was feeling winded. Breathing heavily herself, Remmy stopped at a cross street and pointed to a white house on our right. I was taken aback by how familiar the old-style place looked, though I had no recollection of ever having seen it before.

"This place reminds me of those old manors in England," I said, mostly to myself.

"Totally," Remmy laughed. "Except those manor houses are, like, massively huge."

"Yeah, well…just the same…it just reminds me of them."

She gave me a look of surprise that evolved into a knowing smile.

"Then you are *so* going to fit in here."

"What do you mean by that, exactly?"

"You'll see," she laughed before dashing across the street.

I followed and nearly plowed into her when she stopped abruptly at the brick path leading to the front door.

"*What* will I see?" I asked while looking at the house again. "Who lives here?"

Her expression was one of frustration and impatience.

"Will you just, like, trust me on this?"

I felt an overwhelming fear as the world around me grew hazy and distorted. I was preparing to cry out when I suddenly found myself back in the *room*, sitting in a canopied bed, looking at the ordered cluttered. Even so, I felt oddly happy to have these things, well, most of them anyway. I was trying to figure out what I was doing there when a black-and-white something moved on the floor next to the bed. I started to lean over to see what it was, and...

"Gerry?"

The sound of Remmy's voice pulled me partway back to the present, leaving me half there and half here.

"Uh…yeah?" I asked stupidly as a ghostly hound, its paws on the edge of my bed, overlaid her body.

"Where were you this time?"

The dog vanished, but it left me feeling desperate and humiliated.

Why can't I stop myself from going back there?

To cover my confusion, I looked at the house again to see an auburn-haired woman appear in the doorway.

"Is that who we're here to see?"

In one fluid motion, Remmy faced her, waved, and turned back. "Yeah. It's my Aunt Jasmina."

I looked at the woman again and was surprised to see how much she looked like an older version of my girlfriend.

"That figures," I sighed.

Her head bobbed. "She's my mom's sister, and I totally think she can help you."

"Help me? How?"

"I told her about your dreams, and she, like, thinks she knows where they are coming from."

When I looked at the woman again, she gave a quick wave. Not sure what else to do, I reflexively held up a hand and waggled it.

"Where is that?"

Without responding, Remmy grabbed my arm and pulled me toward the house.

"She's not, like, some kind of witch, is she?" I whispered as we moved down the brick path.

"Does she look like a witch?"

"Don't know. I've never met one before."

"Well, she's not. Even better, she's a miracle worker."

"What kind of miracle worker?"

"The kind who totally helps people sort out their past lives."

Chapter 8

Pressing a hand to the doorframe, Elizabeth gingerly rested an aching shoulder against the cool wood and scanned the silent drawing room, her attention stopping on the piano against the far wall. In her mind's eye, Phillip was crowded next to her on the bench as they played a lively tune together. The curtains were open, flooding the room with bright light, her mood soaring as she imagined them playing smoothly. She remembered the pleasure of those once-happy days before he went off to war, when they were often hip-to-hip on that bench, lost in the moment, blissfully ignorant of time's passage.

Nodding slowly, she happily hummed along, engrossed in the music until he hit a sour note. She, and her younger self ignored it and continued on. Phillip caught up, but after a few bars he missed another note…then another.

The room darkened, and the sudden chill made her look up to see his handsome features were now marred with his war wounds.

"I am worthless," he groaned, his pain obvious as his left hand dropped to his lap.

"You are nothing of the kind," she heard herself say pleasantly as she continued to play. "Simply jump back in where…"

The pain of his forearm striking her shoulder made her cry out as the impact knocked her to the floor.

"Why must you mock me?" he screamed as she struggled to right herself and look at him. "Do you not think I feel retched enough?"

"You are anything but worthless," she pleaded.

"You think me a useless prat. Is that it?"

His tone was sharp and bitter, eyes squinting, face bright red, and both she and her younger self cringed at the biting words. However, part of what troubled her was that even then she no longer disagreed with him.

Struggling to keep her voice calm, she forced herself to say, "I think no such thing, Phillip."

"Liar!"

"I would never lie to you. I honestly mean..."

She jerked left to avoid an ash tray.

"Bitch," he screamed. "Admit it! You want me dead. Why not just say so and be done with it?"

In the present, as her heart pounded and tears trickled down her cheeks, she closed her eyes and saw her younger self staring up at him with mouth open.

I should have agreed with him then and there, she thought, but instinctively knew it would have made no difference.

In her mind, his stocky body loomed over the cringing woman, seeming larger than life as his good eye glowed with a hate that made both her and the younger woman gasp. She wiped away tears as the scene played out, even though she desperately wanted it to stop.

"Why do you hate me so?" he cried. "Why?"

She tried to protest her innocence, to plead for him to believe her, but her tongue would not allow another lie.

When her silence continued, he threw his head back and howled. She shivered uncontrollably when he looked down with a face so contorted with rage she did not recognize it. Seeing his black-gloved right hand rise above his head, she gasped and threw up her hands up in defense, but not before...

"Mistress," Tilley protested from behind her. "Whatever are you doing down here? You'll catch your death in this drafty place."

The piano and its accommodating bench were once again empty as Elizabeth started to turn away, but the many pains in her body and mind made her hesitate.

As her maid placed a warm shawl over her shoulders, she looked back at the piano, no longer hearing the notes, but just their sad echo in her mind. When Tilley gave her shoulders a gentle, but insistent push, Elizabeth sighed and let herself be ushered back upstairs.

"Where is Beauregard?" she asked hoarsely when fading energy forced her to lean on the railing, feeling weak and vulnerable.

"While the master is napping, William has taken Master Beauregard for a bit of a run on the lawn," Tilley responded. "He'll be back soon enough."

"No," Elizabeth countered as she struggled to take another step up. "Never soon enough."

Chapter 9

"Oh my goodness," Jasmina stated as she sat next to me on the couch in her office, her eyes closed, one hand lightly gripping my own. "This is really intense!"

"What do you mean?"

Her eyes popped open and she gave me a look of genuine surprise. "I usually just get a sense of the person my clients are connected to, but with this woman...it's...it's like I'm looking in a mirror."

"What do you see?" Remmy asked excitedly.

Taking both of my hands this time, she closed her eyes and responded, "I see a woman. She's a little over five feet tall, slender, and quite attractive."

Remmy was standing behind the couch, her elbows on the back so her face was close to mine. I felt some comfort when she put a hand on my right shoulder and squeezed.

"Any idea where this person lived?" she asked.

"England, I think."

I didn't know what to say. This was so outside my experience, I had no idea what was expected of me...or her, for that matter.

"There's a room...a bedroom. She's been badly hurt and is in a bed looking at...a dog?"

When Remmy sucked in a breath, I blurted, "What kind of dog?"

Her eyes still closed, Jasmina shook her head. "I don't know. It's only a puppy, but it's already bigger than most dogs ever get. When it grows up, it will be huge!"

Remmy gave my shoulder a shake. "That's what you saw, isn't it?"

I jerked a nod. "A Great Dane, or something like it."

"This is interesting," Jasmina said slowly. "This is you with the dog." She opened her eyes and looked at me. "And you are a woman."

Remmy barked a laugh, but I was in shock.

"A woman?"

Jasmina shook her head. "Don't worry. It's not at all uncommon." She patted my hand lightly. "It's often a good thing for a man to have been a woman in a previous life. It makes him more compassionate and very respectful of women in this one."

Feeling both confused and a little embarrassed, I looked up to see Remmy smiling, but to my relief, it wasn't an I-told-you-so kind of smile. She was nodding in agreement with her aunt.

Then her expression turned somber. "But it couldn't have been, like, all good. Why would Gerry be having nightmares?"

Jasmina release me, closed her eyes, and folded her hands together as though holding a small ball.

"Remmy is right," she said softly. "I'm sensing a dark element in your life. Your former life as a woman, that is."

I suddenly felt someone-is-holding-a-gun-to-my-head alarmed. Faker or not, this woman had my rapt attention.

"What do you mean, dark element? Like in something bad?"

She shook her head. "It's hard to see specific details. It's something you've really suppressed, but it has to do with your sense of duty, like maybe you were trapped in an unhappy marriage. Yes, that's it. You were married to a man you didn't love, and he wasn't kind to you. That would explain the woman's injuries."

"What year was this?" Remmy asked.

Jasmina's hands jerked again. "I'm sensing it was...late...eighteen hundreds. Shortly after the first Boer War. Whenever that was."

"Divorce was, like, nearly impossible to get in those days," Remmy shouted.

Jasmina nodded. "Your family had some kind of title, or property, but they were having financial problems."

I felt my chest tighten, and was surprised that it felt so personal. More than that, it really pissed me off.

"I was *sold off* in marriage to some rich guy so my parents wouldn't lose their land?"

When Jasmina's eyes opened again, she was smiling. "Exactly!"

In that instant, I was suddenly two different people. One part of me felt trapped, claustrophobic, and defensive. This was a real threat, though how it could be I couldn't say. The other part wanted to laugh out loud at the absurdity of it. After all, my Christian upbringing had taught me that there was no such thing as past lives.

Mediums are fakes! My mother's voice exploded in my head so powerfully it made me blink. *It's all just trickery designed to pull you away from the True Word! Don't let these devil worshipers deceive you!*

But how did Jasmina know about the dog? I argued. *Did Remmy tell her?*

I looked down to see my hands shaking. Though I quickly folded them together to hide it, that didn't stop the ache in my gut or the desperate need to get out of there.

"I think I need to..."

Jasmina's eyes snapped shut as her head flew back. "Oh my!"

I tried to rise, but Remmy's grip on my shoulder held me down. "What is it?"

Jasmina was looking at me again, but a frown had replaced her smile. "I sense a very angry, very powerful presence nearby."

Releasing me, Remmy flew to the nearest window.

"Oh my God," she exclaimed. "Someone's out there."

Without another word, she did a quick one-eighty and ran from the room. It took me a moment to gather my wits and follow.

For reasons I couldn't articulate, I felt a raging sense of panic as I bounced off the hallway wall and sprinted toward the open back door. My feet didn't even touch the small porch when I flew over it to land on the concrete path. To my utter relief, Remmy was standing at the bottom of the driveway looking first one way then the other.

The sound of my shoes slapping the sloping driveway made her turn toward me, her face the epitome of frustration.

"I saw someone running, but by the time I got down here, he was gone," she exclaimed.

"It was a man?"

She looked confused. "I think so, but it was hard to tell. He was wearing a long coat."

"Is everyone OK?" Jasmina called from the porch.

We both turned toward her, but it was Remmy who spoke, "Someone's after Gerry."

Her statement struck me as absurd. "Why would anyone be after me?"

"We can't put Jasmina in danger."

"What?" I blurted. "Danger?"

Ignoring me, Remmy waved at her aunt. "I so need to get him home. His parents should know about this."

Jasmina shook her head. "This doesn't make any sense."

I wanted to agree, but Remmy was pushing me down the sidewalk. "We'll talk with his folks, and they can decide what to do."

Chapter 10

Shaking her head, Elizabeth stared into the mirror at a face that constantly frustrated her. In her opinion, her eyes were too wide, and nose too small, even disgustingly pert. Sighing, she pinched her thin lips together and picked up a powder puff from her dressing table to carefully pat a creamy compound over the greenish remnants of a fading bruise, smoothing the makeup carefully to make it appear that she had applied nothing at all. It had been two months since she had "fallen" from the roof, but these bruises, though fading, were newer than that.

"That's an ever so pretty dress, Mistress," Tilley said cheerfully as she carried a vase of flowers into the room. "The green suits you."

She watched the girl place the colorful bouquet on the end of her dressing table before returning her attention to the mirror. However, instead of seeing her carefully arranged hair or the effects of her makeup, she fixated on the weary face staring back at her.

"I hope Phillip likes it," she muttered for Tilley's benefit.

The absurdity of the comment forced her to stifle a laugh. She no longer cared what Phillip thought. Truth be told, she had never loved him. At least not the love she had imagined as a young woman. Her mother had insisted it "would come in time," but even before he was injured in the war, she only felt her obligation to him as his wife. Then when he came back so damaged he could not look at himself in the mirror, it was all about loneliness and regret.

She suddenly realized Tilley was talking.

"...these flowers might go well in the..."

"Tilley?" she interrupted while adjusting the silk roses on her bodice. "Have you given any thought to marriage?"

When the maid did not respond, she turned to find the girl gawking at her.

"Was the question inappropriate?"

Her mouth opening in surprise, Tilley hesitated briefly before asking, "Mistress?"

Elizabeth shook her head. "Forget I asked."

A rap on the door made them both turn toward it, thankful for the interruption.

"Yes?" she asked as a blushing Tilley rushed to open the door.

As was his usual habit, Phillip stayed outside the room, peering in as though it were forbidden territory.

"Are you decent?"

The question ignited years of pent-up frustration, and to hide her irritation she looked into the mirror. Though her hair was perfectly arranged and her makeup now hid the fading bruises, she still saw the hint of bags under her eyes, and wrinkles to come. Old age was creeping up on her, and there would be no children to brighten her days.

Pushing down the urge to cry, she replaced her frown with a smile and faced him again.

"Yes, Dear," she chirped as pleasantly as could be managed. "Please do come in."

When Phillip entered, Beauregard rose and moved toward him. Though not yet a year old, the dog's size was true to his breed, and Phillip barely had to stoop to scratch his ears.

"The Wellingtons are early, as usual," he announced, his eye on her.

She caught a look of hunger on his face, which she found perplexing. He must have seen her confusion, because he quickly turned his attention to the dog.

"I suppose it is the stables for this big fellow," he said as casually as though he were commenting on the weather.

The suggestion sent Elizabeth's heart thumping, and she struggled to keep her voice light. "He is no bother, really. People adore Beau, and the Wellingtons especially. I must say, he is wonderful for starting a conversation."

Phillip's head came up, the anger expressed by his good eye being emphasized by the disfigured half of his face.

"Nevertheless," he said with a coldness that made her muscles freeze. "Our guests shall be dressed in their finest attire. Surely they will not wish to be covered with dog hair. He should stay outside while they are here."

As his wife, she should agree, but she could not. When her hand automatically started to move to the most recent bruise on her face, she successfully resisted the urge to touch it, moving instead to pat at her hair as she glanced at Beauregard. The dog's unquestioning devotion to her had surprised them both, even more so when he interrupted her husband's last attack.

Since the incident on the roof, there had been a short reprieve, and a flurry of gifts, before Phillip's outbursts started again. She knew him well enough to see most of them coming, and her usual tactic was to simply gather up the dog and leave the room, letting him scream and smash furniture until his rage was spent.

When Phillip's outbursts were confined to yelling and throwing furniture, the young dog cowered alongside his mistress, eager to follow her away from this raging maniac. However, when a sudden shift in mood caught Elizabeth off guard and her husband finally struck her, the dog transformed from a cowering victim into her shining defender.

Her stomach cramped as she felt her head shake, and knew if she gave in to Phillip's request, her beloved Beauregard would never be allowed to return.

And I will be defenseless once again.

Her eyes flicking to Tilley, she jerked a slight nod toward the door. Though a look of panic flashed across the girl's face, she silently bobbed a curtsy, and hurried out, closing the door behind her.

Except for his head rotating to follow the maid's progress, Phillip stood like a statue, his left hand resting just above the cuff on the opposite arm. Beauregard's whimper brought her attention down to see the dog was looking at Phillip.

When she could hear Tilley's footsteps on the stairs, Phillip's head jerked around, his face flush with anger, fists clenched. Despite the powerful dog nearby, it took an enormous amount of effort for her to speak.

"Beauregard does *not* belong in the stables," she said firmly, her eyes locked on his. "His place is with me, and he is loved by everyone." *Except you.*

Straightening to his full height, Phillip took a quick step forward, but stopped when the dog scrambled back to stay between them. Though Beauregard made no sound, the look in Phillip's eye made it clear he understood what would happen if he took another step. His good hand instinctively moving to a still-tender spot on his other arm, Phillip's lips quivered, his eye jerking from the dog to her and back.

After a tense moment, he took a step back.

"Th…thiiiss is…my…hhhhhouse…" he howled.

She winced at the outburst, and cringed when she saw the frustration and pain on his face. He opened his mouth again and froze, his good eye squinting angrily at her, strained gargling sounds coming from his throat until he turned and marched from the room.

Though the slamming door made her flinch, it also brought a physical sense of relief as Elizabeth let out an unintentionally-held breath. After Beauregard's butt thumped to the floor, he swung his massive head in her direction, his tongue now hanging from the side of his mouth as though he were laughing.

The threat now gone, she suddenly felt weak, and fearing she might faint, leaned against her chair back and took a moment to compose herself before looking at the dog again.

"You are my knight in shining armour," she sighed, her heart aching as her attention returned to the door. "Would that my husband could fill that role."

Chapter 11

"I saw her," I announced while dropping into the chair next to Remmy in the Marion County Community College library.

After looking quickly around the room, she pressed a finger to her lips to silence me and rose. I was so eager to tell her, my head felt like it would burst, but I kept my tongue and watched her shut her book, gather her notes, and stuff the lot into her backpack.

"Outsssside," she hissed angrily.

I was barely to my feet when she started pushing me toward the door.

"What do you mean? You, like, saw her?" she asked even before the library door closed.

"I was in math class. One minute the professor was explaining factoring, and the next, I'm totally looking at this woman's face."

Remmy's head shook. "It wouldn't be her. People can't see their own faces."

I shook my head as well. "I was looking at a mirror...or rather, she was."

"How do you know?"

I shrugged. "Well, I...she was putting something on her face to cover some old bruises. I watched her for a bit and then there was, like, this knock on the door and that strange guy came into the room."

"The dude with the messed up face?"

I nodded slowly. "But she was totally not afraid of him this time. Well, I guess she was, but she was more angry than scared."

Chewing on her lower lip, Remmy looked at her hands. "How do you know?"

"I don't know. I just felt it. They were throwing a party and he wanted to take the dog away, but she said he couldn't. He was so totally pissed he started to go after her. If the dog hadn't moved between them, I'm sure he'd have hit her."

She looked up at me, her face taught, body tense.

"So what happened?" she asked angrily.

Confused by her reaction, I could do nothing but shrug. "The dog didn't bark or anything, but it made the guy stop and give her a really nasty look before he stormed out of the room."

Turning away, Remmy quickly rubbed her hands together before facing me again. "The dog is her protector. He's keeping her abusive hubby away from her."

I felt myself nodding, but found her sour look confusing. "And that's a good thing, right?"

"Yeah. So?"

"I don't know. You don't really seem…happy about it."

She moved a step away and looked down at her feet. "A big dog attacked me once. Even now, they totally make me nervous."

"Whoa! I didn't know that. You must have been…"

"So why is the dog back now?" she interrupted, though still not looking at me.

"What?"

Her eyes rose to meet mine. "You, like, saw him at Taco Brothers, right?" When I jerked a nod, she asked, "Just after you had your daydream about her?"

I wasn't getting the connection. "Huh?"

Shaking her head slowly, she moved close and put a hand on my arm. "If you are this woman, and the dog was her protector, why would it suddenly, like, appear right after you start remembering that past life?"

I felt my jaw sag as a sudden flash of fear shot through me, but I didn't want to vocalize it.

Remmy's eyes locked on mine. "The dog's back because…" She hesitated as though trying to decide something. After a moment, she looked away and added, "Your husband's spirit is also here. Now."

Sudden panic froze my thoughts, but I managed to blurt out, "How can that be?"

"That woman is connecting with you, right?"

"Well, yeah. I guess."

"So there's no reason to assume he can't do something like that too."

Her statement was like a slap in the face. In fact, I was equally stunned that my right cheek started aching as though someone had hit it. The thought that a ghost from my past -- a past I hadn't even known I had -- was coming after me, boggled my mind.

"What…what am I going do?"

Her head shaking, Remmy shoved an arm into a strap on her backpack and heaved it over her shoulder. Slipping the other arm into the remaining strap, she pushed me toward her car.

"We need to find Jasmina."

Chapter 12

A gentle evening breeze fluttered the frayed scrap of parchment in Elizabeth's hand. Squinting at the flapping document, she leaned toward a nearby lamp and read the cramped writing.

Dearest Elizabeth,

Death and hope are a curious mix,
Yet together shall they play
A perplexing role in our torn lives
Over which we have no say.

I have to wonder if ever I'll see
The world from which I came.
The arms of Death will hold me here.
And drive my soul insane.

To find me is no work for Him.
I cannot hide away
Death is ne'er far from me
He may well come today.

So why then does He hold me so
And deny me what I long?
I beg Him please to set me free
For here I'll ne'er belong.

But escape I cannot do alone.
Others must come too.
Another thing I know for sure:
This will be true for you.

With five, at least, we must try
To pass the barrier there.
With less than that, we surely fail
To be lost in who-knows-where.

For they need me, and I do them
Of this we do agree.
Find your others, those your own,
And likewise you'll be free.

So now I say goodbye to you
Before we ever meet.
You'll find your way, of that I'm sure
And then you will be complete.

"Sorry to give you this as I'm leaving, Dear" the elderly Spinster Peterson said as she watched her carriage approach the front of Phillip and Elizabeth's home, "but I recently found this amongst my papers, and thought it important that you had it straight away."

"This is most peculiar," Elizabeth said while turning over the parchment to see if there was more on the back. "I have the feeling that I might have read this before, but have no recollection of when or where." She looked at her guest. "Whatever does it mean?"

"The meaning escapes me completely, but it is doubtful you ever saw the like of this. It was penned by your great grandmamma only a short while before she was laid to rest, and I have never shown it to anyone before now. You will think it even more queer when I tell you, she made the particular point that I should deliver it to her great-granddaughter Elizabeth."

"But she passed more than twenty years before I was born."

"That is why I set it aside and forgot about it. Even after your birth, I could hardly have given it to a mere babe, now could I?"

"And yet, I know almost nothing about her except her name was Margarette."

Mistress Peterson frowned. "Most thought her strange, to be sure, but I found her a pleasant woman, quite unlike that dour brood of daughters she brought into this world. To my recollection, she had a zest for life so often missing from her generation."

"Yes," Elizabeth said distractedly as she held up the scrap of parchment. "Thank you so much for this, Mistress Peterson, but I have never understood why Grandmother never spoke of her mamma."

"Ah, well," the spinster laughed as she started to leave. "She wouldn't have now, would she?"

"I beg your pardon?"

Turning back, she leaned close and whispered, "She was a foreigner, you see." She tilted her face up, looking skyward as she tapped her chin. "Belgian, if memory serves. Of course, it was very sad about…" She stopped abruptly, looking behind Elizabeth only briefly before jerking a nod and adding, "We must have tea some time, so that I may enlighten you further."

Without waiting for a response, she turned and motioned for Jason to help her down the steps.

"I would very much like that," Elizabeth said to the woman's back.

Leaning against Jason, Mistress Peterson waved a free hand.

"Very soon then," she sing-songed cheerfully, but then stopped and turned, her face now serious. "There is much to tell you, and I am not certain how much time I have left."

Though puzzled by Mistress Peterson's strange behavior, Elizabeth could not stop staring at the odd poem.

"What do you make of…" she started to ask Phillip.

To her dismay, the space he had occupied while they were bidding goodnight to the last of their dinner guests was now empty. Sighing, she waved at Mistress Peterson's departing carriage and moved into the manor to hear his irregular footsteps echoing down the hallway. She knew from experience where he was going.

There is alcohol in the library.

She crossed the entryway toward the stairs, feeling relief at not having to face him. Though she was sure their guests had no clue, he had been ugly to her all evening: angry, glaring expressions when no one else was looking; demeaning remarks out of earshot of the others; pretending not to hear when she spoke to him. He was quite adroit at presenting the myth of marital bliss to their friends while making it clear only to her that he wanted to beat her to within an inch of her life. Or worse.

Sadly, she was equally good at hiding her feelings: covering her deepening depression with a glowing smile, laughing when he talked down to her in front of others, and pretending she did not have a care in the world. She practiced in front of her mirror for hours, working expressions until she had perfected the lie that hid their misery behind the façade of the ideal couple.

How long can it last?

She was only thirty-five, her mother an active, though dour fifty-four, and her still-living grandmother, seventy-two. Shaking her head, she stopped at the base of the stairs and looked up toward the safety of her room: her sanctuary/prison.

One of us will surely be dead long before I reach that advanced age.

Sighing, she hiked her skirts and prepared to climb but the sound of a crystal stopper rattling into its decanter stopped her with a shoe suspended over the first step. After closing her eyes for a moment, she stepped back and turned to face the open library door.

Which of us will it be, I wonder?

She was so focused on the door, she jerked in surprise at the sound of Beauregard's claws ticking against the entryway tiles. Looking at his large, blocky head, she could see that though he had stopped next to her, his beautiful brown eyes were also on the library door.

He knows something is wrong.

Sighing again, she reached down to pat his thick neck, feeling comfort in both his size and the softness of his fur as he turned his attention to her, his eyes questioning.

"You are the only one who truly understands."

Feeling incredibly sad, she shook her head and took a step forward, but stopped when the dog matched her move. Snapping her fingers, she waited until he was looking at her again before using her left hand to motion for him to sit. He did so without hesitation, but his face projected concern as he looked from her to the library door and back.

His reaction made her want to wrap her arms around his shivering body and hug him close, but instead she held a hand flat over his head as a command to stay while she whispered,

"My husband and I need a moment alone."

Looking anxious as she moved away, he nonetheless obeyed, but she drew strength in knowing that one word from her would bring him running. Phillip would be aware of it as well.

Despite the echoing sound of her heels on the polished hallway floor, Phillip's back was to her when she reached the doorway. His broad shoulders were squared as he lifted his drink and downed the contents in one gulp. He was reaching for the decanter when she let her foot slap the floor.

After pouring another drink, he turned casually to look at her, and to her surprise, did not look angry. Not happy, but certainly not angry. Even so, she stayed in the doorway as he watched her for a moment before turning to look into the flames of the fireplace.

"Would you like something?" he asked flatly while returning the decanter to its tray.

Yes. A divorce.

His eyes still on the fire, he lifted the glass to his lips, but when she did not respond, he gave her a questioning look. She wanted more than anything to vocalize her thought, but deeply inbred tradition stopped it at her lips.

"I came to wish you a good night."

His eye on her, he hesitated momentarily with the glass halfway to his mouth. When she said no more, he shrugged and gulped down the remainder of the drink.

Why do you hate me so? flashed in her mind as he continued to stare without responding.

After a long moment, she let out an involuntary sigh and started to leave.

"You wish to be rid of me. Is that not so?" he stated as unemotionally as if he were making a comment about the weather.

She turned back. "I should think it is you who wish to be free of me."

He waved his left hand at the ceiling. "You only married me to save this dreadful place from the collections agents."

She was surprised how much the truth hurt. Love was never a part of her feelings for him. She had liked him well enough before he went off to war, and even enjoyed it when they made love. He had been so passionate, so caring, even when the hoped for child did not come before he was mustered out.

And afterward -- after his long stay in hospital; the many, mostly useless surgeries; the painful, grueling recovery -- she stuck by him, even though the shell of what was left of her husband vanished into the privacy of his room and left her with a deep, aching longing he could no longer fill.

"You are drunk," was all she could think to say.

It surprised her to see him jerk as though slapped, and she suddenly felt torn. Part of her wanted to shake the hatred out of him and bring back the gentle man she married. The other half wished he would die and make her a happy widow. The latter thought filled her with shame, and she could feel her face warm. From his angry expression, it was obvious he saw her reaction.

Fearful of what else she might say, she hurried toward the stairs, hearing his footsteps, but afraid to look back.

"You will never be free of me," he bellowed as she quickened her pace. "I will follow you to the end of eternity!"

Beauregard quickly rose to his full height, but true to his orders, did not approach, even when she broke into a run. Tears blurred her vision as she continued on, not caring if Phillip might follow. Upon reaching the stairs, she paused, started to look back, but stopped when his words echoed in her mind.

What a dreadful, loathsome man he is, she thought angrily as she hiked up her skirts and mounted the stairs. She had managed only a few steps before the reality of his declaration sank in.

I will never be free of him. Ever!

Chapter 13

"Gerry, we should totally call the cops," Remmy insisted as I bit into my second Mano-Mano Burger Deluxe at The Hamburger Hutch. Instead of taking me from Jasmina's to my house, my girlfriend led me to one of our favorite hangouts. Good thing too. The stress of all this crap in my life…uh…lives was making me crazy hungry.

"Wa wd I say?" I argued testily through a full mouth. "An evil spirit from my past life might be haunting me?"

Giving her head a quick shake, she put down her more petite Princess Burger and stabbed a finger at me. "The dog wouldn't, like, be here if you weren't in danger."

Waggling my hand hid the fact that it was shaking. "But that's the point. The dog wasn't really there, so what do I have to show them? My worn-out backpack? They'll think I'm mental."

"We need to talk to Jasmina again," Remmy stated. "She'll totally know what to do."

"Maybe she'll do an exorcism and purge all my evil..."

The uncomfortable sensation of being watched stopped me, but before I could look around, Remmy protested,

"Don't be a tool. She doesn't, like, do that kind of..."

"Mister Patterson?" a woman's voice interrupted. "Gerard Patterson?"

The voice was high and anxious, and I looked up to see cold, calculating eyes hovering just above Remmy's head. The anorexic, angular face wore a curious expression: the mouth grinned nervously, the blue eyes did not.

I was preparing to ask what she wanted when I saw the gray raincoat sagging from her bony shoulders like cloth on a coat hanger. The sight sent my heart racing.

Looking again at the eyes, which didn't blink, I had the distinct impression she was preparing to leap over Remmy and devour me.

The woman ignored my girlfriend in that irritating way adults often do, our eyes staying locked for a long moment before I realized who this might be.

"Gerard Patterson? My name is Elissa Grant, but you might remember me as...."

"What do you *want*," Remmy demanded with an intensity that surprised me.

Sometimes it's good to have an aggressive girlfriend, especially when she is assertively protecting your interests, but at this moment I had to wonder.

Taking a step back, the woman blinked and looked flustered. "I don't...you see..."

My instincts took over before she could finish. Without even thinking, I scooped up my backpack, stepped around the table, grabbed Remmy's arm, and pulled her toward the exit.

"No," Elissa cried. "Wait!"

My head shaking, I continued on, trying to keep the resisting Remmy moving with me. As we struggled, she crashed into me, I stepped on her foot, and felt myself falling forward. Releasing her arm, I jerked my feet under me, rose up, and grabbed her again.

"We have to get…"

"He was a Great Dane!" the woman shouted.

The air went completely out of my lungs as panic put a pincer on my brain, muddling me so thoroughly I hardly felt my girlfriend break free of my grip.

Nor could I respond when Remmy asked, "What's she talking about?"

Straightening, I turned slowly to see the woman looking anxious, as Remmy moved between us.

"The dog! White...with black patches," the woman continued haltingly as I remembered the black and white beast behind my chair.

All color drained from my vision, as wild, raging panic made me abandon my girlfriend, drop my backpack, and run. I managed two off-balanced steps before my shoulder rammed a door frame. My feet still pumping, I did a three-quarter spin, touched one hand to the ground, careened off a concrete garbage can, and kept going.

"Gerry?" I heard someone call after me, but was so focused on getting away I could not register who said it.

"Please," an older voice pleaded. "Let me explain."

I couldn't stop. Nothing mattered more than getting out of there. Couldn't hear, couldn't see, couldn't think. A senseless array of colored lights -- red, green, yellow, orange -- flashed in my vision as my lungs ached, the streets and sidewalks merged into one, people shouted, and horns honked. I sprinted around a blur of bodies, cars, and parking meters, barely aware of where I was until the city transformed into an expanse of grass and trees.

Gasping for air, I finally emerged from the haze of panic to find myself somewhere in Bush Park. On rubbery legs, I stumbled and hyper-extended a knee which pole-vaulted me into soggy, waist-high brush. Crashing onto my left shoulder, I rolled onto my back and sucked in a sharp breath, both from the pain of the impact and the cold water soaking my clothes.

Breathing hard, I closed my eyes, and was quickly overwhelmed with a flood of random images: a dog jumping, a shadowy fist flying at my face, dancing with a handsome man, a blur of stairs, the confusing rush of vertigo, and a sense of falling.

Feeling like I was doing a silent scream, I forced my eyes open as a sudden warmth filled my head. Marshalling just enough strength to roll over, I tried to rise, but thrashing emotions cramped my gut and stopped me at hands and knees. When the spasms slowed, great sobs erupted from me in convulsing waves that almost sent me back to the ground.

I threw up. The suffocating power of it robbing my oxygen-starved body of what little strength it had left. I was close to passing out when it stopped, but the sobbing continued, with wave after wave coursing through my body as though pushing out an unknown poison.

When the sobbing slowed, I collapsed onto my side again, shivering as the soggy ground chilled my skin, and the strangest of thoughts came to me: something I would not have expected in a million years.

I've been here before.

Chapter 14

Fighting a stiffening breeze, Elizabeth struggled to hold her umbrella over her head to protect her feathered hat from scattered raindrops as she moved carefully down the gravel path, tippy toeing to keep her polished boots out of the many puddles in her way. Her olive-green raincoat flapping with each step, she let out a sigh of relief when they rounded a large hedge, and the manor house came into view.

"I know'd we shouldn't a walked home, Mistress," Tilley moaned as she squinted at the dense wall of rain approaching from their left. "We'll surely be soaked to the bone if that storm catches us."

"Hurry along then," Elizabeth chastised while stepping around a muddy pool of water. "I did not force you to..."

She stopped when Phillip suddenly appeared in her path, his dark-gray raincoat open to the wind.

"What are you playing at?"

Elizabeth was preparing to respond when she realized her husband's eye was on Tilley.

"Your mistress should not be slogging through the mud."

The panicked girl squeaked, "I told her we should..."

"Off with you," he demanded, his right arm pointing toward the manor house while his shoulders hunched against the drizzle that was quickly becoming a downpour.

Tilley hesitated only briefly before rushing past him.

"How was I to know the rain would come so quickly?" Elizabeth protested. "Surely you can't blame..."

"I blame you for disobeying my orders."

She blinked in surprise. "Your what?" Suddenly the rain did not matter. "I am your wife, not your servant."

"And damned poor at both, I must say," he shouted above the increasing roar of pounding rain. She blanched when he lunged forward to stab a finger at her face. "How must it look to have my wife mucking about in the rain on a day such as this?"

"I am not *mucking about*, surely" she protested. "We just took a bit of a stroll."

She saw her husband's eyes scanning the bushes behind her. "And where is that slag you left with? Afraid to face me, is he?"

The absurdity of his questions stunned her like a slap in the face. "If you are referring to Colonel Struthers, he was not with..." She hesitated as the realization of what he said sank in. "How did you know he departed when we did?"

He gave his uncovered head a shake, sending raindrops flying. "Because after William returned home alone, I went to see what had become of you and was told you left together."

Taking an exasperated breath, she closed her eyes for a moment before glaring at him. "The colonel drove directly off in his carriage. Tilley and I went our own way."

"And I am supposed to believe that?"

When a gust of wind nearly yanked the umbrella from her hands, she pulled it down, snapped it closed, and stamped a foot. "I don't care one wit what you believe," she shouted before continuing her march to the house.

As she passed him, his left arm shot out and slammed her shoulder. Off balance, she staggered off the gravel path, crying out when her heels sank into the rain-softened soil. Though desperate to keep from soiling her clothes on the wet grass, she managed only two clumsy steps before sprawling onto the ground.

"Whore!"

Rain pelted her face as she struggled to rise with the hope of putting some distance between them, but before she could manage it, he was beside her, his gloved hand slamming her cheek. She cried out at the stinging pain and fell onto her back. When she looked up again, he was a towering hulk against the gray sky, his body shaking, face distorted with rage. Frantic, she again tried to rise, but he took a large step that put one foot on each side of her. When she continued to struggle, he sank to his knees and squatted back onto her thighs, his right arm high and ready to strike.

"No!" she screamed while holding up her arms in a futile gesture of defense.

The impact collapsed her limbs, but deflected the frozen fist so that it slammed her left shoulder.

Instead of continuing the attack, Phillip rose onto his knees, lifted his arms to the sky and bellowed. Realizing his weight was no longer holding her down, she tried to scoot free, ineffectively pushing on the wet grass until her fingers found the umbrella handle. When he looked down again, she swung the thing up at his face, but he deflected it. Before she could try again, he tore it from her grasp and heaved it across the lawn.

Lifting his right arm, he was preparing to strike again when something made him hesitate. Elizabeth was so focused on the coming assault she did not hear the sound that drew his attention from her.

"Woof" Beauregard repeated as he bounded across the grass.

His arm still in the air, Phillip swore, but kept his eye on the dog until Elizabeth turned her own body toward her canine protector. Surprised by the move, Phillip lost his balance, and started to fall forward. Elizabeth screamed again, but he caught himself, scrambled to his feet, and quickly backpedaled to the path. Seeming to realilze his mistress was no longer in danger, the dog slowed, trotted up to her, and sat.

"One day, I will kill that damned beast," Phillip snarled before marching toward the manor.

Shivering from both the shock of the attack and wet clothes, Elizabeth rolled onto her side, tears mixing with rain as she watched her husband vanish into the house without once looking back. Beauregard lowered his head as she released a sob, brushed back wet strands of hair, and stroked his boxy head.

"He can never succeed, my love," she murmured.

As though in response, the dog looked at her, sucked in his wagging tongue, and nodded.

Chapter 15

A cool October mist rained down on me as I tried to push myself up, but my muscles were simply too weak. As I fell back to the ground, despair overwhelmed me.

Who can help me now?

The questions spurred a feeling of panic and the resulting adrenaline rush gave me enough energy to sit up and look around. A red-haired woman in a bright-yellow raincoat was walking her Rottweiler on a trail to my left. Though the dog gave me an interested look, the woman was facing away from my brushy hiding place, and seemed unaware of my presence.

When she was a safe distance away, I crawled onto the path, shivering as I watched them grow smaller. Hearing footsteps behind me, I turned and gasped at the sight of that dark-gray raincoat. Even more daunting was the hunger in her blue eyes.

How did she find me?

I tried to rise, but felt so unbalanced I kept to hands-and-knees and hurried across the bark-mulch path to the grass beyond.

"You don't have to be afraid of me," Elissa said softly as she stared at me. "I won't hurt you."

"Yes you will," I heard myself saying as my arms gave out and sent me sprawling onto the grass.

I looked up to see her hold up both hands, palms out. "No. I promise."

"Go away. The only way you can avoid hurting me is to leave me alone...forever."

"I can't do that," she cried. "There is something we must do..."

"No!" I shouted, though it felt like someone else was speaking. "There is no way to make up for what you've done."

She briefly looked confused then shook her head. "You have it wrong," she insisted while moving toward me. "I didn't mean to…"

"Beauregard!"

The name just erupted out of me, and before either of us could react, I heard a high-pitched yelp of surprise followed by the Rottweiler's deep, threatening bark. When Elissa's eyes jerked up to look behind me, her confusion changed to fear.

Puzzled, I turned to see the red-haired woman running our way. Her dog, his leash bouncing freely behind him, was charging straight at me with teeth bared, and his brown-and-black block of a body moving at surprising speed. Nearly wetting my pants, I tried to push myself up, but my hands slipped on the grass and I fell back to the soggy ground. When the dog let out a thunderous bark, I jerked my head up to see him come to a stop just short of where I was sitting.

It was only then I realized his attention was not on me, and I looked back to see Elissa running away.

"Sorry! Sorry! Sorry!" the redheaded woman cried. "Tyson. Leave this poor man alone." The gasping woman grabbed her dog's leash and gave it an ineffective yank.

The Rottweiler held his ground, his tongue flapping out the side of his mouth, his big, brown eyes looking expectantly at me as though asking if I was OK.

"Are you all right, young man?" the woman asked.

"Yeah," I responded while rising unsteadily to my feet. "But I think your dog just saved my life."

The woman's eyes went wide. "Really? Was that person attacking you? Should we call the police?"

As she pulled out her cell phone, I held up a hand. "No! Please. It was just a misunderstanding. Once she calms down, she'll be OK."

"Why did she attack you?"

My mind raced to think of a way to keep her from calling the cops.

"She's my aunt," I lied. "She's totally freaked out because she's going through a divorce. Calling the police will only make matters worse."

"Are you sure?"

Taking a deep breath to calm myself, I moved to the Rottweiler and scratched his ears, feeling a deep sense of calm when his head leaned into my hand.

"I used to have a Great Dane," I heard myself say, and though I knew it wasn't true, it didn't feel like a lie.

"Really?" the woman asked though she looked skeptical. "They're such beautiful animals, but they're huge."

Nodding, I continued to scratch Tyson's ears while looking into eyes that seemed to know me. "I loved him with my life."

Chapter 16

"I'm sure I don't understand," Elizabeth said as Mistress Peterson handed her a tea cup decorated with corn flowers. "Who are these five people I am supposed to find?"

Elizabeth had worn a long-sleeved blouse, and fought the urge to touch the ugly bruises on her arm where only the day before Phillip had struck her. Unaware of her distress, Mistress Peterson looked cautiously around her sitting room as though expecting to find someone lurking behind a seriously out-of-fashion overstuffed chair, or her well-worn antique writing table. A cheery fire burned brightly in the otherwise dark and dismal room that Elizabeth's delicate nose told her had not been more than dusted in a very long time.

Her hostess seemed hesitant, her moist eyes searching Elizabeth's face for a moment before she leaned forward and spoke in a loud whisper, "I'm told your great-grandmother was weak of mind in her final days. It may well be she simply dreamed the whole thing up, because the last time I saw her she seemed quite confused. Do you know, she kept asking me if I knew about the *Others*."

"Others? Who might these others be?"

Mistress Peterson shook her head slowly. "I had no idea at the time, now did I?"

Carefully putting her tea cup down, Elizabeth sat up straight, placed her hands in her lap, and asked, "What do you mean?"

"She seemed quite obsessed with that bit of finding her *other* people, like the whole world would come to an end if she were to fail." Straightening herself as well, Mistress Peterson pointed a gloved finger at her guest. "And she also made a particular point of saying that you should do the same, just like it says in that poem."

"Me?"

The elder woman jerked a nod. "That is what she said."

"And do what?"

She shook her head slowly. "That is the saddest part."

"Whatever do you mean?"

"Surely you must know."

Trying not to show her irritation, Elizabeth asked, "What is it I am supposed to know?"

"The poor dear did herself in, didn't she? And there were four others as well. It was quite the scandal, as you can imagine."

"Lord in Heaven!" Elizabeth exclaimed. "I had no idea."

"It was a shock to us all, I can tell you."

"Who were these people? Did she know them?"

Mistress Peterson's eyes stayed on Elizabeth as her head shook. "That's the strangest bit of all. She was frettin' and fussin' about how she had to find them, and then one day they started arriving. I am told her happy demeanor returned, and she was like a giddy child with a new toy until the sad day her husband returned home to find the lot of them dead as can be."

"But someone in her family must have known who these people were, surely."

"I was told that even she had not set eyes on any one of them before the fortnight prior."

"And she never mentioned their names to you?"

"Not a sausage."

Elizabeth opened her handbag and extracted the poem. "When did she write this?"

The elder woman sighed. "It was no more than two days prior to that sad day. She came to me looking as giddy as a school girl and announced that she'd found her people. That's what she called them, 'her people'." A puff of air burst from her lips. "You can imagine my confusion when she placed that document in my very own hands. I thought it dark and strange, to be sure, but how was I to know it was a suicide note?"

"Did you show it to anyone in the family?"

She nodded. "After she and the others were discovered, I took it to her husband straight away, but he would have none of it. He refused to even read the thing. I might have pressed him, but what would be the good of it? The deed was done. She was in the arms of the Lord and it was His task to judge her."

"Where is she buried?"

Another sigh. "Who's to know? I always assumed her family took her back to Belgium, but among our people not another word was ever spoken about her. I made inquiries, to be sure, but they acted as though she never existed." She leaned close, and whispered, "I heard they burned all her things, like she had been the carrier of a contagious disease. I must say, I've never seen the like, either before or since."

Shaking her head, Elizabeth held up the poem and read,

I have to wonder if ever I'll see
The world from which I came.
The arms of Death will hold me here
And drive my soul insane.

"Is it possible she was referring to her home in Belgium? Did she ever go back while she was alive?"

Mistress Peterson nodded. "Just once, if I recall. It was a short time after her marriage, and she had a grand time. Unfortunately, her husband found the place quite unsuitable and its people disagreeable. 'Too much like the Frogs,' he'd say. He gave her the choice of staying in Belgium or coming back with him. She returned to England, and to my knowledge, never saw her family again."

So why then does He hold me so
And deny me what I long?
I beg Him please to set me free
For here I'll ne'er belong.

"I think she saw her husband as the devil," Mistress Peterson observed. "She wanted to be with her family and he wouldn't allow it. Is it any wonder she topped herself?"

"Oh my!" Elizabeth sighed. "Such a tragedy." She stared at her hostess for a moment before another thought occurred to her. "You don't imagine there might have been a sixth person. Someone who did them in and then escaped the scene?"

The elder woman shook her head slowly. "No, dear. There's little chance of that."

"Why would you think so?"

Rising slowly, the elder woman moved to a small writing desk behind her chair. Pulling a key from a pocket in her dress, she opened a drawer and scooped out the contents. Returning to Elizabeth, she held out a hand expectantly.

"I had planned to keep this bit to myself," she announced, "but if you are to make sense of what happened, you should know all of it."

Unsure what was expected of her, Elizabeth hesitated before cupping both hands together and holding them under her host's. She gasped when a small crystal vial thumped into her open palms, but quickly held it up to look at the white powder within.

"What is it?"

Returning to her chair, Mistress Peterson plopped down with a loud sigh. "It's what they used."

The sudden realization of what she was holding made Elizabeth suck in a breath and hold it as she examined the vial again.

"She gave you this?" Elizabeth asked. "You knew about her plans?"

Mistress Peterson scowled. "It was delivered in the post the day after the deed was done" She stabbed a shaking finger at the vial. "She left instructions that when you were old enough to understand, I was to deliver it to you along with this."

Elizabeth had not noticed the piece of paper in Mistress Peterson's other hand until she held it out to her. Feeling a distressing surge of nervous energy, she rose from her chair to take it.

Her mind awash with confusion, she froze with the vial in one hand and the note in the other.

"Put the bottle down, dear," Mistress Peterson insisted. "You must read what she has written. I am sorry to say, you may find it unsettling."

As she slowly lowered herself back into her chair, Elizabeth sat the vial on the coffee table between them and unfolded the paper.

Dearest Elizabeth,

The English I speak poorly still, I think, but this I must write for you. We are from a place much different, you and I. A place without the limits we find here. As I say in the poem, you must find others like us. Very possible they are nearby already, and it is only for you to open your mind to them.

Do not have fear, mon petit. When the time is right, you will know, and then you must gather together your people, and mix in wine the contents of this vial. It will take you on the adventure grand, and it will be magnifique!

Farewell, my belle arrière-petite-fille.

I will always love you,

Margarette

Her mouth open, she slowly lowered the note and gawked at her host.

"She wishes for me to kill myself?"

The elder woman nodded slowly. "But only if four other people will do the deed with you."

"This is preposterous!"

Mistress Peterson reached over and patted her guest's arm. "Now don't trouble yourself, my dear. I am certain you will not be as foolish as your great grandmamma."

"No," Elizabeth said slowly, her eyes fixed on the vial, her heart aching as though it held a great secret that only she could understand.

Ridiculous! she thought angrily as she jerked her eyes from the vial to her hostess.

"Most certainly not."

Chapter 17

"My God," Jasmina cried as I stood on her back porch and shivered like a newborn kitten. "You're soaking wet!"

I was at a loss as to how I should respond.

What am I doing here?

For as long as I could remember, my mother had lumped mediums with fakes, con men, drug addicts, atheists, and minions of the devil. It was hard to go against a lifetime of teaching, even when the actual truth was chasing me around town. I just knew Mom had to be wrong, because at this moment, Jasmina seemed to be the only person who could help me.

"I'm in a real fix, and don't know where else to turn."

"Come in! Come In!" she insisted as she jumped back and waved me into the house. "Just a minute," she added as I closed the door. "I'll get you something to dry off with."

She returned a moment later with a large towel, and a concerned expression. "What happened?"

"He's here," I gasped while looking at my shaking hands. "He's totally here."

"Sorry?"

Taking the offered towel, I gave my hair a quick rub.

"You remember my past life as a woman?"

I looked up to see the light of recollection flash in her eyes. "*He's* here? Now?"

There is no way to explain the sudden relief I felt when she didn't laugh in my face.

I jerked a nod. "He's a woman now, but it's totally him."

"How do you know?"

"She told me about the dog, and even described it."

"Oh my. We need to think this through." She started to lead me into her office, but stopped and turned back. "Where's Remmy?"

The question threw me into a panic again, but all I could do was shake my head.

"We were together downtown when the woman approached me, but got separated."

Jasmina looked out the window beside the back door as though expecting to see her niece coming up the driveway. "You don't suppose she has her, do you?"

I looked as well, and my chest constricted when I didn't see her. "I don't think so," I answered unconvincingly while groping in my pocket for the cell phone. "The woman chased *me* to the park."

I didn't breathe until Remmy picked up on the third ring. "Where are you?"

"Where are *you*?" she snapped back angrily. "I've got your stupid backpack and the thing weighs a ton."

I wanted to sprint out the door to find her, but was stopped by the thought that Elissa was also out there looking for me.

"I'm at your aunt's. Come here and I'll fill you in."

"How did you…? Shit! Don't, like, start anything until I get there. I'm two minutes away."

"Start anything? What?"

"Just wait! OK?"

I nodded before realizing she couldn't see me. "Watch out for that woman. She's still out there."

"Right."

After the connection went dead, I turned to Jasmina. "She's fine. She'll be here in a couple of minutes."

"So tell me what happened."

I filled her in on events since our last meeting. When I got to the part about the Rottweiler chasing the woman away, she gave a low whistle.

"Beauregard must have been the name of the dog in your past life," she nearly whispered. "He's still watching your back."

"A dog? How can that be?"

Smiling knowingly, Jasmina shook her head. "This is an intelligent spirit and he or she is devoutly loyal to you."

"Enough to follow me through several lifetimes?"

"Your evil husband did. Why couldn't someone else?"

For a long moment, my mind refused to process her statement.

"So what does this mean? Why would he be haunting me?"

Jasmina shrugged. "I don't quite know, but it's a real game changer."

"Huh?"

Taking my arm, she moved me into her office and sat me on a bench near the door.

"I'll get you some dry clothes and then we can talk this through," she announced and started to leave the room.

"Wait," I cried while pushing myself up. "What do you do about something like this?"

Her back to me, Jasmina stopped and it was a long moment before she turned back to me.

"I'll be honest with you, this is something new. Lots of people make connections with their past lives, and some are even able to communicate with them, most often through people like me." She moved back to me and put a hand on my arm. "I've never had someone from the past actually chase another person through time. As far as I know, no one has."

"So how do we deal with it?"

Shaking her head, she stepped back. "I guess we take it one step at a time and see how it goes?"

I wanted to scream, and it took all my self-control to keep from doing so. "But she might be here to kill me."

Jasmina nodded. "Then we need a plan, and it better be a good one."

Chapter 18

Early morning sunlight flooded through the dining room's tall windows as Elizabeth entered. She was surprised to find Phillip reading the Times, but not to see him jerk the paper up to completely cover his face. Even so, the move made her stomach ache. It had been two days since the attack on the lawn, and he had not spoken to her once. Of course, her concern was also tinged with a sense of relief. If he was not speaking to her, he was also not beating her.

"Good morning," she announced cheerfully, more for the maid than her husband.

"Good morning, Mistress," Tilley said with a curtsey. "Cook will have toast up shortly. Will you be having your coffee now?"

Without looking at her silent husband, Elizabeth moved to her place at the table and nodded. "Yes. That will be fine."

As the girl poured coffee, Elizabeth forced down her irritation, pulled out her chair, and sat, saying, "Have William make the carriage ready, will you? I am off to London to find an outfit suitable for Lord and Lady Argyle's cotillion ball."

"Yes, Mistress," Tilley said while returning the coffee pot to the warmer.

Without lowering the newspaper, Phillip announced, "That will not be necessary, Tilley."

The fact that he spoke at all made both women turn toward him.

"I beg your pardon?" Elizabeth asked.

He shook the paper. "Tell your mistress we shall not be attending."

When Tilley looked as though she would have a seizure, Elizabeth said, "But this is the height of the season, and Lady Argyle is a dear friend. We simply cannot miss it."

"And yet we shall," he stated before folding up his paper and rising without looking at her.

The two women stared at him as he turned and left the room. It wasn't until Elizabeth heard his footsteps echoing in the hallway that she pushed back her chair and rose. Her mind a confusing jumble, she had no idea what she would do as she hurried from the dining room, but found sudden clarity upon seeing him vanish into the library. A flash of anger made her face warm while she marched after him, intentionally clomping her heels on the hallway floor so he would hear her coming.

When she reached the library door, he rushed out to confront her.

"What do you want now?"

Uncomfortable with their closeness, she stopped and took two steps back. "How can you be so cruel?"

"It is you who insists on dragging me to these wretched affairs so you can display your beauty beside my grotesqueness. I am done with it."

"Then I shall go alone."

"You will not!"

"But you can't possibly..."

"I can, and shall."

Confused and frustrated to the point of tears, Elizabeth was still struggling to think of a response when he stepped back into the library and slammed the door. Enraged by his rude behavior, she reached for the knob, but was stopped by the sound of a key turning in the lock.

Tears streaming down her cheeks, she pressed her hands flat against the door and stared blindly at its dark surface. Time lost meaning as she waffled between pleading through the door, or simply giving in and allowing him humiliate her.

She was trapped in that unending mental loop until she heard Tilley ask, "Is...is everything alright, Mistress?"

Jerking around to face her maid, she blinked twice in a vain attempt to clear her vision, but more tears flooded in to replace those running down her cheeks.

Shaking her head, she blurted, "Yes, Tilley," and marched past her toward the stairs.

If living with a monster is in any way "alright".

Chapter 19

"I'm not sure I fully get what's happening," I said to Remmy as we walked to my house. "It's hard to believe that some ghost from my unknown past is haunting me."

"It's not a ghost. It's the soul of someone you knew in a past life, but unlike a ghost, this person is in a real body and can be dangerous."

Much as I wanted to believe what she was telling me, a lifetime of indoctrination by my devotedly Christian mother could not be swept away just because some stranger mentioned the same dog I saw in a daydream. There had to be a connection I wasn't seeing, but as I tried to make sense of it, the whole thing seemed embarrassingly stupid.

"I was a dork for being afraid of that woman. It's not like she did anything to threaten me."

"What if she had a gun?"

"I didn't see one, and she didn't say she had one. She just said she wanted to talk. I don't understand why I ran." I shook my head again. "The next time I see her, I'm going to ask what she wants."

Remmy scowled at me. "Bad idea! You heard what Jasmina said about your abusive husband. She might..."

Remmy started across the street, but I was suddenly overwhelmed with the feeling that someone was behind me. Stopping at the curb, I looked back to see a shadowy figure peeking out from behind a tall bush at the end of the block.

"It's her."

"Gerry? No!" Remmy cried as I started jogging toward her. "You don't know what she'll do."

"Not until I confront her," I grumbled before pointing at the person and shouting, "Hey! Wait right there."

When the figure disappeared behind the bush, I broke into a run, but by the time I reached the corner, she was climbing into a Jeep

Wrangler. Tires squealed and the vehicle lurched out from between two parked cars. Without even thinking, I ran into the narrow street, waving both hands over my head.

"Stop!"

Elissa's eyes were wide, lips moving as her left hand waved me out of the way. I wanted to dive for the sidewalk, but couldn't make myself move. My whole body tensed for the impact, but at the last second the car swerved into a driveway, turning so sharply the rear end slid around and hit me.

The impact sent me flying, and I landed on my back in the middle of the street as the Wrangler tore across someone's lawn.

"You could have been killed!" Remmy wailed as I lay on the hard pavement, and listened to the vehicle accelerate.

Shaking my head, I held up my hands to inspect the damage they had suffered when I hit the pavement.

"I don't get it," I groaned as my girlfriend's pounding feet pulled my attention to her. "She goes to all the trouble of tracking me down, chases me across town, and then runs when I try to approach her?"

The scowling Remmy glared at me. "You totally don't get it, do you? Abusers are all about control. Your running after her must have, like, shaken her confidence."

"But why me?"

"Listen," she snapped before grabbing my hand to help me up. "Get it through your thick head that this woman is a nutter. She'll act sane one moment and do, like, unspeakable things the next. You totally have to stay away from her."

"Easier said than done," I said while leaning against her. "Up until now, she was chasing *me*, remember?"

Chapter 20

"I have changed my mind," Phillip said softly from the open door of the sitting room.

Elizabeth jerked in surprise, nearly dropping her copy of *A House-Boat on the Styx* as she turned to face him.

"I beg your pardon?" she asked because she was too flustered to think of anything else.

"You should attend Lord and Lady Argyle's cotillion," he responded before pushing off the door frame and turning away from her. "There is no reason for both of us to stay at home and be miserable."

Still stunned by his pronouncement, she gaped at him until he took one step out of the room then hesitated, as though waiting for her to respond to his last statement.

Recovering her wits, she stood and moved toward him, her rose-colored skirts rustling as she quickly stepped around a small table, nearly knocking over an ornately framed picture of her parents.

"You should attend as well," she insisted. "Many of your friends will be there, surely. You will have a grand time."

Turning back toward her, he tapped his chin, looking uncharacteristically pensive. "That would be unwise. I shall only be a hindrance to you."

Though the thought of being free of him for an entire evening excited her, she dutifully suppressed the feeling, and gave her head a shake.

"Nonsense. An outing would do us both a world of good."

He initially scowled, but then surprised her by showing the hint of a smile. "You know, you may jolly well be right. Am I correct in assuming we are to come in costume?"

"Why, yes. It will be an All-Hollows-Eve theme with a bonfire and dancing. What would you come as?"

He rubbed the good side of his face for a moment before answering.

"A pirate, I should think."

"Excellent. I very much look forward to..."

She stopped when he abruptly turned and walked away.

Stunned by this change in her situation, she started to walk back to the settee then stopped and turned to look again at where Phillip had been.

Am I dreaming this?

In a daze, she moved slowly around the room until she bumped into a chair. The impact snapped her out of the fog and made her realize she was clutching the book to her chest. After a brief moment of confusion, she took a deep breath to collect herself, put the book on a side table, and left the room, only to find the hallway empty.

"Where could he have…"

Her question was interrupted by the sound of a crystal decanter stopper dropping into place. She hurried toward the library, her chest aching out of fear that she had only imagined his sudden change of heart. Somewhat breathless when she reached the doorway, she stopped and looked inside to see him standing in front of the fireplace, a drink in one hand, poker in the other.

"Would you mind if I take the train to London tomorrow and do some shopping?" she asked when he turned to watch her enter.

"A splendid idea," he responded cheerily. "For what time should William prepare the carriage?"

Still flustered by this sudden turn of events, she watched him stoke the fire for a moment before responding. "If we leave by ten, I shall just catch the eleven-o-five and return on the five-fifteen."

"I will see to it then," he said before downing the contents of his drink.

She stared openmouthed as he lowered the glass, walked to a long cord next to the fireplace, and gave it three tugs.

"If I may ask. What made you change your…"

"Will Colonel Struthers be accompanying you to London, do you think?" he interrupted with a forced casualness that immediately angered her.

"No. Whatever for?"

Phillip shook his head. "No reason."

"If you mean to imply that Colonel..."

She stopped at the sound of Jason's footsteps in the hall. Turning as he entered, she saw his eyes stop on her for a brief moment before he turned toward Phillip and asked, "Sir?"

Phillip waved a hand in his wife's direction. "Your mistress will have need of the carriage at ten tomorrow morning. She is to catch the London train."

Though she kept her attention on her husband, from the corner of her eye, Elizabeth could see Jason bow slightly. "I shall see to it, Sir."

Without another word, Phillip turned to pour another drink, leaving the butler looking uncomfortable. Elizabeth had noticed that since she had fallen off the roof, both her servants had been more protective of her, but regardless of their feelings, their lowly positions left them unable to do much to help her. Her husband's reversal in mood must have been as puzzling to Jason as it was to her.

Is he expecting Phillip to have another outburst?

When it looked like Jason was not going to leave without being dismissed, Elizabeth said,

"Thank you, Jason. That will be all."

Jason's eyes flicked to her briefly before he bowed slightly and said, "Yes, Madam."

When she was sure he was out of earshot, she faced her husband again, unhappy to see his back was still toward her.

"Phillip. If you think I am having an..."

"Are you getting what you wanted?" he interrupted without looking at her.

His question took her by surprise. "Why...yes, but I do not think..."

"Then why must we argue?"

"We are not arguing about the..."

She stopped abruptly when he turned toward her, his face taught.

"Is it so difficult to be civil to me?" he asked, his level tone contradicting the anger in his eye.

Fear stopped her mind for a moment before she responded, "N...no."

He turned away again. "Then let us make the most of this situation."

She took that as a dismissal, but as she started to turn away, a sense of dread made her stop.

"Phillip. I have always been a faithful wife to you."

His back still to her, he took a drink before responding, "I have never doubted you, my dear."

The absurdity of his statement made her struggle to suppress a derisive laugh, knowing what it would cost her. The resulting confusion in her mind pushed away any appropriate response. When he continued to stand with drink in hand and his back to her, she gave up and moved down the hall, hearing the decanter stopper clatter onto its tray, followed by the clink of crystal against crystal.

Briefly closing her eyes, she slowed her pace and willed herself not to give him the satisfaction of hearing her run away because he would know for certain he had made her cry.

Upon reaching the stairs, she stopped, daubed her eyes with a lace hanky, and looked back. It was then she realized something different in him. Though Phillip liked to drink, he rarely gulped down his liquor, choosing instead to sip and enjoy the flavor. Yet he had finished one drink and was pouring another during the short time they were talking.

That is not like him.

She pulled back from the stairs and turned toward the library when another thought stopped her.

He used Colonel Struthers to stop me from asking why he changed his mind.

Feeling suddenly alarmed, she began to question the wisdom of leaving the house for the day to go shopping.

What is he up to?

She took two steps toward the library, but stopped when she remembered another of Phillip's statements.

Is it so difficult to be civil to me?

Her shoulders sagging, she realized he had drawn a line she could not cross. Any challenges to his reasoning would be taken as an attack on him, and his reprisal, whether against her or Beauregard, would be blamed on her.

Frustrated to the point of tears, she clenched her fists and turned back to the stairs, pausing again at the bottom to look back one last time.

"It must be to do with Beauregard," she muttered angrily. "He wishes to take him from me."

She froze in place for a long moment before taking a deep breath and starting to climb.

"We shall see about that!"

Chapter 21

Beauregard!

I woke with a start, disoriented and sucking in air until I realized I was in my own bedroom. The street light's faint yellow-green glow illuminated my brother as he lay askew of his bed, his head half-hanging over the near side, feet poking out the other, and disheveled covers intertwined with his chunky frame. The fact that he was still asleep meant I had not been screaming, but my hard breathing was proof that demons still haunted me.

Looking quickly toward the bedroom door, I felt a flash of guilt because though I promised Remmy I would tell my parents everything, I had not. My mother's religious beliefs left zero room for past lives or haunting evil spirits, and I had no energy for the fight it would bring on.

"When is this going to end?" I gasped while wiping sweat from my forehead.

My eyes swept to the nightstand where "2:23 AM" glowed in angry red on the clock's face. Groaning, I clamped my lids down tight and tried to go back to sleep, but after my tenth peek showed it was still only 2:43, I slipped from bed and quietly dressed.

Finding the hall outside my room empty, with no tell-tale light coming from my parent's room, I tippy toed over the squeaky hardwood floor to the living room, still unsure of what I was going to do. It wasn't until I reached for the light switch that I saw something glowing across the street.

"What would someone be doing...?" I gasped, my lungs freezing as I left the light switch untouched and moved to the living room's picture window to peek out the partly closed curtains.

Though the car was across the street, it was close enough for me to recognize the occupant's anorexic frame. It didn't matter that the face was too shadowed to see her steel-blue eyes. I still imagined them staring at me, her distorted mind calculating the many ways she would cut me into tiny pieces, and feed me to...

"Son?" my father called as light flooded the room.

Momentarily blinded, I threw a hand up to shade my eyes, and cried out in protest,

"Dad!"

"What *are* you doing?" he asked as though he caught me flashing the neighbors.

"Someone is watching us from the street."

"Where?"

I was pulling the curtain back when the sound of a revving engine reverberated through the glass.

"There she goes!" I exclaimed while pointing at the streak of light accelerating across our view.

"Who is that?"

Letting go of the curtain, I faced him and tried my best to think of a story that would keep the concept of past-lives out of the conversation. It is hard for me to lie, especially to my parents, but I had to try.

"Some crazy lady has been following me."

"What? Why haven't you told us about this?"

I tried to shrug casually, as though it wasn't a big deal. "I think she's harmless, but she seems to have a thing for me."

"Do you know she is?"

"She says her name is Elissa Grant. She first showed up when Remmy and I were eating at Hamburger Hutch. She acted like she knew me, but it freaked Remmy out so we took off."

"*First* showed up? You mean you've seen her since?"

I nodded. "Yeah. In Bush Park."

"And she was after you? You're certain?"

I felt a flash of irritation, but it was tempered by the fact that I couldn't tell him the whole story.

"I'm totally sure. She asked for me by name."

"But why?"

I couldn't think of an answer, so I just shook my head and shrugged again.

"Now that's creepy," he said while moving over to snatch up the kitchen phone. "I'm calling the police."

Not good!

"Do you really think that's necessary?" I asked lamely, my mind racing to think of a reason to stop him. "I mean, she hasn't done anything except try to talk to me. What am I going to tell them?"

"You don't know what might be going on in a pervert's mind. Best to let the cops sort it out after they've picked her up."

Unable to think of an un-lame response except to shrug again, I dropped into a nearby chair and watched him dial 911. When the operator answer, he turned away and spoke softly into the receiver. After a few minutes, he put the handset back into the charger.

"They'll send someone out later this morning," he said. "In the meantime, you're not leaving the house alone."

My mind reeling, I pushed myself out of the chair and pulled the curtain back again. "What can the cops do? It's not like she..."

Movement outside stopped my declaration, but before I could react, the window exploded inward, engulfing me in a spray of glass. I threw up my hands to block it, but something heavy slammed my arms and my feet went out from under me. I howled as pain exploded in my hands, forearms, and face, but that was cut off when I hammered the floor.

You know how they say you can't hear yourself snore? Well it must also apply to screaming too because though my vocal chords were vibrating, all I could hear was Dad's bellowing while I pushed something heavy off my chest. The action intensified the pain, and as the object clunked to the floor, I instinctively pulled a piece of glass from my arm and held it up. The sight of my own blood dripping off that shard made me gag, and I quickly let the glass slip from my fingers. It was only then I realized Mom had added her screams to Dad's bellowing, and then Matt's unique soprano joined the uproar.

The neighbors must have called the ambulance, because we were too busy screaming.

Chapter 22

"William?"

Immediately recognizing the voice, William leaned his pitchfork against the wall of the stall he was cleaning and hurried out to see Elizabeth standing in the entrance to the stables. As he drew near, he could see she was smiling. The sight made him self-conscious, and he quickly rubbed his mop of brown hair, appalled to see chaff flying away from his head.

"Yes, Ma'am."

"I would ask a favour of you."

"Anything, Ma'am."

"I will be away most of the morrow and do not wish Beauregard to be a bother for your master."

"Do not worry yourself, Ma'am. I be 'appy fer the chance to care for 'im."

She looked around warily. "Your master may wish to go riding, and I wouldn't want…"

Fully understanding, he took a quick look around as well before nodding eagerly. "You wants me ta stash 'im someplace safe?"

She nodded. "Only until I return in the evening."

Hardly able to contain his smile, William nodded again. "I knows just the place fer 'im, Ma'am. Master Beauregard won't come to no 'arm while in my care."

"I am sure he will not."

"You can depend on it, Ma'am."

She looked around again. "And if the master were to inquire, we have been discussing the carriage."

William winked. "I'll 'ave it fer ya at the stroke of ten, Ma'am."

He felt a sense of gratification when his mistress smiled. "Thank you, William."

Leaning against the stable door, he watched as she returned to the house, walking as gracefully as any woman he had ever seen. There was no question in his mind that a relationship with her was impossible, even laughable, but that did not stop him from fantasizing about being alone with her, wrapping his arms around…

The hand on his shoulder shocked him like a bolt of lightning, but he received an even bigger surprise when he jerked around.

"Master Phillip," he cried while taking two quick steps back. "Ya startled me, sure."

Scowling, Phillip held up a hand, palm out. "Not so loud, William. It would not do for your mistress to hear."

His face warm, William gulped in a deep breath and struggled to fight the panic constricting his chest. Unsure as to how much the master knew, he had no choice but to play dumb.

"Sir?"

"What is it your mistress wanted?"

His heart thumping loudly in his ears, it took William a moment to remember what he was supposed to say.

"She…uh…were asking after the carriage, Sir. She wanted to make sure I had it cleaned off before we left in the morning."

William could feel a trickle of sweat running down the side of his face, and was relieved to see Phillip's attention was on his departing wife.

"I have a bit of a surprise planned for her," he explained conspiratorially. "And I need your help."

"'ow can I be of service, Sir?"

Phillip's attention returned to his stableman. "Your mistress' dog is a bit mangy, and needs a good washing."

"A bath fer a dog?"

His master nodded. "It is done in all the finest houses."

His knees weak with relief, William bit his lip for a moment before doing his best to smile convincingly. "Well then, Sir, I reckon it couldn't do no 'arm fer Mister Beauregard to 'ave one as well. I'll get right on it after I deliver the mistress to the station."

Phillip's head shook slowly. "Not to worry. Just clear out the space in front of the last stall. After she leaves tomorrow morning, I will bring the dog out here, and someone will collect him."

"Collect 'im, Sir?"

William jerked with surprise when his master barked a laugh. "It is not enough to simply pour water over the beast and rub him down. Special soaps must be used, and scented oils applied."

The stable boy shook his head. "If you say so, Sir.

Holding a single finger in front of his scarred lips, Phillip whispered, "Not a word to anyone, hear?"

Feeling confused and embarrassed, William struggled to keep himself from looking at the manor house. "No, Sir. Not a word."

Though Phillip seemed to be smiling, William was never sure because the scarred side of his face distorted it so badly.

"Grand! Your mistress will be thrilled beyond all reason."

William watched as his master turned and headed toward the back of the barn. After exiting the building, Phillip slipped behind a hedge and disappeared from sight, but William knew the path lead to an extensive garden at the back of the house, making it appear to anyone inside that Phillip had been nowhere near the stables.

"No good is gonna come of this," he muttered while moving back to the stall he had been working in. "An' you're smack in the middle of it, Lad."

Chapter 23

"Ohmygod! Ohmygod! Ohmygod!" Remmy cried, her hysteria palpable even before she popped through the curtain surrounding my bed in the emergency room.

Stopping just short of me, she held both hands over her mouth, a half whine, half moan filling the air as her bulging eyes scanned the various bandages covering my arms and face.

"I can't believe this!"

I only knew my head was shaking because it hurt.

"It was that lady. I thought she drove off, but just after Dad called the cops, a honking-big wrench came through our picture window."

Looking somewhat surprised, she flicked her eyes from my face to the bandages and back before asking, "That lady at the restaurant? Are you sure?"

"Who else could it have been?"

"Yeah, but she...I mean, she didn't..." She gave her head a sharp shake before clinching both fists in front of her chest and crying, "Oh My God! She could have killed you."

Pain kept me from shrugging. "Why did that window break into such large pieces?"

"It's an old house," Dad explained. "It was probably put in before regulations required safety glass."

"Well, it should have, like, been totally replaced before now," Remmy stated angrily.

Looking guilty, Dad shook his head. "I never even thought about it. Who does?"

"Mister Patterson?"

We all turned to see a police officer standing in the curtain opening, holding a clipboard with both hands.

"Yes? I'm Alvin Patterson."

"The nurse tells me your son is going to be OK. I'm glad to hear it."

Dad's eyes closed as he nodded. "Thank you. Did you find anything?"

"No fingerprints on the wrench. Was it yours?"

"Never seen it before."

"Any idea who would do something like this?"

Rather than respond, Dad looked at me, and I told the officer as much about Elissa as I dared.

"Why would she drive away and then stop to throw something through your window?" he asked.

I shrugged. "I don't get it either, but she's been weird since I first met her."

He looked from me to Dad and back. "Did either of you actually see this woman throw the wrench?"

I carefully shook my head. "It was dark outside. All I saw was some motion before the window exploded in on me."

"Who else could it be?" Dad asked. "This woman has been stalking my son."

The officer shrugged. "That is what we hope to find out, Sir."

"What else can we do to help?"

"Any idea where she's from?"

I felt a twinge of guilt as I shook my head, frustrated that I couldn't really explain what was going on. Instead, I gave him a description and answered a few more questions before he lowered the clipboard and excused himself.

Dad stared out through the gap in the curtain for a moment before turning back to me.

"Why didn't you mention the nightmares?"

"What for? I don't remember anything about them, and they started before I met the woman."

I didn't consider the daydreams to be nightmares, so I wasn't lying...technically.

"Are you sure?"

OK, I lied. Daydreams are pretty much the same as nightmares, but being called out on it pissed me off.

"What difference does it make? He's not investigating my sleep problems. He just wants to know who threw a honking big wrench through our living room window. Can we go home now?"

Dad stared at me for a long moment before shrugging. "I'll see if I can find the doctor."

It wasn't until after he left that I realized Remmy had moved to a chair on my left, towards the head of the bed.

"You OK?" I asked while carefully turning to see her sitting rigidly, her eyes on the floor.

After jerking a nod, she pushed out of the chair and took my hand.

"This is totally my fault," she whispered. "I should never have introduced you to Jasmina."

"What does she have to do with this crazy lady?"

"If we hadn't confused things with this past-lives stuff you might have gone to the cops sooner."

"That's nuts. I still had nothing to tell them. She only said hello. Is that a crime?"

Jerking back, she glared at me. "How can you defend her? She, like, tried to kill you."

I held up my bandaged arms. "I'm totally not defending her. I want her arrested as much as anyone, but who knew she'd do something like this?"

Remmy slapped her hands over her cheeks and started to cry. I reached out and touched her arm, but my injuries stopped me from pulling her into a hug.

"They'll catch her and this will all be over soon."

"And what if they don't?"

I sighed. "Dad wants me to stay with his sister in Keizer until she's caught."

"Bad idea," Remmy exclaimed. "You, like, need to stay here so we can catch her and kill her."

Her statement took me by surprise.

"Listen. I want to see her put in jail, but we don't need to off her just because she trashed our front window."

Remmy's eyes went wide. "You're not taking this seriously!"

I lifted my arms again. "How is that possible? I'm totally covered in bandages."

Surprisingly, my declaration seemed to calm her, and after I lowered my arms, the smile I've always loved returned.

"You're right," she said before taking my hand again. "A little time away from here might, like, do you a world of good."

"They're finishing the paperwork right now," Dad announced as he pushed through the curtain. "Your mother is at the house packing your things. We'll get your medicines and then pick her up on our way to Aunt Susan's."

"In Nehalem? That's over a hundred miles from here. I thought I was staying in Keizer. What about school?"

"Keizer doesn't seem far enough away. I'm sure it won't be for that long."

Remmy held up a hand. "Jamie's taking the same classes as you are. I'll get your assignments from him and send them to you."

I looked from her to Dad. "And you'll both let me know what the police come up with?"

They nodded eagerly.

"Just rest up and heal," Remmy said as she squeezed my hand.

Dad barked a laugh. "His aunt won't let him do otherwise."

Chapter 24

Looking into her dressing-table's mirror, Elizabeth watched Tilley fuss with the leg-of-mutton sleeves ballooning out from the top of her shoulders down to her elbows. Taking her eyes off the maid, she snapped the clasp of the wide belt around her narrow waist before admiring the smooth green-and-white skirt as it flared out to completely cover her feet.

She had not noticed Tilley moving away, and was mildly surprised when she returned with a pair of white, elbow-length gloves.

"You'll be the prettiest woman ever they saw, Mistress," the girl gushed.

As she pulled the gloves on, Elizabeth shook her head. "I wish Phillip would permit me to wear a tailor-made suit for these outings. They are so much more convenient. "

"Oh no, Mistress. That would simply not do. "

"I don't care if men see them as unladylike. Why must we women always give in to them? "

When Tilley did not respond, Elizabeth released a heavy sigh and looked at her maid.

"Then bring my hat and let us be on our way."

"Yes, Mistress!"

Despite her protests over the limits of her wardrobe, the dress made her feel almost like royalty. Her spirits soaring, she pinned on a bonnet festooned with flowers and a large white feather. With a sense of anticipation, she hurried to the room's door, but stopped when she heard Beauregard's nails tick-tacking on the floor.

She motioned for the dog to sit before turning to Tilley.

"William is to take Beauregard to the barn as soon as he returns," she insisted before adding lamely, "The master does not approve of him wandering the house alone."

The maid's scowl made her feelings obvious, but Elizabeth knew the girl would not be so foolish as to voice them when there was a chance someone beside her mistress might hear.

"Yes, Mistress."

Opening the door, she was surprised to find Phillip standing just outside.

"Hello, Elizabeth," he said cheerfully. "You look utterly radiant this morning."

His presence and demeanor caught her off guard, but she quickly recovered. "Thank you. I look forward to my little outing. Are you certain there is nothing you wish for yourself?"

Smiling, he shook his head. "Only that you return safely home to us."

She felt herself gasp at his statement, but before she could respond, he jerked a nod and strolled away. Puzzled by his abrupt behavior, she stepped through the door, and turned to watch him disappear into his room without looking back.

"What is he...?"

"Madam," Jason announced as he reached the top of the stairs. "The carriage is ready."

In that instant she felt torn between the urge to investigate Phillip's sudden change in behavior, and the certain knowledge that confronting him would only lead to another row in front of the servants.

Is it so difficult to be civil to me?

The words hurt more than the most biting putdown. *Her* being uncivil with *him*?

"Yes, Jason," she finally responded, her eyes still on her husband's door. "I am coming now."

She turned to see her maid also staring at Phillip's door.

I must leave before I change my mind.

"Come, Tilley. We shall be late."

The flustered maid looked from her to the closed door and back. "Yes, Mistress."

Her two servants in front of her, Elizabeth started down, but after only two steps, she stopped to take one last look before shaking her head and continuing.

Chapter 25

I snapped awake, confused and disoriented until I looked out the car's window and realized we were halfway down the long driveway to Aunt Susan's pale-green house: a small A-frame structure, with large windows, T1-11 siding, and a composition roof. It seemed an inadequate defense against an invading hoard, even if that "hoard" was only one person. Strangely enough, despite the limitations of the house's design, the color had a calming effect on me.

As Dad parked the car next to her tan Volvo station wagon, my aunt appeared on her narrow stub of a front porch, her face awash with concern, arms wrapped tightly across her chest.

"Gerry," she cried as I carefully extracted myself from the car. "My God, it's worse than I thought."

Shaking my head I held up a wounded wing. "Not really. It's mostly a bunch of small cuts."

Rushing to me, her arms outstretched, she was preparing to give me her traditional bear-hug greeting when I pulled back just out of reach. She barked a self-conscious laugh and pulled her hands to her chest.

"Ohhh. That would hurt, wouldn't it?"

"Yeah," I responded, smiling weakly. "Pretty much."

She pressed her hands together and turned to Dad, her eyes wide as she bounced on the balls of her feet like a two-year-old waiting for a cookie.

"How could this happen, Alvin?"

Dad glanced back at the highway before pointing at the house. "Let's talk inside."

Seeming to understand, she jerked several quick nods. "Of course. Of course."

My whirlwind of an aunt snatched my bag, and ran up the porch steps with enough nervous energy to power a lighthouse. Though normally hyperactive, news of the attack had apparently ratcheted her up several notches, and I felt tired just watching her.

"Miriam told me about Gerry's stalker," she blurted after she closed the door behind us. "Is she the one who did this?"

Dad nodded. "Looks like it."

She turned to me, her eyes full of pity. "My poor nephew. Why would she do something like that?"

Almost believing the lie myself, I gingerly shook my head. "No idea."

"But surely a stalker would try to talk to you, wouldn't she?"

Dad shrugged. "She tried, but Gerry told her to go away." He turned to me. "Isn't that right, Son?"

I nodded mutely, afraid of saying too much. Unfortunately, my aunt continued to stare at me with expectant eyes.

"How did you meet her?"

I told her about the encounter at Hamburger Hutch, Elissa following me to the park, and the dog chasing her off, but not my visit with Jasmina.

"Why were you afraid of her?"

I felt my eyes widen as the panic came alive again, rising from my gut like a wild beast that clamped its claws around my lungs as its teeth gnawed my brain.

But I stood up to her, flashed in my mind, quelling some of the panic, but leaving enough to keep my gut tight as I shook my head.

"Not exactly sure," I exhaled after regaining the use of my lungs. "She just creeped me out."

The room went dead silent for a long moment before Aunt Susan took a deep breath and gently placed a hand on my back.

"Let's get you settled in," she said while guiding me to a chair in her small living/dining room. "Would you like something to eat?"

After I sucked in a breath of my own and eagerly nodded, she motioned for me to sit. As I did so, she gave Dad a concerned look. He was behind me, so I couldn't see his response, but considering the events of the last few hours, it couldn't have been any less serious.

Her expression brightening, she looked at me again, and said, "You stay here and I'll bring something out."

Dropping my bag, she grabbed Dad's arm, and hustled him into the kitchen. The sudden relief of not having someone watching over me, combined with the muffled voices in the kitchen made me realize how tired I was. I took a deep breath, closed my eyes, let it out, and was suddenly back at the Manor, climbing into a carriage. The butler was saying something I couldn't make out but I felt a sense of impending danger.

I was preparing to ask what was going on when I was snapped back to the present by my chirping cellphone. Though now wide awake, it still took some effort to extract the phone from my pants pocket.

"R U ther yet? :;:-)" Remmy's text appeared, along with her signature emoticon, which she calls the "winking face".

"jst arrived," I typed back.

"wen cn I c U?"

I wanted to respond with *Come right now!*, but knew it was a two-and-a-half-hour drive from Salem.

"Come dis satdy."

"rgr dat! :;:-)"

"Who was that?" Dad asked.

Turning to see him leaning through the kitchen doorway, I held up the phone as though it confirmed my response.

"Remmy's coming up on Saturday with my homework."

After moving further into the room, Dad nodded, but his presence irritated me, like I was on suicide watch and he couldn't leave me alone for a minute. Feeling hugely conflicted, I tucked the phone into my shirt pocket and pretended to get comfortable, all the while wanting to bolt and run.

"The cops should have that woman in custody before the weekend," he said with a self-conscious smile before waving a hand toward the kitchen. "I'll give your aunt a hand."

My head was so full of confusing thoughts, I could do little more than sink back into the chair and stare at the closed door until the microwave dinged. The sound of food being prepared made me realize how hungry I was, and brought my thoughts more into focus. Unfortunately, before I could begin to organize them, Aunt Susan appeared with a plate in one hand, and a glass of milk in the other. The delectable smell of sizzling bratwurst flushed away my irritation, despite my munching father being only a step behind her, his eyes on me even as he stopped at her small dining room table to set his plate among the many books, framed pictures, and knickknacks nearly blanketing its surface.

"Your favorite," Aunt Susan announced needlessly as I nearly drooled on my shirt.

Eagerly biting into the steaming sandwich, I was nearly overwhelmed by the heavenly sensation of sausage, onion, hot mustard, and relish exploding on my tongue.

"Tanks," I muttered through a full mouth.

"You are very welcome."

I was preparing to take a second bite when I looked up to see that Dad had moved up beside his sister and both of them were staring at me.

"Aren't you guys going to eat?"

Aunt Susan looked at Dad. "I ate just before you arrived, but you guys go ahead."

Moving back to the table, Dad picked up his plate and motioned for her to join him in the kitchen. She started to follow, but stopping at the door and turned back.

"If there's anything you need, just holler."

My mouth already filled with another bite, I jerked a nod, kept chewing, and listened to her chuckle as she pushed through.

I was licking mustard from my fingers when the cell chirped again.

"R U solo?"

"yeh. what's up?"

"i tnk she's wotchN me."

"no way! wher R U?"

"home, bt there's a weird car owtsd. i tnk it's her."

"call d cops!"

"w@ do i tel em?"

"Tell them she's the one who tried to kill me," I typed in unabbreviated form to make sure I wasn't misunderstood.

There was a long pause before she responded, "OK. I will."

I stared at the last message for a long moment before being brought out of my trance by the sound of laughing in the kitchen.

"Lt me know w@ dey sA."

I pressed send and waited anxiously for her response. When none came, I started to dial, but stopped when Aunt Susan pushed through the kitchen door.

Returning the phone to my shirt pocket, I turned toward her.

"Would you like another?" she asked.

Since I still had half a sandwich left, I started to shake my head, but turned it into a nod in the hope of keeping her busy long enough for me to make the call.

Before the kitchen door closed, I grabbed the phone and was punching in numbers when Dad came out, plate in hand.

"These are really good," he declared with such forced sincerity I wanted to gag.

Feeling overwhelmingly frustrated, I dropped the phone into to my pocket again, and nodded while angrily thinking, *Why don't you leave me alone?*

"Listen," he said while putting his plate on the table. "I know this is stressful, but the cops will catch this woman soon and things will return to normal."

My anger was replaced by fear when I realized how ridiculous his statement was.

Normal? How is that possible? Someone from my past life wants to kill me.

Seeing Dad peer at one of the many framed photos on the dining room table reminded me that Aunt Susan was the family historian, and that collection showed who our ancestors were. My past had become much more complicated, not only because I might have many other family histories to consider, but those people weren't staying dead.

With crystal-clear, terrifying clarity I realized that there was nothing Dad, Mom, Aunt Susan, or even the police could do to help.

Struggling to breathe, I grabbed my phone and hammered out another text to Remmy,

"on satdy, brng yr aunt Jasmina."

Chapter 26

"Beau is to go to the stables while I am away," Elizabeth instructed as Jason helped her into the carriage. "William will watch over him."

"He will be fine, Madam," he assured her while taking a small satchel from Tilley and hoisting it up to William in the driver's seat. "No harm will come to him."

Once seated, she turned to Jason. "I know, and thank the both of you for doing it."

"It is our job, Madam," he said while helping Tilley into the carriage. "We are only too happy to see to Master Beauregard's needs."

"Yes. Just the same." She turned to watch her maid seat herself before facing him again. "I have a disturbing sense of foreboding, and Beauregard is..."

When her voice trailed off, Jason nodded.

"Do not worry yourself another moment, Madam. He will be here to greet you upon your return."

She hesitated for a long moment before jerking a nod, at which point Jason closed the door, and stepped back to wave at William.

"Best hurry along now. It will not do for your mistress to miss her train."

Nodding, William slapped the reins to send the carriage down the drive.

Jason watched until the carriage turned onto the lane before moving to the side of the house to see two figures heading toward the stables. Beauregard was anxiously looking around for his mistress, but Phillip kept his eyes on his destination and a firm hand on the dog's collar.

Shaking his head, Jason hurried to the manor's front entrance, moved inside and carefully closed the massive ornate doors before quickstepping to the stairs leading down to the kitchen. At the bottom, he looked toward the servant's area on his right. Seeing no one, he turned left and ran to the end of the hall, swapping his polished shoes for rubber boots before pushing through the outside door. The oversized boots slapping the floor, he walked to the back stairs leading to ground level, and climbed until he could just see the stables. When Phillip reappeared, Jason moved back down the steps to watch his master limp briskly past him and enter the manor through a door on the main floor.

Hearing the door close, Jason rose again and looked around. Seeing no one else, he ran up the steps and jogged to the barn. The distance was thankfully short, and his breath caught when he found an anxious Beauregard tied next to the far stall.

Moving further in so he would not be seen from the house, he snorted derisively as the great hound wagged his entire body and whined.

"Washing a dog? That is as lame a tale as pigs floating on the breeze."

Chapter 27

A flaming arrow shattered against the rock wall near Phillip's head, its splintered remains stinging his cheek, and forcing him to duck. When he looked up again, light from the burning building behind him revealed dark shapes at the edge of the night. He knew that a few enemy warriors had crawled in close enough to fire their arrows, but the bulk of them were still waiting in the darkness, beyond the range of their rifles.

"Company at the ready," his sergeant cried.

Though Phillip already had a good grip on his heavy Martini-Henry rifle, he squeezed even tighter when a guttural roar from the oncoming shadows drowned out all other sounds.

"Load," the sergeant shouted.

As he complied, he was struck by the distinct sound of other levers being ratcheted down, and the cartridges shoved in before the levers snapped back into place. If he survived this battle, he doubted he would ever forget those sounds.

The dark shapes were now five-hundred yards away and running fast, the roar of their voices rising as they drew closer, their numbers so vast he could not even begin to count them.

When the Zulus reached a small rise in the ground, just four-hundred yards out, he heard the sergeant shout, "Fire!"

Aim. Fire. Eject. Load.

Aim. Fire. Eject. Load.

Aim. Fire. Eject, Load.

Phillip repeated the routine automatically, each time picking out a new target from the mass of charging bodies. He had no idea how many of the enemy he hit because all of his attention was focused on repeating the process again and again.

Firing, he ratcheted the rifle's lever down to eject the spent cartridge, this time noticing that the 45-caliber bullet hit a warrior's chest, knocking him off his feet. Even at two-hundred yards, the bullet had enough velocity to pass through the first attacker's body and embed itself in the skull of the man behind. Before either corpse struck the dusty ground, other black bodies were racing around them, their open mouths emitting a shrill war cry as they held their spears high.

The sight briefly unnerved him, and his mind stopped for half-a-second to process the bizarre spectacle. When the moment passed, he shoved in another cartridge, and pulled the lever back up. Unfortunately, his adrenaline-muddled mind did not notice that it resisted more this time than last. Pulling the rifle to eye level, he hardly felt the heat on his cheek as he pressed the gun's butt tight against his shoulder, aimed, and squeezed the trigger.

The confusion of battle, the overwhelming odds, and the impossibility of fighting black men in near-total darkness brought on an intense moment of exhilarating terror. It also produced a strange sense of clarity. He could hear men screaming, guns firing, and the crackling and popping of the building burning behind him.

As familiar with the rifle as he was with his own body, he yanked the lever down and did not have to look to know it had not gone far enough to eject the cartridge. His eyes on the charging Zulus, who were now within fifty yards, he tried again but the lever would not budge. When his third attempt failed, he jerked his eyes down to see the hot cartridge had not ejected.

"Damned hog!" he swore before he stabbed a finger into the breach, hardly feeling the hot metal singeing flesh as the tip of his digit barely hooked the end of the cartridge, but could not budge it. Movement at the top of his vision made him look up to see a screaming warrior shaking his spear and quickly closing the distance between them.

True to his training, Phillip did not panic, but instead leveled his weapon, yanked it back, and lunged forward, the movement throwing off his attacker's timing as Phillip's bayonet pierced the sweaty black chest. Letting out a dying grunt, the warrior released his spear and the weapon's momentum carried it forward to slam into Phillip's right shoulder, slicing through flesh and nerves, piercing his collarbone, and protruding out the back. Howling from the pain, Phillip let his rifle fall with his dying opponent and grabbed the spear shaft.

His fellow soldiers were fully engaged with the enemy now, and it was unlikely anyone noticed Phillip sinking to his knees or heard his cries. Pulling on the spear only made the pain worse, but he tried all the same until his vision cleared enough to see another warrior separate from the crowd, his large white eyes wide with excitement at the prospect of an easy kill. Too incapacitated to defend himself, Phillip watched helplessly as the man drew closer, his gritted teeth a ghoulish smile, legs pumping, white feathers flapping, spear held high.

His eyes locked on the attacker, Phillip tensed in anticipation of the coming blow. The warrior jerked his weapon up for the final thrust, but just as it was coming down, a rifle roared over Phillip's head and a large hole appeared in his enemy's forehead. The warrior went limp, but movement carried him forward to crash onto his intended victim.

Knocked backwards, and nearly delirious with pain, Phillip was struggling to push the dead weight off when a very distinct smell made his breath catch. Something cooled the skin on his right arm, making him twist his head around to see that the tip of the Zulu's spear had punctured a nearby kerosene can. Panic very briefly overcame the pain in his shoulder when he saw the volatile fluid wicking into the right side of his red jacket. He fought to move away from the source, but the body on top of him forced the spear's tip into the ground, and even a surge of fear-driven adrenaline could not counter the overwhelming agony that kept him trapped.

Muzzle flashes brightened the surrounding darkness only to be followed by the yellow streaks of burning black powder. A soldier above Phillip's head released volley after volley, his mind obviously so focused on the attacking Zulus he seemed unaware of the spilled kerosene.

Clamping his jaw against the pain, Phillip howled through gritted teeth as he desperately pushed at the body. His hand slipped on sweat-slicked skin as the corpse's bladder emptied onto his legs.

"Help me, damn you!" he screamed, but his voice blended uselessly into the din.

Having no other options, he continued screaming until someone appeared next to him.

"We'll get ya out'a there, gov," the soldier was saying as the heavy body was pushed off him.

A rifle discharged nearby, and Phillip felt a flash of heat. An instant later, his entire right side exploded in pain, making him jerk his head around to see flames rising from his coat. His savior slapped ineffectively at the fire with his hat, but was forced back by the heat.

He tried to roll over in a vain attempt at putting the fire out, but was stopped when the long spear shaft struck the ground. When he rolled onto his back, someone appeared over him, pressed a boot against his chest and yanked the spear out. He screamed, and continued screaming as searing flame bubbled his skin. A blanket dropped over him, but when it was pulled away he saw more black bodies rising up behind his saviors.

*   *   *

"Behind you!" she cried, throwing off covers as her body convulsed into a sitting position at the edge of the bed. Air hissing through clenched teeth, she gripped her right side in response to the remembered pain.

When the memory started to fade, she kicked off the remaining covers, pushed herself out of the bed, and stumbled through the dark room until her hip slammed the sharp corner of the bedside table.

"Damn!"

She grabbed the injured hip, but the movement threw her off balance and only a lucky grab of the offending table kept her from falling. Though she continued to lean on the table for support, she was now sobbing so hard she could barely breathe.

After regaining control, she flicked on the light and scanned the small room, blinking several times before realizing where she was.

"Gerry has to help us," she stated adamantly. "He has to!"

Pushing off the desk, she took another quick scan of the room before moving to the window to peer out.

"The time is right. Once I get her, he won't be able to say no."

Chapter 28

"Whoa," my aunt exclaimed as she looked at my empty plate. "You scarfed that right down."

I shrugged as the pleasing taste of bratwurst lingered on my tongue. "Guess I was hungry."

"If you'd like more, I'd be happy to get it for you."

Leaning back in the chair, I patted my full belly and shook my head. "I'm feeling really tired."

"Your room is ready," she said softly while waving a hand down the hallway. "Why don't you get some sleep?"

I felt guilty because I knew I should trust her and Dad enough to tell them what was really going on.

They won't understand. How could they?

I gave a sleepy nod, but knew even that was a half-truth and the conundrum threw me into a mental tizzy. My drained and sore body wanted sleep, but my mind was spinning erratically like a bipolar merry-go-round. I needed to be alone, but was certain there was no way I was going to sleep until I heard from Remmy.

After Dad and Aunt Susan escorted me to the room, I kicked off my shoes and sat on the bed. They watched from the doorway as I lay on top of the blankets and closed my eyes.

The next thing I knew, my cell was chirping and the room was dark.

"call me," displayed on the screen.

I sat up to discover that someone had put a blanket over me, but couldn't see anything because the room was pitch black. People who live in the country might be used to not having streetlights at night, but I found it disorienting until I saw a soft glow coming from under the room's door.

Fumbling in the darkness, I found the lamp, switched it on, and snatched up my phone to see it was after nine o'clock.

It's been five hours?

I tapped in Remmy's number and waited anxiously as it rang, feeling even more stressed when it went to voicemail.

"Yeah, it's me. Leave a message, or if it is important, text me."

"Remmy," I blurted. "This is Gerry. I just got your message. I'll send a text in case you don't get this."

I hung up and sent the promised text. When no response came back I started to panic. How would I get to her? I had no car, and the nearest taxi was probably in Tillamook, some thirty miles to the south.

I was trying to work out how to steal my aunt's car when my cell began playing Remmy's favorite tune. I almost dropped the darned thing as I struggled to answer it.

"Remmy?"

"You want to see your girlfriend again, do as I say."

The voice was low, but it sounded like a woman pretending to be a man, and there was little doubt in my mind who the woman was.

"OK, but I don't have a car."

"I'll meet you at the end of your aunt's driveway at midnight."

"How do you know where I am?"

"If I see cops, I'll dump her body in the river."

The sudden silence was like a vacuum, sucking the phone tighter to my ear, but when she said no more, I yanked it down to see, "Call disconnected" on the display. Panic overwhelmed me. My first impulse was to climb out the window and go after them. A bonehead idea because I had no clue as to where they were.

I started to throw back the covers, but was stopped by the sound of slippered feet in the hall. Turning off the lamp, I pulled the blanket over me and closed my eyes.

When light flooded in from the hallway, I tried to remain still, which is hard to do when every muscle in your body is crying for action. After a long pause, I heard a sad sigh and the door clicked shut.

When the footsteps continued on, I sucked in a breath, and looked at my phone. The display read, 9:15.

Midnight was a very long way away.

Chapter 29

Pushing back the sitting-room window's heavy curtains, Jason looked out as a small wagon pulled up to the barn. He shook his head when two disreputable-looking men in long, heavy coats jumped out and hurried inside. In less than a minute they reappeared carrying something large wrapped in a wool blanket, and Jason automatically released a low whistle when he realized the something wasn't struggling, which meant it was probably dead.

With William's help, Jason had swapped his mistresses' beloved dog with an older hound a neighbor was going to put down. His only fear was that Phillip might escort these men to get the dog, but his master had gone to the library immediately after delivering Beauregard to the barn, obviously distancing himself from the dastardly deed.

"The day of reckoning will surely come," he whispered angrily as the men unceremoniously heaved their load into the back of the wagon, climbed in, and drove off.

Turning away from the window, he looked down at his pants, muttering a complaint when he spied a spattering of mud just above the right knee. Swearing under his breath, he was walking toward the kitchen when a voice stopped him.

"Jason?"

He looked up to see Phillip standing at the bottom of the stairs to the upper rooms. The sight confused him, as he had not heard his master's uneven gait, his labored breathing, or the tick-tick of his walking stick when he moved from the library to his present location.

"Sir?"

"I need your assistance in sorting out my costume for this All Hallows Eve party your mistress and I will be attending. I am to be a pirate of some kind."

Of some kind? Jason thought angrily. *What you just did is worse than any pirate I've ever heard of.*

Remembering the mud, he tried to think of a reason for putting him off long enough to change his pants, but when none came to mind, he sucked in a breath, made sure his face was neutral, and changed direction to follow his master up the stairs.

"I have just the arrangement in mind, Sir."

"Will it look authentic, do you think?"

Thankful that Phillip could not see his reaction, Jason nodded as they reached the top. "Everyone present will surely believe the infamous Black Bart has risen from the grave to plunder them, Sir."

At the door to his room, Phillip hesitated a moment before looking back as Jason. "Say, what is that on your trousers?"

His heart in his throat, Jason did his best to act innocent as he looked down. "My apologies, Sir. I must have brushed up against the carriage wheel whilst seeing Mistress Elizabeth off. With your permission, I will go to my room and change straight away."

His master's good eyebrow rose, and he hesitated again before asking, "Have you been to the paddock today?"

Hoping his face did not reveal the panic he felt, Jason pointed at his polished shoes. "In these, Sir?"

Phillip's good eye flicked from Jason's feet to his face several times before he finally jerked a nod. "Well, clean yourself up then, and show me what you have."

"Very good, Sir," Jason responded. "I will be up directly."

Returning to the stairs, he raced down, going first to the kitchen for a damp cloth, and then to his room next door. Stripping off the pants, he pulled on his only other pair before using a damp rag to clean off the mud. Once done, he carefully spread the wet pants flat over his bed, and paused to suck in a deep breath and slowly release it. Though he dreaded the idea of doing so, he exited the room, carefully closed the door, and hurried to Phillip's room to find his master whistling so off key Jason had no idea what the tune was.

He could feel Phillip's eye following him as he moved to a wardrobe near the small room's door. Unlike Mistress Elizabeth's room, this one was sparsely furnished with a single bed, small desk, a woefully undersized wardrobe, and not a single mirror. Worse yet, even though the curtains over its only window were pulled back, it was poorly lit.

Though he should be used to it by now, he still had to struggle to hide his disdain for his master's meager accommodations.

"I took the liberty of acquiring a pirate's jacket and hat for you, Sir," he said while opening the wardrobe and pulling out the described items. "For the pants, Cook is preparing an oversized pair of trousers, properly cut to appear frayed and well used."

"But what about my cutlass?"

"William is making a wooden sword to round out your costume. He will paint the hilt black and the blade silver."

"Why not use a real sword? There are plenty around the place, surely."

Though it was difficult, Jason managed not to gasp at the suggestion.

"The swords on display are medieval, and quite cumbersome. In addition, I assumed you would not wish to use your military saber."

At the mention of the saber, Phillip's head jerked back, his expression so mixed, Jason could not read it.

To his relief, only a moment passed before Phillip nodded, and said, "You seem to have thought of everything."

"Thank you, Sir."

Resisting the urge to sigh, Jason closed the wardrobe, but his breath caught when he turned to see that his master's angry expression did not match his praise.

It was all he could do to keep his voice calm while asking, "Will there be anything else, Sir?"

Phillip stared at him for a long moment before turning away. "That will be all."

"Very good, Sir."

Upon reaching the main floor, Jason touched his brow to find it wet with sweat.

"You've made your choice, old boy," he muttered as he continued down to the basement. "Let's hope you can live with it."

Chapter 30

A milky fog had settled in and completely engulfed me as I crossed Aunt Susan's front porch and took slow, cautious steps down her driveway, stumbling several times in the darkness and coming close to falling on my face. There was no flashlight in my room, and I was afraid I might wake my aunt if I started digging through drawers and cupboards to find one.

Though unable to see, I used the grass border on the driveway as a guide and slowly worked my way along. Unfortunately, the gravel road was uneven with numerous puddles and weed patches, and when my foot splashed into water, I jumped aside, only to trip on a clump of grass. It took a quick move to keep from falling, and the effort made my many wounds ache.

"I could totally use that flashlight right now," I complained before pulling out my cell and checking the time.

It was only eleven-thirty-seven, but I was too stressed to wait any longer.

Light from the phone's screen gave me an idea, and I turned it around to shine its faint illumination on the road.

"Better than nothing."

The phone's ghostly glow produced only a small bubble of light that made the space beyond its reach appear even darker and spookier. I stumbled along, cursing the still-painful cuts in my arms and occasionally tripping over uneven ground because even though the faint light helped me avoid puddles and clumps of grass, it gave me no sense of depth. It also distorted distances, leaving me with little idea how far I'd come or needed to go.

Hearing a car on the highway, I quickly hid the phone and froze in place. When the vehicle finally appeared, its headlights created a glowing ball of fog that moved across my vision until it vanished around the next corner.

Once my brain started working again, I realized its passing showed how far I was from the roadway. Eager to get this over with, I quickened my pace, high stepping to avoid invisible obstacles, and no longer caring about getting my feet wet.

It was eleven-thirty-eight when I reached the road, breathing hard as much from panic as exertion, and unsure of what to do next. The light from my cell was far too weak to penetrate more than a few feet into the blackness around me, so I dug into my memory and tried to think of a place to hide as I inched my way toward the other side of the road.

I tried to concentrate on my objective, but kept getting distracted by the sense of another presence that was kind of like Remmy, but not her. I swept the light from my cell phone around, but only saw milky fog. The light barely reached three feet, so if someone was standing much further away, I'd never see them.

My right foot was just coming down onto the road's center line when a burst of light stripped away the darkness and left me exposed in a glowing bubble of fog. I immediately panicked, and started to run, but stopped when I remembered why I was there. My shoes still skidding on pavement, I turned to squint at two glowing orbs about thirty feet away, and understood for one long terrorizing moment how a forest-creature would feel when trapped in the glare of those blinding lights.

The car's engine roared to life and it lurched forward, the engine hissing loudly as it accelerated. When it was nearly to me, the driver slammed on the brakes, bringing it to a stop so quickly its front end bounced several times before settling down with headlights glaring, engine at idle, me gaping at it.

"Are you armed?" Elissa asked, her voice taught and high pitched.

Speechless, I held up both hands and shook my head.

"Police?"

I shook my head again.

Lifting a hand to block the bright lights, I saw the woman behind the wheel, her head turned as she briefly spoke with someone in the back seat before leaning her head out the window again.

"Get in."

Climbing into that car meant certain death, but the desire to run was checked by my need to save Remmy.

Two heads are better than one, but not when they're on corpses.

"Get in!"

I closed my eyes and took the first step.

This is soooo stupid, I thought before opening my eyes and walking hesitantly to the passenger side of the car.

To my surprise, Elissa had both hands on the steering wheel and there was no weapon on the seat.

"In the back."

Opening the door, I was both distressed and relieved to see my best friend sitting on the opposite side and waving a hand at me.

"Hurry up. Get in!" she demanded.

Only then did I see the gun in her other hand.

Chapter 31

"Beauregard is missing?" Elizabeth asked anxiously as she handed her coat to Tilley and turned to face Jason.

Feeling his face warm, Jason briefly watched the departing hack that had returned his mistress from the train. Only he and William knew where Beauregard really was, and it had been their plan for William to "find" him while searching the fields. Unfortunately, neither of them expected Master Phillip to uncharacteristically involve himself in the search. If the master believed the dog to be dead, how were they going to resurrect him without Phillip realizing he had been duped?

Though it made his heart ache to do so, he had no choice but to play along until something could be arranged.

"He ain't nowhere to be found, Mum," Cook blurted as tears dribbled down her cheeks.

Elizabeth kept her eyes on Jason. "But he was locked in my room, surely."

Jason was so moved by the pleading in her eyes, he wanted to blurt out the truth, but looked away instead, hoping she would not see his discomfort.

"I went to collect him for delivery to the barn, but he was nowhere to be found."

"Did you search the house?"

As Cook whimpered, Jason briefly looked at her before taking a big breath and turning to face his mistress.

"Yes, Madam. Cook, William, and I searched from attic to cellar, and he is nowhere on the premises."

"But then who could have..." She hesitated while briefly looking toward the library. "Surely someone would have seen him?"

Jason cleared his throat. "If I may, Madam. Cook was in the kitchen, doing her weekly cleaning, and I was helping the master with his costume from shortly after you left until he retired to the library at a quarter past eleven. He was still there when I brought word of Master Beauregard gone missing."

She walked toward the stairs and waved a hand in the direction of her room. "But my door was closed. How could he have escaped?"

Jason also pointed toward the second level. "The door was ajar when I arrived, Madam. It would seem Master Beauregard found a way to open it."

"But how did he get out of the house?"

Cook let out another whimper and quickly put a hand over her mouth as Elizabeth turned toward her, but when she said nothing more, Jason answered for her.

"He may have escaped when Cook left a rear door open to clear the air whilst sweeping the pantry."

"I didn't know 'e was out, now did I?" Cook wailed. "I'd never wish no 'arm to Master Beauregard. Not in a million years."

"Who is looking for him outside?"

"William has been out for some hours now," Jason responded, "but we have no news of him."

"And where is your master?"

"He has taken the wagon to inquire at the neighbors."

Slapping both hands over her mouth, Elizabeth closed her eyes for a moment, her staff silently watching until she turned toward the windows to see a wagon coming up the drive. Uttering a cry of alarm, she hurried to the main entrance, exiting in time to see William driving, with Phillip next to him.

Elizabeth moved off the steps into the wide expanse of crushed gravel in front of the house, walking slowly, her eyes on the approaching wagon, one hand over her mouth, the other on her stomach.

As he followed her, Jason became acutely aware of everything around him: her shoes crunching gravel, the rustle of skirts as she moved, water splashing in the central fountain, birds chirping overhead. She was standing on tiptoes, as though hoping to see Beauregard's head over the side of the wagon, and it bothered him greatly to see her obvious disappointment when it did not appear.

"Did you find him?" she asked desperately, her hands now clasped tightly over her chest as the wagon slowed.

Phillip shook his head. "The dog was nowhere to be found, but all our neighbors are on alert and will report to us if he should show."

She turned her attention to William who glanced nervously at Jason before looking down. "Sorry, Mistress."

After the wagon stopped, Phillip dismounted.

"We will not be needing the wagon again today, William," he said abruptly as he walked around the horse. "Give horse a good rubdown and an extra measure of grain for his hard work."

"Yes, Sir."

While the wagon moved away, Phillip walked to his wife, but stopped an arm's length away and made no effort to touch her. "The dog is most likely off chasing a bitch in heat. He will return soon enough."

"And if that is not the case? My poor boy may well be trapped somewhere, or injured. We simply cannot stop looking."

"What would you have us do? I have canvassed the neighbors, and William searched the fields and forests around."

"It is not enough! We must search again."

Phillip waved a hand dismissively. "And will you be slogging through the fields as well, or must others postpone their necessary duties to do it for you?"

She glared at him. "I will do it alone if I must."

"That will not do," Phillip insisted angrily. "We will wait until morning. The dog will surely be back before then."

"And if he is not?"

Phillip was preparing to respond when a whimper from Cook brought his attention to the three servants watching them.

His face turning red with rage, he grabbed his wife's arm and pushed her toward the house.

"We should not be rowing in front of the staff."

The sudden shove threw her off balance. Bending at the knees to regain her balance, she took a quick step to one side, but the heel of one shoe landed on her hem, tilting her forward. When she cried out,

Phillip brought up his maimed hand to catch her, but her left foot rolled, pitching her forward so quickly his hand slammed her face.

Screaming, she lurched from his grasp and sprawled backwards onto the gravel, cutting her hands as she landed.

"Damn it all," Phillip shouted. "That is not what…"

"Mistress!" Tilley screamed and started to move toward her, but stopped when Phillip angrily waved her off and finished his sentence.

"…I intended to do."

Obviously flustered, he reached down to help her up with his good hand, but unbeknownst to either of them, her right heel had punched through the inner lining of her dress. Trying to rise, she failed to get her feet under her, and fell backwards again while still gripping Phillip's hand. The sudden shift in weight threw him off balance, and he tried to stabilize himself by swinging his stiff right hand inward, hitting her in the middle of the chest, and knocking her flat.

"Please no!" Cook wailed as Jason rushed forward. "Don't kill 'er, Master!"

Jason grabbed Phillip's right arm, but as he pulled his employer back up, the master stepped on Elizabeth's flailing foot. She screamed just as Jason yanked hard, only to lose his grip and fall onto his butt. The sudden release sent Phillip toppling forward to drive his shoulder into his wife's abdomen.

He quickly rolled off, but the impact had knocked the wind out of Elizabeth.

"Lord in Heaven," Tilley screamed as her mistress gasped in short, choppy breaths. "She's a gonner!"

Still on the ground, Jason turned to Cook. "Send William for the doctor."

Whimpering, Cook hiked her skirts and hurried her plump form toward the barn as Phillip and Jason rose to their feet.

"Why in blazes did you interfere?" Phillip shouted angrily.

Jason scowled at him. "I was hoping to avoid what just happened, Sir."

"Well you bloody well made it worse, damn it!"

"Help her," Tilley cried. "She's turning blue."

As Elizabeth desperately gasped in short breaths, she looked up at the two arguing men.

Seeing her distress, Jason quickly dropped to one knee beside her.

"Calm yourself, Madam. Try taking a deep..."

Phillip's good arm slammed into the butler's shoulder, knocking him onto his side.

"Get away from my wife!"

Suddenly enraged by the assault, Jason lunged at his master. Both men went down, but Jason's attack was so forceful, his momentum carried him over his employer to roll on the gravel.

Furious beyond reason, Jason bounced back up and charged.

"You damned idiot," Phillip bellowed as he clumsily struggled to rise. "I'll have you whipped to within..."

Though off balance, Phillip turned aside Jason's charge with a roundhouse punch. The blow slammed Jason's cheek, but his momentum carried him into his master. The action so surprised Phillip, he reflexively stiffened, arched his back as he fell, and his head slammed the brickwork at the base of the fountain.

Quickly rolling away, Jason rose to his feet, fists clenched, ready to continue the fight, but Phillip did not move.

"Lord in Heaven!" Tilley moaned. "What've ya done?"

"He will not beat her again," Jason responded angrily while glaring down at his master's prostrate form.

Hands over her mouth, Tilley let out a loud wail that rose in pitch until it peaked and faded away.

Jason's eyes jerked from the now-sobbing girl to the blood pooling on the paving stones behind Phillip's head. He froze for a moment until his attention was drawn to Elizabeth when she gasped in a desperate breath.

Tilley also looked at her mistress and exclaimed, "She's breathin' again!"

Though the pair continued to watch their mistress struggling to breathe, Elizabeth's eyes were on her husband.

"Why does he not move?" she asked anxiously as though she did not see the blood.

Jason wetted a finger and briefly held it under Phillip's nose before straightening and shaking his head.

All three stared at the corpse in silence until the sound of rumbling wagon wheels drew their attention to it.

"What must we do, Madam?" Jason asked.

Her mouth silently opening and closing, she looked from her husband to Jason.

"I fear this will be the end of us," she finally said.

Jason locked eyes with her for a long moment before turning to look at the approaching wagon. He rose without speaking, walking briskly toward it while waving a hand over his head. When William reined the horses to a stop, he hurried up beside him.

"The master and mistress have both been injured."

"Mistress Elizabeth?"

"She is no longer in immediate danger, but I fear we have need for both a doctor and the constable."

"What in 'eaven's name 'appened?"

Jason shrugged. "Master Phillip had a fit of apoplexy. He fell and bashed his head."

William's eyes went wide. "Lord in 'eaven. 'e ain't dead is 'e?"

"It would seem so, yes."

"Lord in 'eaven," William repeated an octave higher. "What should I tells the constable, do ya reckon?"

"Tell him only that there has been an accident, and he should come at once to investigate."

"An' if 'e wants to know more?"

"He should come to the house and speak with Mistress Elizabeth."

"But Mister Jason..."

The butler stopped him with an upheld hand. "At present, you know only that your master and mistress have been injured and the master may be dead. If that is all you tell him, then you shall not be lying."

William shook his head. "Cook said the master was beatin' 'er."

"Keep that bit of business to yourself. We will address it when the constable arrives."

"Yes, Sir."

"Now off with you, and be quick about it."

As Jason moved toward the women, he looked back to see William slap the reins and race down the drive. When he turned back again, he was surprised to see an unearthly glow around Tilley and Elizabeth. He blinked twice in an attempt to disburse the apparitions, but they remained.

While struggling to take in the sight, he felt the urge to move quickly to them, but was stopped by an alarming sense that he must do something unspeakable.

Murder? Me?

Frozen in place, he stared at the women: Tilley speaking in hushed tones as the dazed-looking Elizabeth sat quietly next to her, her eyes on Phillip's inert form.

Bring harm to Tilley and Mistress Elizabeth? Impossible!

Despite his mental protests, the feeling was so strong, he turned to watch the wagon continue down the drive, and was almost overcome with the urge to call William back to include him in that thing he could hardly bring himself to vocalize.

Closing his eyes, he clamped his mouth shut and fought the powerful urge until he was back in control. When he looked again, the wagon was out of sight, and the feeling gone. Taking a deep breath, he turned back to see the unearthly glow around the women had also disappeared, but the sight brought no relief.

Had it been my intention to kill my master? Would I have done the same to these women?

Repulsed by the thought, he straightened his back, clenched his fists, and continued on to where Elizabeth sat.

"I know it was not my intention to harm anyone," he muttered to himself unconvincingly, "but I will most certainly hang for this anyway."

Chapter 32

"What's going on?" I asked while sliding into the car next to Remmy. "I thought *she* kidnapped *you*."

The car suddenly accelerated, slamming my door shut and making me look toward the front to see Elissa's surprised eyes in the rearview mirror.

"I'd never do anything like..."

"Shut *up!*" Remmy screamed as she pointed the gun at her. "This is all your fault."

We all went silent as the car raced down the twisty North Fork Road, Elissa expertly managing the turns while Remmy shook her head in silence. It took me a long moment to build up the courage to ask,

"Remmy? What's going on?"

Her cheeks wet with tears, she lowered the gun and looked at me. "It's all lies."

"It is not," Elissa insisted.

"What's a lie?" I asked cautiously, my gaze jumping from Remmy to this strange woman.

Elissa barked a laugh. "You don't remember, do you?"

I watched in fascinated horror as she pointed over her shoulder at Remmy.

"She does."

"Shut up!"

"She does? What?"

Elissa's eyes were all I could see in the mirror, but they were squinting angrily at me. "She's the one who threw you off the roof."

"No!" Remmy protested. "That was an accident"

I gasped as my mind filled with a flash of sensations: something hitting my face, my hair hurting, fighting for my life until I was overcome with the feeling of falling that was so real, I slammed a hand against the seatback to stop myself.

My lungs literally ached as I tried to take in a breath.

"That was you?"

"I'm not that person anymore."

"And yet you are," Elissa countered.

"No!" Remmy protested, tears spilling down her cheeks. "I'd never hurt Gerry like that."

"You have to understand," Elissa said as she looked back at us in the rearview mirror. "It no longer matters what happened in the past. It is really all about…"

"Stop it!" Remmy sobbed as she leaned forward to jam the gun into the back of the woman's head. "That's not the way it was supposed to be."

The car lurched forward, sending us both back into the seat, and because my seatbelt wasn't fastened, the next turn threw me into Remmy. The gun exploded like a canon, the windshield cracked, and Elissa screamed.

I felt the car shudder as it missed the next corner, went briefly airborne then plowed through a barbed-wire fence. All three of us screamed as it slammed down onto a narrow patch of grass, and with us howling in perfect triple harmony, it bounced up to let the river bank pass beneath us. The sudden weightlessness shut us up, producing an eerie silence as the car did a slow-motion arc through the air, slowly rolling forward until it nosedived into the Nehalem River.

I heard Elissa groaning, "Son of a b…"

The windshield exploded inward, slamming her with a wall of glass and a torrent of icy-cold water. I was thrown forward into the seatback in front of me, and immediately knocked back by a shocking coldness that cramped my muscles, and forced much of the air from my lungs. Completely disoriented in the pitch black car, I struggled for a moment to regain control of my body before kicking out with my feet until one of them found a foothold. It was only by chance that my head ended up in an air pocket near the rear window. Coughing and spitting, I managed to suck in a desperate breath then found the flailing Remmy, and yanked her up next to me.

"God that's cooollld," she howled, but before she could say more I was back under the water, trying to orient myself while being distracted by the pain in my head brought on by the cold.

With spasmming muscles making it impossible to hold the air in my lungs, I lasted only seconds before being forced to struggle my way back to the moving air pocket. Gasping in a breath, I barely registered that Remmy was still there before going under again. The shock of the cold water so disoriented me, it wasn't until Remmy pushed me away from her that I found the right side door, my already-numb fingers desperately searching its surface until I yanked the release handle and pushed.

The damned door didn't budge.

Despite the ache in my lungs, being punched and kicked by the flailing Remmy, and being colder than I've ever been in my life, I managed to find a foothold and pushed with all my might until the door slowly started to move. Sensing an opportunity, I grabbed the edge of the seat and tried to pull myself through the opening, but the pressure of water rushing past our sinking car was working against me. My body was stretched as far as it could go with my current foothold, and I could find nothing closer, so I groped around until my fingers wedged into some kind of groove. However, when I started to pull myself out, Remmy grabbed my belt and yanked me back, my stiffening fingers slipping on the wet metal as I fell back into the car.

Working only by instinct, I jerked my body around to break her grip, pulled my feet under me, and pushed up until my head was again in the shrinking air pocket, now barely large enough for two people. Seconds later, a screaming Remmy appeared as well. I barely felt her hands gripping my shoulders before I was under water again.

I managed to resurface, and was preparing to tell her to calm down when the car hit the muddy bottom and I was suddenly under water again. Remmy had fallen away from me, and as the car rolled, all sense of direction vanished.

I struggled fruitlessly in the tiny space for a moment before Remmy's flailing hand slapped my face, making me realize that my eyes were closed. Opening them, I could make out ghostly images in the faint glow of the car's interior lights.

Having reoriented myself, I made for the door again, only to have Remmy wrap her arms around my thighs, making it impossible to kick. Finding the door now open, I was trying and failing to pull both of us out when something grabbed my left arm. I looked up to see Elissa's ghostly figure in front of me. She pulled, I pulled and we were quickly through the opening.

The current grabbed us as soon as we were out of the car, but I was having trouble swimming with Remmy hanging onto my legs. Within seconds, the car had vanished into the murky gloom behind us, robbing me of all light. Before I could even react to the sudden darkness, we did a slow-motion crash into something large and prickly that snagged my clothes and held me against the current.

When I realized that Elissa's hand was no longer gripping my arm, I panicked, and for a long second was frozen in place, yet still fighting a strong urge to open my mouth and end it right there. I might have too, if the struggling Remmy, her arms still wrapped around my legs, hadn't brought me back into focus. Desperate to have my legs free, I reached down, broke her stranglehold, and yanked her up to bear-hug my waist. The action broke us free of the prickly colossus, and we were once more floating in the current. I felt Remmy's feet kicking me, so I matched her as best I could and started digging at the water with my hands, pulling us, I hoped, in the right direction.

The cold so numbed my skin I no longer felt pain, but each pull of my hands through the water felt like it would be my last as my lungs threatened to burst. Despite Remmy's dead weight, I somehow found the strength to do one stroke, then another and another until I broke the surface to gasp, choke, spit, and gasp again.

Reaching down, I yanked Remmy up, but upon surfacing, she went all wild-animal on me, gasping in air before letting out a primal roar as she slapped and clawed at my exposed head. Unable to speak, I grabbed at her arms, but the gasping, spitting, bellowing woman was too quick and I was under water again. Slapping her hands away, I swam a short distance from her, and came up for air.

When her head popped up again, I shouted, "Head to shore."

She disappeared for a second before surfacing again, her arms windmilling.

"Can't…swim!"

Though desperate to get out of there, I could not leave my best friend to drown.

Swimming to her, I slapped her hands away, and tried to move behind her, but the coughing-spitting girl kept grabbing my shirt and pushing me under.

"Leave her," another voice yelled as I surfaced for the fourth or fifth time.

When the flailing Remmy reached out to grab me again, I back-paddled and shouted, "Trust me."

Her mouth opened, but she slipped under the water again, appearing only seconds later to cough out a mouthful of liquid, her eyes wide with fear.

"Stay where you are, and don't grab me," I commanded before swimming around behind her. She sputtered and cried as I snaked an arm around her chest, but didn't resist when I pulled her toward shore.

The current was still carrying us down river, and when I looked up, my heart sank as the faint glow of moonlight illuminated a vertical wall of mud. With no more strength left to battle the numbing cold and Remmy's dead weight, I desperately needed something to grab onto.

Unable to think of anything else to do, I swam until we were nearly rubbing against the mud wall, and was just about to give up when we floated into a large pile of dirt that had sloughed off of the wall, giving us a small, narrow island to climb onto. Barely able to stay above water myself, I heaved Remmy toward the mound and let go. She slipped, went under but quickly bounced up coughing and gasping as I pulled myself up beside her.

The water was freezing, the mud was freezing, the air was freezing, and I could barely feel anything beyond my elbows and knees. My body shivered violently as I slogged on hands and knees through sticky mud toward the highest point. When I finally sat with my back against the impossibly-vertical wall of mud, a hacking, moaning Remmy crawled up beside me.

"We've g…g…got to…g…get out of heeerrre," I stammered while looking up at over ten feet of vertical dirt wall above us, and seeing no way out.

The faint moonlight illuminated Remmy's shivering form, her arms now wrapped tightly around her knees, face turned toward me, mud and hair plastered across it.

"Let's t...try to c...climb out," I stammered while pulling her close for warmth.

Her only reaction was to slowly shake her head.

"We'll d...die d...down here," I insisted.

"I...I'm already d...dead. Re...remember?"

Her comment reminded me of Elissa, and I looked around for any sign of her, but could see little more than the black water rushing past.

"That w...woman m...might not have m...made it."

Her teeth chattering, Remmy pressed her shaking body against mine.

"G...good r...ridd...ance!"

Chapter 33

Still struggling with the shock of his most recent experience, Jason approached the two women sitting next to Phillip's corpse. He could hear Tilley sobbing, but his attention was on Elizabeth, who continued to stare blankly at her husband.

Touching a stinging spot on his own cheek, Jason flinched, and pulled his hand away to reveal bloody fingertips. Though it should not have, the sight shocked him, and it was a long moment before movement brought his attention back to the women.

Eyes still on her mistress, Tilley rose to her feet, her black dress splattered with dirt, apron and cap askew.

"What are we to do?" she sobbed.

Before he could think of an appropriate response, Elizabeth turned slowly, mechanically to face him, obviously unaware of a stray lock of hair dangling over her right ear, or the blood dribbling from her lower lip as she spoke in a near-whisper,

"Should we summon the constable?"

It took Jason a moment to realize what she said before he nodded. "William is off to fetch him."

She looked back at the corpse, reaching out a hand as though to touch him, letting it hang in the air for a moment before slowly pulling it back to cover her mouth.

"Would the doctor be of any use?"

"I fear the master is beyond his help, Madam, but I have summoned him for you."

"Me? Whatever for?"

"You took a hard blow, and have cuts that need tending. It would be prudent to have the doctor examine you."

Shaking her head, she looked again at her husband. "Please take him inside. It will not do for him to be lying on the ground like this."

"I will do so at the first opportunity, but I fear the constable would not be pleased if we moved him just now. However, I shall have Cook fetch a blanket and see that he is covered."

Nodding slowly, Elizabeth tried to rise, but lost her balance and fell back onto her rear. An elbow brushed her dress, smearing blood across the smooth surface. Tilley let out a cry at the sight and quickly reached down to take her mistress' arm.

"Careful how you go, Mistress. Best we get you inside and tend to that injury."

Rising with her maid's help, Elizabeth took several steps toward the house before turning to look at him.

"Thank you, Jason," she said softly as the loose curl bounced pathetically over her ear. "I cannot begin to…" She hesitated, her eyes unfocussed, jaw slack for a moment before she shuddered. "Thank you," she added before unsteadily continuing on with her maid's help.

His attention moving from the women to the prostrate body, and back, Jason felt the urge to catch up with them and put his own arm around Elizabeth's narrow waist, to shove that stray hair back into place and restore her dignity, the dignity her husband tried to beat out of her.

Confused, he continued to watch them until Cook's footsteps in the gravel reminded him that he had duties to perform. Turing toward Cook, he waved her over. She quickened her pace, but stopped when she saw the two women.

Seeing her confusion, he moved toward her.

"Please find a suitable blanket to cover the master until the constable has had the opportunity to examine him."

When she looked past him, Jason did not follow her gaze.

"This is a sorry business, Mister Jason," Cook said sadly. "Very sorry indeed."

Shaking his head, he looked at the unmoving figure, the blood drying on the paving stone, and wished that somehow he could make it go away. He knew his fate was sealed. Regardless of the circumstances, he had attacked his master and would be called to account for it. His only concern was that Elizabeth not be tainted by this catastrophe.

"Yes," he muttered distractedly. "I could not have expressed it better."

Chapter 34

I was balancing precariously on the brink of an infinite abyss, listening to a sad song I'd never heard before, but was intimately familiar with. The darkness pulled at me, and I was about to let go and fall in when the distant wail of a siren pulled me back. I was too numb and cold to feel anything, unable to speak, or even open my eyes. I hugged Remmy closer, mostly because I could barely feel her next to me. For a moment, I thought I was slipping back into the void, because mingled with faint noise of the siren was the soft purring of a kitten.

"Over there!"

It took a moment for the words to make sense, and even longer to realize the purring was the sound of a small outboard motor. When I finally managed to force my eyes open, the sight of the small boat, blurry faces, and bright lights barely registered. A moment later, someone pulled Remmy from my stiff arms and carried her away. Then a woman's soft voice assured me I would be OK while she laid a blanket over my shoulders. My shivering muscles didn't want to respond, but she somehow got me to my feet and into the boat without my ending up back in the water.

By the time we reached dry land, the dense fog was awash with a confusing haze of flashing red and blue lights. The beam of a flashlight was pointed at my face, as though that would somehow help me see. The next thing I remember, a shadowy figure was asking for my name, where I lived, if I'd been drinking, and who was driving the car. I don't know what I said, but when someone put a steaming cup of something in my hands, I gulped it down, unable to taste it, but glad for the warmth.

I could sense that Remmy was nearby, but couldn't see her. Of course, there were lots of people rushing about, too many vehicles crowded into a small space, and my soggy brain couldn't absorb things fast enough to keep track.

I spoke with a paramedic, then a cop, and sometime after that, a nearly hysterical Aunt Susan was hustling me off to her car.

"What in heaven's name were you doing out here?"

"Where's Remmy?"

"Was that who was with you?"

"Yeah."

I was still too much in shock to really register what we were talking about. My initial responses were automatic, but as she continued to probe, and I tried to explain that which made no sense, I began to feel defensive.

"But you were safely tucked in bed," she protested. "How did you get in that car?"

I didn't respond at first, feeling irritated at having to explain myself, because it was my business, not hers.

"I got a call," I answered testily.

"From who?"

"That strange lady I told you about."

"The one stalking you?"

My annoyance at her questions flashed to anger, as I shook my head.

"I totally had to meet with her," I argued. "She was going to kill Remmy if I didn't."

"There was someone else in the car? Did you tell the police?"

I jerked a nod. "She said she'd kidnapped Remmy, but that didn't explain the gun."

"There was a weapon?"

I shook my head, but not in response to her question. I was trying, and failing, to reason this out.

"Yeah."

"Where is it now?"

Frustration and fatigue increased my irritation, and I wanted to give her a snappy retort, but the energy it required exceeded the little I had left. I slouched down in the seat, and struggled to keep my eyes open.

"Probably still in the car. There was *so* much water, and it was *so* cold. All I wanted to do was get out of there."

"Well, thank the Lord, you did. Let's get you home and out of those wet clothes."

I was about to nod when I suddenly remembered my friend.

"What about Remmy?"

Without looking at me, Aunt Susan shrugged.

"The paramedic wanted to take her to the hospital, but she refused, so she'll be transported to the police station in Nehalem where her parents can pick her up. But don't, for a minute, think this is over with, young man. You both still have a lot of explaining to do."

I started shivering, and even though I pulled the blanket tightly around my body, I couldn't stop.

"I'll call your parents as soon as we get home," she continued. "They're not going to like this one bit."

Her comment infuriated me. After all, I hadn't kidnapped Remmy, or fired the gun, or run the car into the river. I was trying to save my friend, and now everyone was pissed at me. I looked up, intending to protest, but the expression on her face diffused my own anger. It was then I realized she was more scared than pissed.

"Sorry for all the trouble," I said dully. "But there's more to this than meets the eye."

"I certainly hope so. You almost got yourself kill..." She wiped her eyes with a free hand before taking a big breath. "Can you imagine how upset your parents are going to be? And not only with you."

"Why would they be angry with you?"

She glanced at me, her eyes wet with tears, mouth pouting. After taking in a deep breath, she let it out and briefly looked away.

"Your mother hasn't been particularly thrilled with my life choices. This is just going to confirm her worst fears about me."

"But it wasn't anything you did? That's not fair."

"It's not about fair. It's about me protecting you from harm."

"But what could I have done? Remmy's life was in danger."

"You could have trusted me."

I tried to think of a response, but this added guilt trip sucked out the last of my energy reserve. It was all I could do to reach out and turn up the car's heater before pulling the blanket even tighter around me.

Thankfully, the drive to my aunt's house was short.

Chapter 35

"Thanks," Remmy said as she took the steaming Styrofoam cup from the officer who then waved at the door of the small room they were in.

"The Sheriff will be here shortly. I expect he'll have more questions for you."

Her journey from the edge of the freezing riverbank was a blur of distorted faces, garbled voices, and painful cold. Gerry had been next to her in the mud, but she had been so cold her brain had almost completely shut down and the only thing she could hang onto was her own body.

Her next memory was sitting in the back of an ambulance, wrapped in warm blankets, a paramedic shining a light in her eyes, and Gerry nowhere around. Despite a hot cup of coffee, it still took some time for the shivering to stop, and longer for her mind to start functioning again. Even then, so many confusing thoughts and memories filled her head she had trouble telling past from present.

The events of the last twenty-four hours had not only exhausted her, but stripped away her sense of who she was, and filled her with an overpowering need to be with Gerry. There was something unreal about their relationship, like they had been together a hundred years…or even longer.

A hand on her shoulder shocked her back to the present, and when she opened her eyes she was surprised to see a different officer's face. Sleep had snuck up on her and the sudden awakening left her confused and disoriented. Looking around the small, sparsely furnished room, she shifted in the stiff plastic chair until she was sitting more erect. Voices outside the room were echoey and indistinct, but she could make out some of the words.

"She's fragile…barely has it together…be gentle with…think she was driving?"

"Hi there, Miss," the officer said pleasantly. "Sorry to bother you, but I need to get some information."

She was suddenly overwhelmed with panic.

Are they talking about me?

Taking a clue from what she had heard, she let her eyes droop, and pretended to be sleepy. Slumping in the chair again, she pulled her feet under her, and snuggled into the blanket.

"Could you tell me your name?"

It had surprised her that she had lied to the EMT earlier when asked the same question. This time, she resolved to tell the truth.

Totally. Without question.

"Ellen Myrsten."

"Thank you Ellen," he said while scribbling on his note pad. "And how can I contact your parents?"

Though her heart beat rapidly, she let her head bob forward and forced her eyes closed.

"Ron and Sally Myrsten."

"And their number?"

"503…381…" She mumbled the rest before pulling the blanket tighter around herself and sighing as she lay back into her seat.

"I didn't quite catch that, Miss. What was that number again?"

Keeping her eyes closed, she let her head loll to the side as though she'd fallen asleep. Thankfully, he didn't try to rouse her.

After a long moment, she heard the crackling of leather as he rose, and then footsteps that grew softer with each impact. Without moving, she opened her eyes just enough to see she was alone. The urge to run away was overwhelming, but a tug on her still-damp blouse made it clear she would not last long roaming through the county's fields and forests in wet clothes, with no food, and nearly exhausted.

If I stay here, how will I find Gerry again?

Slumping sideways, she released an involuntary sob.

I've really screwed this up. Again!

Desperate to do something, she almost pushed herself out of the chair, but her boost of angry energy quickly dissipated, leaving her weak and sleepy, her mind drifting to a place she didn't want to go. Black and white shapes swirled around her. Long spears stabbing at her heart. Shouts of the terrified, screams of the dying. Though terribly afraid and wanting to scream herself, she couldn't. She struggled to run away from the shapes, but they kept getting closer and closer until…

"Excuse me, Miss."

Gasping she jerked awake to find a female officer looking down at her, but her uniform was not military red, and the room was flooded with light.

"Where am I?"

"You're at the station house, in Nehalem," the officer explained. "We couldn't raise anybody at your house, but someone in Salem is going to drive by and make contact."

Still disoriented, she sat up and looked around, her eyes stopping on the empty coffee cup beside her.

Picking up the cup, she held it out. "Can I have more coffee?"

Smiling, the young officer nodded. "Sure."

As soon as she was out of sight, Remmy rose and moved to the room's only door to give the station's small lobby a quick scan. Hearing footsteps again, she hurried back to slump down in her seat and pretended to be dozing. When the officer entered, she slowly opened her eyes and took the offered cup.

"Thanks," she said, holding it with one hand while using the other to keep the blanket over her shoulders.

"My sergeant's gone to get you some dry clothes. He'll be back in a few minutes."

"Did they find the other woman?"

The officer shook her head. "Nah, but they did find where she climbed out of the river. It's doubtful she'll get far before they catch her."

Knowing that Elissa was still alive gave Remmy a confusing anxiety rush, because she was not sure if she was happy or unhappy that the woman had survived. She knew Elissa's presence threatened to drive a wedge between her and Gerry, but she also had this unshakable feeling that they needed this woman.

How could that possibly be?

The question left her feeling desperate and alone, and the lonely feeling reminded her that she had not yet asked about her friend.

"Where's Gerry?"

"The boy who was with you? I'm not sure. He's not here, so they might have taken him to the hospital in Tillamook."

It was all she could do to keep herself from jumping out of the chair.

Stay calm! He's OK. I know it!

Despite the reassuring thoughts, she had to ask, "Was he badly hurt?"

The woman officer shook her head. "I don't think so. They said you both walked from the boats to the ambulance. It was probably just as a precaution, to make sure there weren't internal injuries."

A shudder rippled through her and she tried to hide it by slowly nodding as she pointed past the officer. "Restroom?"

The woman twisted at the waist and pointed. "Just take a right at the hall. It's the first door on your left."

Taking a sip of the coffee, she set it down, and rose, forcing the deputy to take a step back. Though her legs barely supported her, Remmy cinched the blanket tighter, and forced herself to walk past her.

Weaving on her way to the hallway, she could hear the officer following a short distance behind. When the footsteps stopped at the room's door, Remmy's sense of relief was countered by the struggle to keep her caffeine-infused body from bolting for the nearest door. She briefly squeezed her eyes shut to fight back the panic then straightened her path and continued on, feigning a weariness she no longer felt as she continued to search for a way out.

Finally reaching the restroom door, she glanced back to see her escort had not moved. Without hesitating, she pushed through the door, locked it, and walked quickly to the only toilet.

Sitting, she did her business while searching for an exit, but the only window was high and small.

"Totally bogus thinking, dork," she chastised herself. "This is a police station. They wouldn't, like, make it easy to escape."

Finishing with the toilet, she pulled up her pants, but didn't flush. After making a quick circuit of the tiny room, she stopped at the sink to look at her mud-smeared image in the mirror. The ambulance attendant had given her a warm towel to wipe her face and hands, but without a mirror, she had no idea how bad a job she had done.

"Shit. Even Mom wouldn't recognize me."

Dipping her head close to the faucet, she splashed water onto her face and hair, pulling out a half-dozen paper towels to dry herself before wetting another handful to scrub mud from her clothes. After using the blanket to finish drying off, she tossed it on the floor, combed her hair with her fingers, and stood back to look in the small mirror.

"I totally smell like river mud, but it will have to do," she sighed before digging into her pocket to extract a still-wet wallet containing three twenties, two ones, her driver's license, and student body card.

Holding up the card, she muttered, "I won't need this anymore."

She was preparing to toss it into the trash, when a thought stopped her.

"Since you gave them a fake name," she muttered while sliding the ID card back into the wallet, "it would be totally idiotic to leave the stupid thing behind." Stuffing the wallet back into her pants, she moved to the door. "Let's hope that oaf isn't, like, still watching."

Slowly pulling the door open, she peered out, thankful to find the lobby empty.

Her heart in her throat, she slipped out and quietly closed the door. After another quick look toward the lobby, she headed in the opposite direction, her heart thudding as she walked carefully on tiptoes to keep her sneakers from squeaking on the linoleum. A few steps later she saw an exit at the end of the hall. Though inviting, she dismissed the idea when she spied the alarm unit on the release bar. Shaking her head, she turned into the first office on her right, thankful to find the door unlocked and the space empty.

Tiptoeing through the dimly lit room to its only window, she released the lock, and yanked it open. It was only then she thought of alarms, and the idea made her hesitate a moment to see if she had been discovered. Hearing no cries of alarm or pounding feet, she hefted her legs over the sill, and dropped to a squat. Though the sky was still dark, a single green yard lamp buzzed overhead, giving a ghostly glow to the two cars in the small parking lot.

This is so totally crazy, she thought while briefly closing her eyes to steel her nerves.

Finally looking around to make sure the coast was clear, she reached up and closed the window.

What is happening to me? she wondered as she sprinted across the lot, and pushed through an eight-foot hedge to find herself on the edge of downtown Nehalem. *Why am I doing this?*

The questions vanished unanswered as she scouted the area like an experienced soldier, her attention moving from car to car, house to house, looking for the most logical place to hide. It wasn't until she spotted the glow of moving lights several blocks away that she realized what that meant.

"The main highway!"

Taking off at a sprint, she ran down the middle of the empty street until she was almost to the busy highway. At the end of the street, she moved to the corner of a building, and looked around it to see cars and trucks speeding in both directions. Her breath caught at the sight of a flatbed truck idling on the side of the road, its turn signal indicating it was about to pull into traffic.

At first, she thought of asking the driver for a ride, but nixed the idea because he could later identify her.

I need a change of clothes.

The revving engine made it clear she had no time to find other clothes. Yanking off her jacket, she tossed it behind a dumpster, and ran to the back of the now-moving truck. Easily catching up with it, she hopped onto the bumper rail, dropped to hands and knees, and scrambled in to slip under the edge of canvass covering the load. She could feel the truck accelerating into traffic before turning right at the main intersection where the highway headed south toward Tillamook.

After she stopped moving, the chill set in, making her want something more to wrap around herself. She started to peek out from under the tarp, but quickly pulled back when light from a following car blinded her. Afraid they might somehow alert the truck driver to her presence, she wrapped the canvass around her wet, shivering body, which continued to shake uncontrollably even in the confined space.

The night's events had exhausted her, and when the air inside her improvised cocoon started to warm, she closed her eyes, and was near to falling asleep when a sharp jolt jarred her entire body. A moment later, the truck hit another rough spot, and its stiff suspension transferred the impact directly to the hardwood bed on which she lay.

"Damn," she sighed as she rolled onto her side. "Why did I leave that blanket behind?"

Chapter 36

"You say your master were prone to fits of apo…uh…apo-poxy?" Constable Higgins asked as he sat opposite Jason in the drawing room, notebook in one hand, pencil firmly gripped in the other. "What brought them on, do you suppose?"

Jason looked into the plump constable's dull eyes and wondered if the man even knew what the word meant, but it was not the man's ignorance that irritated him. For reasons he could not explain, he had the overwhelming feeling that he had missed an important opportunity by not killing the mistress and Tilley…and himself. The thought repulsed him, but would not go away.

Resisting the urge to give his head a sharp shake, he answered, "It is apoplexy, Constable, but I cannot rightly say. I would assume his fits were the result of war injuries. He was in the first Boer War, you know, and sustained his injuries fighting the Zulus."

The constable looked briefly at his note pad. "Terrible business that," he said solemnly. "From the look of 'is body, it seems 'e were badly burned. Is that where they come from, would you say?"

Still struggling with the unwanted feelings, Jason nodded. "His survival was a true miracle, but the scars went much deeper than skin."

"I reckon so," Higgins said sadly before his eyebrows shot up. "Is it your opinion that this 'ere apoplexy was what caused 'is death?"

"I can think of no other reason. As for today's incident, Madam Elizabeth was just back from London, and was quite upset because her dog had gone missing, and…"

"Dog? What kind of dog?"

Taken aback by the question, Jason hesitated for a moment before answering. "He is a Great Dane."

"And 'e went missing, you say?"

"Yes. It appears he escaped from the house sometime after the mistress left for the London train."

"Did anybody try to locate this missing dog?"

"Yes. As a matter of fact, Master Phillip returned from his search soon after the mistress arrived home."

"Did 'e find 'im?"

Jason shook his head. "Unfortunately no, and they were discussing the next course of action when he flew into a sudden rage and struck her."

The constable shook his head as well. "Terrible business. Terrible business. She were badly bruised, you say?"

"The doctor can tell you more, but I should think so."

"I trust 'e will." Pursing his lips, the officer gripped his pencil and pad as though trying to inscribe the words in stone, his head shaking the entire time. "Terrible business."

"Most certainly."

"And 'ow is it your master came to be killed?"

"I was attempting to get between the master and Mistress Elizabeth when he appeared to seize and fell backwards, bashing his head on the ground."

The silent constable continued to struggle with his writing utensil for a moment before he looked up.

"And 'e struck you as well?"

Jason rubbed a sore spot on his arm and nodded. "He was not himself at the time."

"Are you sure you didn't strike the first blow?"

He shook his head. "My only concern was that he not harm anyone further."

Higgins returned to his scribbling. "'arm anyone further," he muttered as the pencil scraped across paper.

"Well, then," he finally said. "It looks like a tragic accident, but that is not for me to decide, now is it? That'll be up to the coroner, I reckon."

Jason nodded and motioned toward stairs to the kitchen.

"If there is nothing more, I must attend to the rest of the staff. As you can imagine, they are quite upset over this."

"Quite right. Quite right. Such a terrible business."

"Thank you," Jason said as he turned to leave.

"Uh, one more thing, if I may."

"Yes?"

"Well, it's just that I 'ear tell there might be something between your mistress and a Colonel Struthers. I suppose, working so closely with the family as you do, you'd know of such things?"

His anger flaring at the slander, Jason struggled to keep his face neutral. "Colonel Struthers? I should think not."

"'e ever come 'round when the master were away?"

"The master is...or was only rarely away from the manor, and on each of those occasions, Mistress Elizabeth accompanied him. As far as I am aware, Colonel Struthers has never been here."

"Why is that, do you suppose?"

"Master Phillip found him unsuitable company."

"And did your mistress also find 'im...unsuitable?"

"I believe she did, but you would do well to ask her."

"And did she never go out on 'er own?"

"She did, on occasion, but I did not accompany her, and therefore am unable to comment on what transpired."

"And 'er maid never mentioned 'im to you, in passing, as it were?"

"If she had, I would be remiss in mentioning such a confidence to anyone else, but be assured, Constable, no such conversation ever took place."

"Then I guess I'd best have a word with the maid. Would you be kind enough to send 'er up?"

Nodding, Jason continued to the stairs, his mind reeling with the implications of what Tilley might say. Halfway down, he stopped to take a deep breath in an effort to contain the growing panic compressing his chest.

Finally regaining the strength to continue, he entered the kitchen to find Cook sitting on the floor in front of the hearth. Tilley lay with her head in Cook's lap and a wet towel on her forehead. As he approached, Cook looked up, her face sad, head shaking, but when the girl saw him she started sobbing.

"How is she faring?" he asked.

Cook continued to shake her head. "Blubbering like a babe all this while."

"Be that as it may, she must pull herself together. The constable wishes a word."

"Saints preserve me," Tilley wailed. "I'm in no fit state fer the likes of him."

"Fit or not, you are to go upstairs at once."

Pulling the towel from her forehead, she sat up. "And what am I to say? That I saw you murder Master Phillip?"

Jason felt his stomach sink. "You saw nothing of the kind. I was trying to prevent him from bringing further harm to your mistress."

"Right as rain, that is," Cook exclaimed. "It was certain 'e'd 'a killed 'er."

Tilley looked briefly at Cook before turning again to Jason. "That ain't how I seen it. You needn't have hit the master so hard."

He lifted a hand with the intent of debating the issue, but another thought made him stop.

If we row, who will die this time?

Sighing, he let the hand fall to his side.

"You must tell him what you believe you saw," he said in a calm voice that hid the tightness in his chest. "But I never thought to harm him. You must believe that."

Tilley handed the towel to Cook and stood. "I believe you, Jason Smythe, but the master's dead all the same, and someone must come to account for it."

He could think of no response as she moved out the door.

After she was gone, he felt lost and disjointed, his gaze roaming around the kitchen until it stopped on Cook.

"If the constable has further need of me," he said with all the dignity he could musters. "I will be upstairs with Mistress Elizabeth."

She nodded. "That's a right thing to do, Mister Jason, but what're we to do if the sheriff sets 'is mind on murder?"

Shaking his head, he started to leave, but checked himself and turned back toward her.

"Then I fear he will set his mind on me."

Chapter 37

"Not tell your parents? Are you serious?"

I shook my head as Aunt Susan pulled a bathrobe from a cupboard and handed it to me, her face the picture of utter astonishment.

"For only a little while," I argued weakly. "It's just that..."

"You *do* realize how much trouble you're in, don't you? Someone may have died in that river. If I didn't have friends on the police force, you'd probably still be at the station right now."

I felt my argument crumbling, but had to try. "Yes, but if I could only speak with Remmy, I'm sure…"

"Absolutely not! From what you're telling me, she may have participated in your kidnapping, and nearly got you killed."

"That's what makes it all so weird. Remmy would never do anything like that."

"That's not the way it looks to me."

I wanted to respond, but couldn't pull an intelligent thought from the jumbled mess thrashing around in my head. Remmy was more than my best friend, and I was certain she would never do anything to hurt me. On the other hand, I had no explanation for why she had the gun. When Elissa told me Remmy had been my former husband -- a man who treated me like property, to be controlled and abused as suited his whim -- Remmy had not contradicted her. How could that be? How could Remmy have the same soul as that heartless bastard?

I tried again to say something, but though my head was shaking, and mouth moving, nothing came out.

After a moment of uncomfortable silence, Aunt Susan held up her phone.

"While you're in the shower, I'm going to call your folks. After you're cleaned up, you are can start at the beginning, and tell me everything."

I couldn't stop the big sigh that came out. "You're so not going to believe me."

She shook her head. "I'm the best shot you have right now."

Sitting on the stool next to her wood stove, I leaned toward the welcome warmth, wanting to absorb as much as I could.

"I'll tell you now."

"Nope," she said before pulling me to my feet. "You smell like a sewer. Take a hot shower and put on some clean clothes."

I started to resist, but a whiff of river mud stopped me.

"Then what?"

"Tell your story, and we see where it leads."

All of the remaining strength in my body melted away, leaving me no choice but to give in and take the most painful, challenging shower of my life. After I was dressed, Aunt Susan put fresh disinfectant and bandages on my wounds while I sat next to the wood stove and told my tale until the sky started to brighten. Aunt Susan remained silent as she listened, her expressions ranging from incredulous, to understanding as I rattled on.

"That's some tale," she said after I finished.

I shrugged. "If someone else had told it to me, I wouldn't have believed them, but I'm telling the truth."

To my utter surprise, she nodded. "I believe you."

"You do?"

She waggled a hand. "Maybe not the past-life stuff, but this Elissa person sure seems to believe it."

"But she knew about the dog."

"You've always liked big dogs. She may have been following you, and overheard you say you liked Great Danes. Now that is scary."

"You're telling me."

"Your parents will be here in a few hours, but I still need to tell the police about that woman. If she didn't drown, they need to find her and figure out what she's up to."

I felt the urge to protest, but her determined expression stopped me.

"OK," I sighed. "Let's get this over with."

She grabbed the phone and dialed. Holding it to her ear, she tossed her cell at me.

"Call your friend."

When I nodded, she turned away and started talking. Shaking my head, I dialed Remmy's number, and wasn't surprised when it went immediately to voicemail.

"Remmy," I said after the beep. "I hope the cops haven't confiscated your cell, because I need to speak with you about..."

The river!

The thought forced out an involuntary groan. Remmy cell would be worthless because it went into the water with us.

I was suddenly cold again and my aunt's phone felt like dead weight in my hand. Impotent is a word I rarely use, but it applied here. On the other hand, what I felt didn't really matter, because at that moment, wherever my friend was, whatever trouble she was in, she was pretty much on her own.

Chapter 38

"What are we to do, Madam?" Jason asked as he looked out from an alcove off the entryway toward the drawing room where the constable was still speaking with Tilley.

Elizabeth looked up at him with empty eyes. "What? Do? Sorry. Were you addressing me?"

He started to respond, but hesitated when he realized she was hardly aware he was in the room. After following Tilley to the main floor, he found his mistress standing in front of the library, her face blank, hands crossed over her heart. When she refused to go inside, he tried to take her upstairs, but they only made it to the small bench in this alcove before she would not go any further.

"May I get you tea, Madam?"

Her chin resting on her folded hands, she shook her head slowly.

"Is he still out there?" she asked without looking outside.

Jason nodded. "I am afraid so, Madam. They are waiting for a detective inspector to examine the circumstances of his death."

"I cannot cry for him," she whispered. "Is that the way a wife should act when her husband has...?

He was alarmed by how much he wanted to take her in his arms and comfort her. That the feeling was not new mattered little. She would be offended by advances from a person of his lowly station, and that was something he would never do.

And yet, he could not explain the powerful connection he felt for her. Not just affection, but something equally strong, equally strange, yet familiar.

He gave his head a sharp shake to dispel the feeling.

"You are in shock, Madam," he heard himself saying. "The doctor has given you a sedative. When the constable has finished with Tilley, she can escort you up to your room."

"Yes. I am very tired."

"It will only be a few..."

She rose suddenly and held out an arm, crooked at the elbow, as though expecting him to take it and steady her.

When he hesitated, she announced, "I wish to go to my room now."

"But Madam. Tilley is with the constable."

"Oh," she responded distractedly while looking toward the next room. "Then I shall go myself."

She took two steps, stumbled, and started to fall. Jason rushed to her side, and pressed a hand into the small of her back while the other took her groping hand.

"If you will only wait until..."

"Please help me. I must go now."

He looked pleadingly toward where the constable was speaking with the maid, but neither was looking their way when Elizabeth took a quick step forward, pulling herself from his grasp. When she stumbled, he quickly caught up and grabbed her outstretched hand to stop her from falling sideways.

"My husband used to take me to my room," she said dreamily as she gripped Jason's hand. "He was much gentler in those days: such a kind, tender man."

"Mistress Elizabeth," he pleaded anxiously as they reached the stairs. "Your maid is not available to assist you. It would be most inappropriate for me to..."

He stopped when she gave her head a determined shake. "I do not want Tilley. I want my husband before he was..."

Her words faded away as she mounted the stairs, but her gait was so unsteady, Jason kept a hand on her waist and let her lean against him. He closed his eyes briefly as her perfume aroused feelings he struggled to suppress. At first the pressure was slight, but by the time they reached her bedroom door, it was all he could do to keep her from falling.

He steered her toward the bed, but two steps into the room she started sinking to the floor. He grabbed quickly, but upon realizing one hand was on her breast, he shoved both hands under her arms and lifted.

The position was awkward, and when he reached down to wrap an arm around her waist, her body turned around, putting them chest-to-chest, like two drunken dancers attempting the Flamingo. When she continued to slide down his body, he wrapped both arms around her and struggled to move her toward the bed, grunting as her body pressed tightly against his, her legs splayed out, with one knee on each side of his, and her head lolled back.

"Well, this 'ere *is* a pretty picture, I must say," the constable said warily.

Jason felt his heart freeze as he turned toward the officer.

"It appears Mistress Elizabeth has fainted," he said as calmly as he could. "Please help me get her to bed."

"From the looks of it, you've got 'er 'alfway there already."

"Mistress!" Tilley cried as she rushed past the constable and glared at Jason. "What are ya doing to her?"

As the girl threw her arms around Elizabeth's limp form, Jason protested, "She insisted on coming up for a lie down, but it seems she succumbed to the sleeping draft before reaching the bed."

"You could have had her wait fer me."

"I made the suggestion, but she would have none of it. In light of her condition, I could hardly allow her to climb the stairs alone."

As the two of them clumsily hefted the limp woman onto the bed, the constable said, "So you say, but seeing as 'ow you're the one who topped 'er 'usband, a different sort of explanation comes to mind."

"How could you?" Tilley protested, her accusing eyes on Jason.

The absurdity of the situation struck Jason mute for a moment before he regained his composure.

"I did not *murder* Master Phillip. It was an accident, and my only intention with Mistress Elizabeth was to get her safely to bed before she fainted."

Shaking his head, the constable lifted a hand and motioned for him to move toward him. "Be that as it may, Sir. It would be best if you came with me to the station. I reckon the detective inspector will want a word with you."

Chapter 39

I could hear Aunt Susan's landline ring as I stared at the cell phone she'd given me to call Remmy's parents.

"We need to know if your girlfriend has contacted them yet."

Why wouldn't she? I wondered. *And what am I going to tell them if she hasn't.*

I hesitated for a long moment before lifting the phone and pressing buttons. My finger was punching the last number when my aunt held her phone out to me. There were tears in her eyes.

"Your father was in the shower when I called earlier."

Fear and confusion made me hesitate, but her insistent shaking of the phone forced me to take it.

"Hi," was all I could think to say.

"What the hell is going on over there?" he demanded angrily. "You drove a car into the river?"

"I wasn't driving when the…"

"We're on our way," he interrupted. "You are not to leave Susan's house for any reason."

"But Dad, I need..."

"No arguing, Son. It'll take us a couple of hours, and I expect you to be there when we arrive."

"Yes, but..."

I stared at the buzzing receiver for a moment before handing it back.

"He's totally pissed."

She sighed. "What did you expect?"

I closed my eyes and exhaled. "Yeah."

"Did you get ahold of your friend's parents?"

"No," I said while returning both phones to her. "I tried Remmy's cell first, but when I got her voicemail, I remembered that her phone went into the water with us. I was just about to call her parents when Dad called."

My legs went suddenly weak, and it was all I could do to stagger to a chair and sit hard. When I looked at my aunt, the whole scene felt distant and unreal, like I was inside someone else's body.

"You OK?"

My head was bobbing like an overstimulated dashboard doll.

"This is all just too much. I'm in trouble with the cops, and my parents. Some crazy woman is stalking me, and my best friend is stuck in a police station, cold and alone."

Moving next to me, Aunt Susan squatted down to eye level. "Your friend should be reunited with her parents soon, and if this woman is still alive, the police will find her." She shook her head as well. "Your folks aren't so much angry as scared. You could have died in that river."

"I didn't know what else to do."

She sighed. "You should have trusted me."

My laugh was part hysterical, part giggling child. "I know...it's just...there wasn't time to..." I felt my shoulders slump. "All I could think about was saving Remmy."

She was about to respond when her phone rang again. After patting me on the shoulder, she straightened and answered.

"But I don't think that's her real...just a minute." She turned toward me. "You said your friend's name was Remmy? What's her last name?"

I felt a sense of panic as I answered, "Reed."

"Is Remmy a nickname?"

"Yeah. It's really Remiah."

She lifted the phone again, but kept her eyes on me.

"Remiah Reed, but her friends call her Remmy. She did? Are you serious?"

Lowering the phone, she shook her head. "What is her parent's phone number?"

"Why?"

She scowled at me. "Do you know it?"

I hesitated for a long moment, not wanting to give it to her, but knowing from her expression that not doing so would bring on even more trouble. I finally gave in and recited the number, turning away as she repeated it to the caller.

"You're friend has taken a runner," she announced as I heard the receiver smack into its cradle. "She also gave them a false name."

Jerking around, I looked for the smile that would tell me that this was some kind of sick joke.

No smile.

"No way! Why would she do that?"

"You tell me."

I froze for a moment, trying to recall the previous day, but could only see flashes of short scenes that lurched backwards from when the car went into the river until I reached back to the memory that bothered me most.

"She had a gun when I got in the car."

"That strange woman? What was her name?"

"Elissa."

"She had a gun on you?"

"No. Remmy had the gun."

"But the woman was driving."

"That's the weird part. If Remmy was being kidnapped, why did she have a gun? I didn't see a weapon on the driver's seat, or in Elissa's hands, which were on the steering wheel."

Aunt Susan shook her head. "And now your friend is on the run. I'd say she's got a lot of explaining to do."

I jumped up. "I need to find her first."

Matching my move, Aunt Susan stabbed a finger at my face. "No!"

"I know we can sort this out."

"There will be no sorting, or running, or hunting on your part, Mister. You're staying put until your parents arrive. Is that clear?"

When I hesitated, she waggled the finger.

"Trying to get between her and the police will only make things worse. I want your solemn oath you'll not meddle in things you don't understand."

I wanted to laugh at the total absurdity of her statement, but knew that would not go over well. When I paused to think of an appropriate response, she lowered her hand and glared at me. My mind still blank, I glared back, but she held her ground and I could tell this wasn't going to end well.

"Gerry!"

"Yeah. OK," I finally conceded while slumping back into the chair." I'll stay put until my folks get here."

"Promise?"

"Yeeessss," I hissed angrily. "I promise."

Looking up at her, I wondered how many decades I'd be grounded for breaking that promise. Of course, odds were pretty good I'd be grounded for the rest of my life anyway, so what did I have to lose?

Chapter 40

The morning sun was not yet over the surrounding hills when they reappeared: black bodies everywhere Phillip looked. The laudanum the medic had given him was numbing the pain, but not enough to let him sleep during the lulls in the fighting, and now that the Zulus were moving, even that would be impossible.

"Hey Sarg," a nearby soldier called. "What's it they call this bloody place again?"

"Rorke's Drift."

He could not move, but from his position in the bed of a wagon parked against what remained of the Mission House -- their final defensive position -- he could see his comrade's helmet shake.

"Rorke's Hell'd be more like it."

Without comment, the soldier turned to watch the Zulu warriors, many nearly naked except for white plumes in their headdress and hanging from strings around their necks. The entire mass flowed partway down the slope, a black and white wave that stopped just out of range of their rifles. These were the same savages who massacred over a thousand British soldiers only two days earlier, but the small troop at Rorke's Drift had inexplicably held them off…at least for now.

Phillip's remaining good eye blurred with tears, but his vision was clear enough to see uncountable black bodies lined up to the horizon. From the conversations of the soldiers around him, he knew they were completely surrounded, ammunition was low, and their position perilous. When they attacked this time, it would all be over.

The medico had told him the building they referred to as the hospital was still burning from the previous night's attack. He remembered the hand-to-hand combat: bayonets flashing, guns firing. He had wanted to scream and run away, but there was nowhere to go.

And then his rifle jammed.

He tried to move his arm, but screaming pain forced a howl from him. A medico, wounded himself, appeared beside him.

"'old on there, Gov," he said anxiously. "I'd give ya' more laudy, but we're plumb out." His head turned as he looked at the line of enemy warriors. "From the look of it, it ain't gonna be much longer now."

He heard the distant report of a rifle: one of the enemy's few ancient flintlocks, but if he could just sit up enough for them to see him, one might just put him out of his misery.

Shoot me, you soulless blaggards, he thought as the growing pain in his right side kept him immobile. *Don't leave me like this.*

"Steady on, lads" the sergeant shouted. "Wait for my command."

How does that bastard keep his voice so calm?

A deep, guttural roar rose up from the wall of Zulus before they stomped the ground in unison and took several quick steps forward. There were so many of them, the sound of their spears against rawhide shields was like rolling thunder. His heart racing, he listened intently as they grunted something undecipherable, and retreated.

Phillip gasped from the pain as he tried and failed to rise. To his dismay the Zulus repeated the ritual three more times. Through the increasing roar of chaos in his head, he heard the sergeant say,

"Any minute now, boys. Hold your line."

He found the last order divinely ridiculous. There was no line. After fighting through the previous afternoon and into the night, his comrades had retreated to a ragged circle around what was left of the mission house, protected only by stacks of bagged mealie flour. There was no place to fall back to.

A scream rose from the mass of bodies and the black wall started moving.

"And now we die," he muttered as he waited for the sergeant's order to fire, but to everyone's surprise, the enemy continued their ritual -- moving forward, slapping shields, shouting, and stepping back.

"What are they playing at?" someone cried.

"Quiet there," the sergeant commanded. "We held them last night. They'll get the same today."

Unable to stand the stress, Phillip tried to shift his position, but the pain was like a million knives stabbing at once into the entire length of his side, and it was growing, and growing, and...

*   *   *

A body-jarring bump shocked Remmy awake and left her feeling disoriented and afraid as she momentarily fought the canvas she was wrapped in until she remembered where she was, and why.

Closing her eyes, she gave her head a violent shake to clear it. "How can I make the dreams stop?"

They were like invading sugar ants: an unpleasant surprise each time they appeared, and nearly impossible to get rid of. The battle scenes were the worst, but there was also the manor in England with a beautiful young woman in 19th-century dress, a silly maid who could not stand still for a moment, and a bumbling butler not much older than the young woman with an obvious crush on her. For most of her life, Remmy was clueless as to her role in the ridiculous melodramas randomly haunting her dreams.

No clue, that is, until Gerry began recalling his own day-mares. Even then it took her a while to realize they were both dreaming about the same people, but seeing them from different perspectives. The one face he remembered, but she had never seen, was the badly-scarred husband.

That's what the battle was about, burst into her head. *Was I that deformed bastard?*

Her aunt Jasmina said Gerry had been a woman, but the idea of her also switching genders was too disturbing to accept. Even worse was the suggestion that she had been a domineering abuser.

Is that why I tried to kidnap Gerry?

Since the day they met, she felt an overpowering attraction to him, but there was more to it than that. She needed him for something she did not understand: something to do with an escape, but to where and why she did not yet know. She just knew they had to stay together and wait for...whatever.

Until now, that had not been difficult. Since she and Gerry started hanging out together he showed little interest in other girls at school. However, when he mentioned that huge, black-and-white beast of a dog, she immediately made the connection. The dog had been a faithful companion to the young woman in her dreams. Remmy's character hated it.

That damned beast is trying to tear us apart. I gotta keep Gerry away from him.

A hard bump reminded her that not only was she cocooned in canvas on a flatbed truck, but she was a fugitive from the law.

She opened her eyes and sighed, "You're a total loon, girl."

When the truck rolled to a stop, she snapped out of her self-derision and rose to peer over the sidewall of the flatbed.

"Tillamook," she sighed wearily while massaging an aching shoulder. "I thought we'd never get here."

She moved stiffly to the back of the truck and hesitated until she heard the driver swear. Quickly jumping off, she ran across the oncoming lane to a gas station.

Knowing the truck driver could not follow her against the intersecting one-way street, she let out a sigh of relief, but her breath caught again when a police car moved slowly past. Turning her face away, she pretended interest in the gas station, relaxing only when the patrol car continued on.

"Gotta find a bus," she muttered anxiously before turning right at the next street.

After walking a block, she stopped to look down the intersecting street and spied a small shuttle-like bus. The sight sent her heart racing, and she walked toward it as fast as she could without attracting attention.

"Is this the ticket office?" she asked a plump woman waiting outside a small building next to the bus.

The woman nodded. "Where you goin'?"

"Salem."

"The only destination outside this county is Portland." She looked at her watch. "The eight-ten to the Portland Greyhound station should be here any minute. From there you can get a ride to Salem."

"But where do I, like, buy a ticket?"

Shrugging, the woman motioned toward the small building behind her. "The office isn't open yet, but you can pay the driver. If I recall, it's only fifteen bucks one way, but you gotta have exact change."

Remmy was reaching for her wallet when she remembered it contained only twenties and ones.

"Thank you," she responded distractedly as she scanned the area for somewhere to get change, and was still looking when she heard a police radio.

"Suspect is female, five-foot-five, about one-hundred-and-ten pounds. Auburn hair, wearing a blue jacket, blue jeans, and red tank top..."

The rest was blotted out when the engine of the nearby bus roared to life. Hurrying behind it, Remmy turned back to peer at an officer moving toward the enclosure. She held her breath, and watched him approach the woman she had spoken to, but before he reached her, his radio burped,

"…accident at the corner of..."

The bus's engine revved again, and it started to pull away as the officer hurried back to his car. The threat now gone, Remmy returned to the sidewalk to watch a larger bus, with a Tillamook/Portland banner on its front, pull in to take its place.

The bus rolled to a stop and disgorged a line of people onto the sidewalk. Unsure what she should do, Remmy watched the group mill around until they organized themselves for whatever they were going to do next. The woman she had spoken with rose and hugged a man before leading him away as Remmy weaved through the crowd.

"Going to Portland, Miss?" a thin, elderly man asked from the top of the steps.

"Yes. What time will this bus arrive?"

When the man stepped aside to let a rider disembark, Remmy looked down to see that her clothes were still splattered with mud.

The driver seemed to take no notice as he answered. "We're keeping a good schedule today, so I'm pretty sure we'll make it by ten-twenty."

"And how long before you leave?"

Looking at his watch, he answered, "Departure is in twelve minutes."

"Then I guess I'll get a bite to eat."

Jogging to a nearby service station, she slipped into the bathroom and pulled off both of the tank tops and her blue jeans. With a fistful of wet paper towels, she quickly scrubbed the pants, cleaning off dried mud and additional debris she'd picked up from the bed of the truck. She then wiped dirt from her face and hair before putting the green tank top back on, and stuffing the red one into a trash bin.

After pulling the jeans on, she went into the gas station's convenience store, and grabbed a packet of beef jerky priced at just under five dollars. Passing the clerk a twenty, she fidgeted nervously as the old woman took her time ringing up the sale and counting out change. With cash finally in hand, Remmy jogged back to see a short line of people boarding. When the driver spied her, he waved and followed the last person inside.

Her breath caught at the sight of a second police car approaching. It was all she could do to keep her panic under control as she bounced up the steps, and handed the driver three fives.

"Good timing, young lady," he said as he pushed the bills into a locked receptacle. "Once you're seated, we'll get this show on the road."

Hurrying to the first available seat, she dropped into it and anxiously watched as the driver closed the door and started the engine. The bus was almost to the highway by the time the Sheriff's deputy exited his car to look around the empty loading area. Suddenly realizing she was holding her breath, Remmy gasped in air as the bus turned onto Highway 6 and accelerated toward Portland.

Chapter 41

Awaking with a start, Elizabeth quickly looked over to see Tilley picking up a dropped handkerchief.

"Mistress! You're awake," the girl said needlessly.

"What happened?" she asked, but as soon as the question left her lips, the memories flooded back. "Oh Lord. My husband is dead."

"Yes, Mistress."

Unable to think of a response, she scanned the room, surprised to find sunlight pouring through her east-facing window.

"What is the time?"

"The clock in the hall has only just struck half nine."

"In the morning?"

"Yes, Mistress. The doctor gave ya a sleeping draft."

She felt the urge to correct the girl's English, but did not have the strength. "And you have been up the entire night?"

Tilley curtsied. "I've been ever so worried about ya."

"Have Jason bring up tea. As soon as I am dressed, I wish to..."

"The constable took him away, Mistress!"

"Jason? Whatever for?"

"For killing the master. They say he done it so he could have you."

The statement struck Elizabeth dumb for a long moment. She had always felt a certain connection to her servants, but it had never been of a romantic nature.

"That is patently absurd," she stated adamantly. "There has never been anything of that sort between us."

The maid began to cry. "The constable sees it different, Mistress, and so do I."

Shocked again by her maid's declaration, Elizabeth glared at her.

"You think I would..."

"No, Mistress! Never! But the constable and me come to yer room to find Jason holding ya in a very unsuitable way."

Swinging her legs over the side of the bed, Elizabeth tried to rise, but a bout of dizziness forced her to grab the bedpost.

"Help me," she demanded. "We must sort this out, and quickly."

"Shall I send William for the detective inspector?"

Elizabeth shook her head. "No. We will go directly to the police station. I will not have them arresting my staff without reason."

"But Jason admitted he done in the master."

Unsteady after reaching her feet, Elizabeth gave her head an exaggerated shake.

"He was trying to protect me," she protested, her body swaying. "Does that warrant prison?"

The girl moved quickly to support her mistress. "Please, Mistress. You should be in bed. As unsteady as ya are, you'll fall down the stairs, and then they'll be laying the blame on me."

Elizabeth was so unstable a slight push by Tilley sent her back onto the bed.

When the room continued to spin around her, Elizabeth sighed loudly and said, "It might be best if the detective inspector came to us."

Chapter 42

The mental tickle, though distracting, did not fully register with Jasmina as she entered the book shop. She often got random feelings from people. When she was alone with a person, she knew who it came from, but in a crowded space, like this bookstore, it was anyone's guess.

Moving inside, she focused on the books she would sign, the people she would speak with, and more importantly, the predicament that Gerry and her niece had gotten themselves into. She wanted to cancel the reading, but her husband, Tim had insisted she go, if only to give her a break from a situation over which she had no control.

But this reading was unlike any of the many others she had done. Her muscles were tense, concentration unsettled, mood dark. That tiny tickle slowly grew, as though she were hearing a far-off tune that was moving toward her. But this was not a tune. No. More like the rumbling of many large boulders bumping together.

Even without the distracting noise, the reading had not gone well. Only a handful of people showed up, and most wandered off soon after she finished reading, not even waiting to ask questions about her book. And without the chatter of eager fans, and the focus their questions might bring, she tried to idle away the time, but still felt out of sorts and uncomfortable until the bookstore owner thanked her for coming and helped her carry her books to the car.

On the last trip in to pick up what remained of her supplies, she lingered at the back of the store, browsing the science fiction section, but her attention was not on the titles. The rumbling had transformed, not into words, but feelings. She was interested then angered; curious then afraid; confrontational then timid.

Unable to stand it any longer, she thanked the owner and hurried from the store, pulling up her collar against the rain as she ran to her car, but before she reached it, another feeling hit her: despair.

Jerking around, she scanned the few faces nearby, but saw nothing that expressed the sensation taking over her psyche.

Such sadness!

She put the last of her supplies into the car, and was preparing to open the driver's door when the sensation became so strong she almost dropped her keys.

Someone needs help, but where is he?

She felt drawn to a nearby alley, and before she could stop them, her feet were moving in that direction.

"This is *not* a good idea," she muttered as she rounded the corner and stared down the relatively tidy alley, void of anything other than a large dumpster.

It took her a moment to realize that something, or someone was pressed into the corner created by the alley wall and one side of the dumpster. She intended to leave at once and have the store owner call the police, but her feet carried her up to the soggy, shivering, wreck of a person scrunched into a fetal position on the barren concrete.

"Are you OK?" she heard herself ask as the little girl inside her cried for her to run away.

She gasped in horror as the head slowly rose to present vacant, hollow eyes; snot dripping from his nose; and quivering red lips scowling on a canvas of gray-green skin.

"M…mmmake them g…g…go away," he pleaded.

"Them?" Jasmina asked as she looked around. "Who?"

The creature lifted a shaking hand, extending his index finger before slowly stabbing it into his forehead again and again.

"They won't ssstttooop," he whined. "Please mmmmake them ssssstop!"

Now even the adult woman in her wanted to run, to escape this miserable sight, and it was quite a shock to find her own hand reaching toward the man's forehead.

"It's going to be OK," she heard herself saying, though she had no idea why.

The instant she made contact, something dark blocked her vision as a powerful, yet desperate force surged through her fingers.

The sensation paralyzed her, keeping her in contact until she too could hear the many voices, all talking at once, all sounding insistent, angry, belligerent, frustrated.

She tried to straighten, to pull away, but her muscles froze. It was then she realized that one of the voices was growing louder, even more insistent, sounding even more frustrated.

I must get to them! it demanded.

"Get to whom?"

You know. You know them!

The intensity of the statements made her want to cry out, but she could make no sound. Whatever this was, it was desperate and would do anything to accomplish its goal. She wrenched her hand back, finally breaking free, but as she stood, the man jumped up, spraying water as he lunged at her.

She tried to scream as his arms wrapped around her, but the sudden lurch toward the middle of the alley made her throat close. For a long moment they clumsily danced in a circle, the man clutching her like a long-lost friend, and she trying to keep them from falling down.

In that tiny interval between hops -- him squeezing and her struggling for stability – she felt something change. The blackness was gone, as well as the desperate intensity. The man abruptly released her and jumped back, but instead of looking confused and desperate, he was beaming.

"You did it," he shouted. "You made them stop."

She felt dazed as the strange man danced around her in the pouring rain, seeming to care little about the cold, or the wet, or the pathetic condition of his soaked clothes.

"You did it! You did it! You did it!"

Stunned, she hardly reacted when he gave her another hug before hurrying down the alley to vanish around the corner.

Bewildered by what had just happened, she stared at where he had gone for a long moment, surprised to see him reappear, a smile still on his face.

"Where am I?" he laughed.

"Uh. You're in Salem."

"Salem, where?"

"Salem, Oregon."

"Really?"

When she nodded, he looked at his clothes as though seeing them for the first time.

"I need to get cleaned up. Where can I do that?"

Hesitating a moment to let the question sink in, she motioned to her left. "Two blocks down to Commercial Street, then go right for about ten blocks to the mission on your left. They can help you."

Nodding, he took two steps into the ally, his arms crossed tightly across his chest.

"I don't know how you did it, but thank you."

She wanted to ask him what she had done, but was stopped by the sudden sense of someone else sharing her consciousness. Looking down at her shaking hands, she thought of a question, but when she looked back up, he was gone.

Running to the end of the alley, she turned the corner to see him sprinting across Liberty Street against the light. Horns honked, tires squealed, but he seemed not to notice.

Shaking her head, she looked back to see something on the ground next to the dumpster. Even though she was wet and cold, she retraced her steps and picked up the small damp book. Opening it, she found most of the pages blank, but the first hundred or so had scribbling in them. Looking closely, she gasped when she realized he had written the same poem over and over again.

Death and hope are a curious mix,
Yet together shall they play
A perplexing role in our torn lives
Over which we have no say.

"I've heard this poem before, but how could I?" she wondered as she turned the pages.

You have not. Another voice in her head answered. *I have.*

"And who are you?"

Your destiny.

Chapter 43

I stared at my aunt's phone.

"How can I get in touch with Remmy?" I asked the empty room.

"Don't use the phone," Aunt Susan yelled from the kitchen. "In case your parents call."

"Right," I heard myself respond loudly before whispering, "And who would I call if I did?"

"I'm going out to the compost pile," she announced through the kitchen door. "I'll be back in a second and then we'll call Remmy's parents."

I was nodding when an idea came to me: Jasmina.

Even before the outside door clicked shut, I was moving to the dining room table where the contents of my wet wallet were spread out. Finding the right piece of paper, I hurried back to the phone and dialed the number written on it.

"Jasmina," I said when she answered. "This is Remmy's friend, Gerry. Have you heard from her?"

"Gerry? Remmy? What?" she asked distractedly. "Has something happened?"

"There was an accident. We're not hurt, but Remmy has disappeared."

"Disappeared? What do you mean?"

"Our car went into the river, and the cops were holding Remmy until her parents could come pick her up, but when they went to check on her, she'd vanished."

"Gerry. What aren't you telling me?"

I shook my head while looking at the kitchen door.

"I can't talk now, but if you hear from her, please call this number and let me know she's OK."

"Have you spoken with her parents?"

"I'm going to call them, but if the cops have already done it, they may be on their way here."

"Where are you?"

"I'm at my aunt's house on the coast, north of Nehalem."

"Gerry. There's something you need to know."

The back door closed, and I could hear my aunt shucking her boots.

"Gotta go. Please call if she contacts you."

"But Gerry. I know what is going..."

I hung up as Aunt Susan poked her head through the partly opened kitchen door.

"Everything OK here?"

"Yeah," I answered while idiotically standing in front of the phone. "I guess."

Her eyes went to the phone and back to me. "Who did you call?"

I thought of lying, but her expression made it clear that I had no future as a poker player.

"Remmy's Aunt Jasmina," I sighed. "I just wanted to know if she had, like, contacted her."

"And had she?"

As she moved further into the room, I shook my head. "I'm worried that Elissa might have somehow kidnapped her and..."

"The woman who was driving? How would she have gotten into the police station without being noticed?"

"Well, Remmy got out without them knowing. Elissa might have grabbed her as she was escaping."

"Good point, nephew-of-mine. So what do we do now?"

I felt a mixed sense of panic and helplessness. My friend was out there somewhere and I could do nothing but wait for word of her.

Word that she was alive and well...

...or dead.

Chapter 44

"Good afternoon, Madam," the brown-suited officer announced after he entered Elizabeth's drawing room and removed his bowler. "My name is Detective Inspector Langdons, with an 's'."

Dressed from head to toe in mourning black, with a gauzy, black veil covering her face, Elizabeth waved a black-lace-gloved hand at a chair near the policeman.

"Yes, Detective Inspector," she said. "Please do have a seat."

Holding his hat with both hands, the inspector moved to the chair, but waited until Elizabeth sat on the settee before lowering himself to the edge of his seat and carefully placing the bowler in his lap.

"I would like to offer my condolences for your loss, Madam, and to assure you that it is my intention to conclude my inquiries as quickly as possible so as to inflict the least amount of disruption possible to your household."

"Thank you. And to that end, I would like to know when you will be releasing my butler."

Smiling grimly, he shook his head. "Not for some time I should think, Missus Montgomery. Truth be told, we are considering charging..." He pulled a notebook from his overcoat and examined it. "...Jason Smythe with capital murder."

Elizabeth felt her jaw drop. "You are not serious, surely. He was defending me."

His head shaking, the detective inspector lowered the notebook. "That's not the way we see it, Madam. Our inquiries are still ongoing, but there are those who believe your Mister Smythe had strong...feelings for you. Had he made them known?"

Elizabeth blinked several times before shaking her head. "He gave no indication whatsoever."

"Thinking back on it, you couldn't say there was anything he might have done to give the impression he was in love with you, or that he had it in his heart to harm your husband?"

She hesitated before shaking her head again. "Never. He was primarily my husband's valet, but also served as butler when circumstances warranted. With his war injuries, my husband had need of his assistance. I seldom saw Jason outside of his company, but on any occasion in which we were alone together, he was most respectful and proper."

"I see. Was your husband's treatment of you also respectful and proper?"

The impudent question raised Elizabeth's ire, and she had to stop herself from making an equally disrespectful response. Clenching her teeth, she waited a couple of heartbeats then squared her shoulders.

"I beg your pardon!"

"My apologies for being so indelicate, but it is relevant to my inquiries."

Feeling her face warm, Elizabeth rose and quickly moved behind the settee to stand in front of the fireplace, her attention on the flames for a long moment before she turned back to the policeman.

"My husband received horrible injures in the war." She pressed her hands together and looked down at them. "His wounds left him crippled and in almost constant pain, but it was the unseen scars that were hardest for him to bear. Unfortunately, he sometimes took his frustration out on me."

"He beat you."

Without looking up, she jerked a nod.

"And did you report this?"

"No, Detective Inspector," she answered angrily while returning to the front of the settee. "After the many painful indignities my husband has suffered, I could not bear to bring such a disgrace upon him."

"Did you ever discuss this with Mister Smythe?"

She shook her head. "Jason is a servant. It is not my habit to share such personal feelings with him, or any of the others in our service."

"And did Mister Smythe ever express his dissatisfaction with the way your husband treated you?"

"He did not."

"He never mentioned that his feelings for you were more than mere respect."

"Never! My husband would have dismissed him at once."

"Would you have told your husband, if Mister Smythe had done so?"

The impertinent question struck her like a blow, but she did not hesitate.

"Most certainly!" she responded more aggressively than she would have liked. "I am not a common strumpet, Detective Inspector. My obligation was always to my husband. Such behavior would not have been tolerated."

"So, it would appear that if Mister Smythe had his mind set on murder, he acted alone in this matter."

"*If* Jason wished to harm my husband, he did not share his intentions with me, or any other member of our staff."

Nodding, Detective Inspector Langdons scribbled in his notebook for a moment before holding up his pencil.

"One more question, if I may."

"If you must."

"Now that your husband is deceased, who stands to inherit his estate?"

The question momentarily confused her, and took away much of the anger, along with the strength it provided. Feeling unsteady, she lowered herself to the settee, folded her hands together in her lap, and sighed.

"Phillip has no living relatives of which I am aware," she answered softly. "Therefore, I believe his estate comes to me."

"And is it sizeable?"

Feeling her shoulders sag, Elizabeth shook her head. "I should think so, but my husband never confided such matters to me. I expect all will be revealed when the will is read."

"But still, we are talking about a considerable sum, surely."

The inspector's insistence on asking about money, the very reason her parents insisted she marry Phillip, a man who beat her, left her childless and deserted in an empty house she had long since begun to hate, made her angry again.

Shaking her head, Elizabeth cried, "What does this have to do with my butler? Surely he has nothing to gain by my husband's death."

"Unless he hopes to marry you afterwards."

"That is absurd!"

His head shaking, the inspector stood. "To you, maybe, but he may well have thought otherwise."

"I can assure you, Detective Inspector, he thought no such thing."

Slipping his notebook back into his jacket pocket, Langdons rose and took two hesitant steps toward the door before turning back. "I am sorry if this causes you undue distress, Mistress Montgomery, but until I am finished with my inquiries, I fear Mister Smythe must remain where he is."

Elizabeth started to argue, but quickly realized he was just an underling doing what he was told. She would need a more direct approach in order to set Jason free.

"I hope it will be soon," she said tersely while motioning to Tilley. "My maid will show you out. Good day, Detective Inspector."

"Good day to you, Madam."

Her face flush with anger, Elizabeth watched as Tilley escorted the inspector out, waiting only until the front door closed before she hurried to the window to watch him walk to his carriage and climb in.

"Have William prepare the carriage," she announced when Tilley returned to the room. "We are off to the train station."

"Mistress?"

"Since the detective inspector has his mind set on a hanging, our Jason will have need of our solicitor."

Chapter 45

Her feet tangled in the hem of her dress, Elizabeth groped for something to steady herself, but caught only air as she fell forward. A hand grabbed her arm and turned her enough to see it was her husband but he was off balance and his free hand was coming toward her face.

There was no time to shout before the rigid fist struck her cheek and sent her crashing to the ground. She threw her hands out to soften the blow and felt stabbing pain as crushed rock dug into them.

Tilley screamed, "Mistress!"

Her cheek throbbing, she rolled onto her back and saw her husband's hulking form leaning over her. His mouth was moving as he spoke, but Tilley's scream blotted out all but, "…intended to do."

To her surprise, he held out a hand, as though to help her up, and more out of reflex than intention, she took it and let him pull her into a sitting position. When he tried to help her rise further, she could not get her feet under her, and fell back again. To her dismay, Phillip let out an angry howl and pitched forward, his fist punching her between the breasts to slam her back to the gravel.

"Nooo!" Cook wailed. "Don't kill 'er, Master!"

Phillip pulled back as he and Jason briefly wrestled. A moment later her husband grunted and fell forward again, his shoulder slamming her midsection and pushing all air from her lungs. He quickly rolled off, but when she tried to take a breath, she could not.

It hadn't occurred to her that Phillip might actually be attacking her until she heard Cook's lament.

And then Tilley cried, "Oh Lord! She's a gonner."

Panic gripped her convulsing breast as she looked around for help. Her husband was rolling on the ground, and though Jason had his back to her, she heard him shout, "Send William for a doctor."

Still struggling to breathe, she turned to see Cook, her skirts held up, bouncing off in the direction of the barn.

"Why in heaven's name did you interfere?" Phillip bellowed.

"I was hoping to avoid what just happened, Sir," Jason answered, his voice uncharacteristically strained.

"Well you bloody well made it worse, damn it!"

"Help her," Tilley cried. "She's turning blue."

Black spots peppering her vision, Elizabeth tried in vain to refill her empty lungs.

*   *   *

I awoke with a start, gasping in air and surprised by the sudden darkness. When I sat up, the painful cuts on my arms made it clear I was no longer in the dream. My breathing slowed when I remembered that my aunt had sent me back to bed, despite my misguided insistence that I'd never be able to sleep.

"Are you OK in there?" Aunt Susan called as a steady rain tapped against the bedroom window.

"Yeah," I responded distractedly while staggering from the bed, throwing on a bathrobe, and opening the door. "Just another bad dream, I guess, except…this time I remember it."

My aunt looked confused. "Dream? About the accident?"

"No. These started before that. It has to do with my past life."

"The one you mentioned earlier?"

I didn't really know what to make of her tone, but since it didn't sound like she was mocking me, I nodded.

"According to Remmy's aunt, I was a woman."

"A woman?"

"And her husband was, like, a total shit."

"He abused her?"

I shrugged. "Yeah. When I first started remembering the dreams, she was in a bed and all banged up. I guess he pushed her off the roof of their home."

"And you believe you really lived this life?"

Suddenly feeling overwhelmed and tired, I returned to the bed and sat. The cuts on my arms ached, my head throbbed, and I felt totally foolish and alone.

"I know it sounds stupid, but how else do you explain what Elissa did?"

"Elissa? The one driving the car?"

"Yeah."

"And she told you about your past life?"

I looked up at her, surprised we were even having this conversation.

"You must think I'm a total idiot."

Shaking her head, she sat beside me, and gently took my hand in hers. "I don't think that at all."

"Do you believe in past lives?"

Aunt Susan barked a humorless laugh. "It doesn't matter what *I* believe. For whatever reason, you believe you were a woman who was beaten by her husband. It is real to you, isn't it?"

I felt myself shudder. "Yeah. Like, totally real. I think that's why Elissa freaked me out. For whatever reason, I know she's part of that story."

"From your past life? How?"

"Remmy says she was probably my husband, but I'm not so sure."

"Who do you think she was?"

"I don't know. I think she was gonna tell me, but the sight of her sent me packing, and I didn't give her the chance."

Aunt Susan put an arm around me and gave my shoulders a gentle squeeze. "If she died in the river, you may never know."

"I don't think she did because it was the woman who pulled me and Remmy out of the car, and after we reached the surface, someone spoke to me. It was all Remmy could do to stay above water, so it totally had to be the lady."

"Did you see her?"

Closing my eyes, I tried to remember, but it was such a confusing blur, I shook my head.

"Why would she help you get out of the car if she wanted you dead?"

Though it hurt to do so, I rubbed a free hand over an uninjured part of my face. "I've been wondering the same thing."

"You think she's still after you?"

I jerked a nod. "And if she has Remmy again, we're, like, back to square one."

"You need help with this, and it can't be me."

"Who then?"

At the sound of tires crunching gravel, Aunt Susan looked toward the front of the house.

"Your father."

Chapter 46

Rain tick-ticked against the bus' windows as Remmy stretched and turned her attention to the brick and concrete façade of the Portland Greyhound bus depot.

After the bus stopped, she rose and followed the other riders splashing through a downpour to the terminal. Once inside, she became cautious and scanned the room for anyone who might be looking for her. Seeing no one who looked like a cop, she moved to the ticket counter and booked a seat for Salem.

"That'll be leaving in two hours," the clerk announced as she handed over the ticket and pointed at where Remmy had just come in. "Right outside that door."

Turning toward her future destination, Remmy saw the Tillamook bus driving off into the pouring rain, and felt a twinge of angst. For the first time in days, she felt safe on that bus, and now she was back in the open where any predator could attack her.

The thought made her shiver, but oddly enough, it also made her realize how hungry she was. Moving to the station's diner, she bought a hamburger and fries before spending the last of her money on a book. Finding an unoccupied bench, she sat at one end and spread out her food.

She was taking a second bite of her burger when a strange feeling made her look up to see a scruffy-looking man with a dirty face and matted hair staring at her. When she returned her attention to the book, he moved closer and sat in the middle of the bench.

"You gonna finish those fries?" he asked expectantly.

She scrunched up her nose against his foul smell, and glared at him. "Go away."

Straightening, he hunched his shoulders. "I don't want no trouble. I was just wondering if..."

"Go away or I call the cops."

Lethargically lifting both hands, palms out, he whined, "OK. OK. Can't fault a guy for tryin'."

She continued to watch as he slid to the opposite end of the bench, but when it appeared he would go no further, she moved to another bench, opened the book again, and tried to focus on it. It was, of course, hopeless, as she could now sense his presence without even looking at him. She felt him moving, and when she looked up, he was right where she thought he would be.

His eyes on her, he moved to the next row over, but he no longer looked timid. Once opposite her position, he stopped.

"Go away," she insisted loudly before looking back at her book.

"Maybe you don't want me to."

She kept her eyes on the book. "I totally do, so, like, beat it."

"I just realized who you are...or were."

The statement struck her as ludicrous, until she began to wonder if he could also sense *her* presence. The thought made her look at him.

"Who are you?"

He shook his head. "Someone who knows what you used to be like."

"Used to be?" she asked cautiously. "What do you mean?"

"Mistress Elizabeth was a fine lady," he said in an entirely different voice. "She didn't deserve what you done to her."

Her book tumbled to the floor as she jumped up and scrambled behind the bench. Though she intended to run away, she couldn't make her legs work and finally turned to face him again.

"What do you mean?"

"I been waitin' fer you a long time."

"Who *are* you?"

The man chuckled, but still made no move toward her.

"My parents called me Albert, but I never liked the name."

She watched as he lifted his hands and stared into the palms.

"What do you...want to be called?"

Smiling grimly, he lowered his hands and looked at her.

"William."

Chapter 47

"I am sorry, Madam," Jason said, speaking loudly to be heard over the hooting and hollering from the crowded prison cells around them. "I should not have struck him so hard."

Scrunching up her nose against the vile smell of poor sanitation, overcrowding, and neglect, she struggled to retain her composure. "It was an accident. You were defending me."

"Be that as it may, Madam. I think the detective inspector is set on sending me to the gallows."

"He will do no such thing. My solicitor will be up tomorrow and this will be sorted..."

"QUIET DOWN YOU LOT," a guard bellowed as he rapped a baton against cell bars. "You never seen a proper lady before?"

When the shouting and catcalls only dropped by half, the guard marched up to Elizabeth, slamming his baton against any exposed fingers and faces he passed.

"Best if you don't tarry, Madam," he shouted above the din. "This lot ain't 'ouse broke. They don't often see the likes of you 'ere."

Elizabeth nodded. "I shan't tarry long."

Scowling briefly at Jason, the guard jerked a nod. "See that ya don't."

As the guard moved away, Jason leaned closer to the bars. "You should leave at once, Madam."

"You will soon be out as well," she responded, her back straight, face somber and only her eyes showing how scared she was.

Jason shook his head. "Not so quickly, I fear."

"You are not a murderer. Your intentions were honorable."

"'ey miss," a large man behind Jason called. "Me intentions be 'onerable as well. Will ya take me 'ome too?"

Several men in the cell laughed raucously as Jason scowled.

"Please, Madam. I fear for your safety."

She smiled grimly. "I fear for yours as well." Lifting a bag hanging from her arm, she started to reach into it. "To that end, I've taken the liberty of bringing you some..."

"No disrespect, Madam," Jason interrupted while glancing back into the cell, "but it would be best if you gave me nothing and did not come here again. These ruffians have a decidedly unique view of honor and having a proper lady delivering amenities to me is not conducive to my wellbeing."

"But surely the guards would protect..."

She stopped when Jason shook his head. "The guards are just as apt to rob me as the inmates."

"Oh dear," she gasped while lowering the bag. "I had not considered that possibility."

He nodded. "I appreciate your intentions, but it is best you leave now."

"But I..."

She stopped when he shook his head more assertively.

"Thank you, Madam, and have a very pleasant day."

When she turned to leave, Jason called, "Madam."

Elizabeth jerked around to face him. "Yes?"

"I forgot to tell you that Master Beauregard is not actually missing. After you left for London, the master set into motion a plan that would surely have resulted in the dog's death. William and I were aware of his plan and found another dog to put in his place. William took Master Beauregard to the Frampton's. Their stable boy, Bobby will know where he is."

"Beau is safe?"

"I believe he is, Madam, but now you must leave."

Her face a mixture of relief and anguish, she hesitated for a moment before she nodded, hugged her hands to her chest, and hurried down the narrow hallway between the overcrowded cells, trying hard and failing to pretend that the whistling and shouting of the other prisoners did not bother her. His head shaking, Jason continued to watch until the guard unlocked the gate and let her out.

"That be a pretty little missus yer gots there, Matey," a gruff voice announced from behind him. "Maybe she'll come all the way in next time, so we can all enjoy 'er many charms."

Without looking at him, Jason leaned his head against the bars and said, "She will not be returning to this place."

"Ohhh, now I ain't too 'appy to be 'earin' that," the large man snarled. "I guess we've no need for the likes of you then, 'ave we?"

Jason turned to face his heckler. "What do you mean, Sir?"

"Well, I 'ears yer mistress is the one s'posed to be in the dock."

"That is untrue. Mistress Elizabeth had nothing to do with the death of her husband."

"An' yer trial will prove that out, will it?"

"Most assuredly."

The heckler chuckled. "An' we can't 'ave somethin' like that, now, can we?"

A flash of reflected light appeared at the bottom of Jason's vision, but before he could look down, pain exploded at the bottom of his rib cage. His scream was cut off when a hand clamped over his mouth and rammed his head hard against the bars.

"Ya won't be 'elpin' 'er now, will ya?"

He tried to protest, but his lungs no longer worked, and the last thing he saw in the fading light was a nearly toothless grin.

Clifford M. Scovell

Chapter 48

"But Dad, you don't understand," I protested as my parents gawked at me as though I'd just announced I was pregnant with triplets.

I had explained as much as I could, but as the story played out, it was obvious they were not buying any of it.

"I know this is difficult, Son," my father finally said with a voice that was far more calm than I would have expected from his expression, "but we need to let the police handle this."

"Remmy may be in danger!"

I could see his jaw clenching.

"And what would you have us do? You have no idea where this woman lives, or what her true intentions are. It's a pretty long stretch to assume she snuck into that police station and kidnapped Remmy. Until we have some hint as to where they've gone, we can't even begin to search."

I felt a flash of outrage that was amplified by my own confusion and fear. How could they not lift a finger to help my girlfriend? How could they be so insensitive?

"You have police connections," I declared angrily. "Ask them what they know."

Dad shook his head. "I do contract maintenance work in the Valley. I don't know anyone in Tillamook County."

Stunned beyond belief by his lame excuse, I was about to blurt out a well-deserved "Bullshit!" but my aunt spoke first.

"I do."

When all three of us turned toward her, she blushed.

"Sorry to interrupt, but I once dated the Sheriff's officer who covers this part of the county." When we remained silent, she smiled and added, "We're still on good terms."

Dad looked from her to me and back before shaking his head. "We shouldn't be butting in on their business."

Aunt Susan picked up the phone. "It couldn't hurt to ask what they know, and besides, I loaned him some garden tools. I've been meaning to call and ask for them."

Looking self-conscious, she dialed the number but kept her eyes on me. Her expression was sad, and questioning, but my attempt at an encouraging smile felt more like a grimace.

"Andrew," she barked self-consciously. "I've been meaning to call you about those tools I...yes...oh thank you, that will be fine." Her eyes shot to my parents before she turned her back to us, as though that would somehow make their conversation private.

"I was wondering if you had any news on the car that went into the river last night. Yes, that was my nephew. No, we haven't heard from the missing girl. Oh really? Did they ever find that woman?" She did a quick spin to smile at us. "You think so? That's good news. Huh? Oh sure, sure. We'll chat later. Yes. Coffee at Wanda's would be nice. See you then."

She lowered the phone and shook her head. "No sign of your friend, I'm afraid, but the other woman got out alive."

A splash of cold fear dowsed my outrage. "They have her?"

"No, but the investigating officer found footprints on the opposite bank, further down river. He's pretty sure they were hers, because as far as they know, no one else went into the water." She looked at me again. "That's right, isn't it?"

I jerked a nod. "Yeah. There was only the three of us."

"Any idea where Remmy might have gone?" Dad asked.

Aunt Susan shrugged. "They think she thumbed a ride on the highway, but there's no way to know if she went north or south. Her description has been sent to all the TV and radio stations. Maybe the person who gave her a lift will call in."

"She'll head back to Salem," I stated with far more confidence than I felt.

"But why did she run in the first place?" Mom asked.

I shook my head as tears of desperation filled my eyes. "No idea, but I can't let her go through this alone."

His expression softening, my father rubbed his chin. Mom seemed to sense that he was about to give in because she quickly put a hand on his arm and turned to Aunt Susan.

"We'll take Gerry home now," she said with determination. "I don't think this strange woman is a threat to him anymore, and we can do a better job of protecting him at home."

From the way my aunt flinched, Mom might as well have shot her through the heart, but when Aunt Susan started to respond, Mom quickly turned away.

"Why would you assume that?" Dad asked.

Mom shook her head. "I don't know why she threw that wrench through our window, but risking her life to pull Gerry out of the car proves she doesn't want him dead. Whatever her thinking, I believe she was just trying to make some kind of twisted point."

"By cutting him to pieces with glass? Twisted is right, and that means he needs to be somewhere safe."

"And last night's incident proves it doesn't matter where Gerry hides. She's going to find him."

My father shook his head as well. "She probably followed us. I wasn't paying close attention when we drove up here, but I'll be more careful from now on."

"Dad," I said insistently. "We have to go back. The cops can watch me. If she tries to use Remmy to get at me, they can grab her."

"I won't use you as bait."

"My friend's life is in danger because of me," I argued. "If you've taught me anything, it is to protect the people I love. That's what I was trying to do last night and what I hope to do by finding Remmy."

"But you don't know she'll be there."

Though I could not explain why, I knew with absolute certainty that Remmy was either in Salem, or on her way there. On the other hand, now was not the time to try to explain the "psychic" connection between us.

"Where else would she go? If she hangs around here the cops will arrest her, and she doesn't have any other family in this state."

"Where is her family from?"

I stopped to think, but found my head so full of other thoughts, it took me a moment to remember.

"New Hampshire, but I know what you're thinking, and no. She might have enough money to catch a bus to Salem, I doubt she'd carry the kind of cash it would take to get her to the east coast."

I locked eyes with Dad for a long moment before he broke away to look at Mom. When I turned to her as well, she shifted her attention from him to me and back before nodding.

"OK. Fine," he announced, "but I'm calling the Salem police from here so they'll be at our house when we arrive."

I felt a sudden sense of relief. "That's fair."

"But no matter what happens, you don't go out alone," Mom added.

I looked from her strained face to an expectant Aunt Susan.

"Agreed, but there's one more thing." My chest felt tight over what I was about to say, but I also felt angry at another injustice I was responsible for.

"I know you're pissed at Aunt Susan over this, but it wasn't her fault." Mom opened her mouth to respond, but I had to continue or I was going to start crying. "What I did was stupid. I know that now, but it was my decision, and there was nothing Aunt Susan could have done to stop me, even if she had planted herself outside the bedroom door."

Mom hesitated for a long moment before saying, "Well, be that as it may…"

"No," I interrupted, knowing where a sentence like that would lead. "You taught me to take responsibility for my actions. Well, I'm doing that now."

"But…you could have been…killed."

"Totally true, but other people were responsible for that, not Aunt Susan. She gave me a safe place to stay and trusted me to do as I was told. I totally broke that trust and deserve any punishment you decide to give me, but not her. To do that would be so totally unfair."

I wasn't expecting the tears in Mom's eyes as she jerked a nod. "OK." She looked at Dad, who looked like he was trying really hard not to smile. Shaking her head, she nodded at Aunt Susan before her gaze returned to me. "Let's get you home."

We all froze for a long moment until Dad broke the spell by pulling out his cell phone and announcing, "I'll call the Salem police."

Both women let out loud sighs as Dad turned away and spoke into his phone. I also noticed that Mom kept her attention on Dad, even though I could see my aunt wanted desperately to speak with her. Before I could think of anything more to say, Dad was waving us toward the front door.

"We'll meet them at our house."

Rushing into the bedroom, I grabbed my bag, and hurried to catch up, stopping only to carefully hug Aunt Susan.

"I'm sorry for all the trouble," I said as she kissed my cheek. "If Remmy calls, tell her where I've gone."

Her eyes still wet with tears, she nodded eagerly. "I hope your friend is OK."

I started to step away when an image flashed in my mind: Jason, William, Cook, and Tilley standing around a person lying on the ground. I looked up at them for a moment before turning my attention to the corpse's pale face. I couldn't help the gasp that came from me. There was more to that corpse than the loss of a person, even if he had been a total ass. All four of us had lost the chance for…

"Gerry?"

Snapping back to the present, I realized I was still holding on to her.

"Yeah," I blurted before running toward the car, one hand waving over my head. "Me too."

Chapter 49

She desperately wanted to run, but to her utter amazement, Remmy stood her ground and gawked at the wreck of a man standing opposite her.

"What do you want?"

"It's your fault we didn't get there the last time," William responded. "If you keep messing up like this, we won't make it this time either."

"I don't know what you're talking about."

He shook his head slowly as she started to inch away from him. As much as she wanted to scream for help, she somehow knew her situation required the opposite.

"It ain't just that we missed our way out, but Jason didn't deserve to die in that grimy cell."

She was surprised at how angry his statement made her. Even more shocking, when she opened her mouth to speak, another voice came out.

"And you think I had a choice in the matter?" a deep, male voice responded. "If he had not shoved me so hard..." The voice stopped abruptly, leaving Remmy unsure as to what to do next.

A more confident William stepped around the bench and moved toward her. Fearing he might attack her, she backpedaled toward the nearest exit.

"You've been having the dreams, haven't you?"

"No," she lied. "I don't, like, know anything about any dreams."

Her heart nearly froze when William slowly shook his head. "Have the others been speaking to you? Have they told you what you must do?"

The questions stopped her. *He knows!*

"What others?" she asked tentatively.

"The ones in your dreams. They told me you would be here."

Black bodies moving in the darkness. Orange flames wicking up her arm.

She gave her head a sharp shake to banish the images, and for a brief moment the room started spinning. *What's happening to me?*

She staggered and caught herself, only then looking up to see she had turned around and was now facing William. The sight made her afraid, but she stood up to the fear and was preparing to ask him to explain when the earlier male voice shouted in her head, *NO! He's a nutter. Get away from him.*

Startled into action, she continued toward the exit, but stopped when she saw a cluster of people standing between her and the outside. Her heart raced when it looked like some of them were watching her.

Are they also from my past? How do I know?

Panic made her desperate to find another way out, but the world around her became a blur with streaks of light and flashes of color. Every face seemed to be accusing, and even if they weren't looking at her, she knew they were watching.

A hand on her shoulder felt like an electric shock that bit into her flesh, and forced a yip of pain from her. She did a quick spin away from William's hand and faced him.

"Don't touch me!"

She did not realize she was backpedaling again until she saw movement on her right.

"Is there a problem here?" a man asked as he approached them.

She was prepared to run, but noticed the newcomer's uniform. Overwhelmed with relief, she stabbed a finger at William.

"He's trying to molest me."

When the newcomer rushed between them, William stopped.

"Sir, I'm going to have to ask you to stay away from this woman."

Flashing a look of surprise, William held up both hands, palms out. "We're just having a friendly conversation."

"That's not what it looks like to me," the man said as he stepped closer to William. "If you don't leave her alone, I will escort you from the building."

His hands still up, William waved them. "Don't want no trouble, Mister." He pointed to the other side of the depot. "I'll just move over there."

Remmy's heart thumped as she watched him move to a table outside the small cafe. She was still trying to catch her breath when her rescuer faced her.

"Are you alright, Miss?"

Though the badge on his arm read "Security", Remmy was now afraid to trust anyone, and simply jerked a nod in response. Holding up her hands, she suddenly realized they were empty.

"I…uh…dropped my book," she announced before hurrying over to snatch it from the floor.

Seeing the man following her, she quickly straightened to face him, but he stopped a respectful distance away and pointed at the ticket counter.

"If he gives you anymore trouble, just let them know and I'll see that he is escorted from the building."

Hugging the book to her chest, she nodded eagerly. "Thank you."

"No problem. We want this to be a safe place for our passengers. Where are you off to today?"

She started to say, Salem, but the word stopped on the tip of her tongue.

"Medford," she blurted. "My grandma lives there."

The man smiled. "I'm sure she is excited to know you're coming. Have a good day."

Unable to make herself move, Remmy watched the man return to the ticket counter and speak with the sales person. When they both looked at her, she grimaced a smile before turning toward where she had last seen William, but found the table empty. Sucking in a sharp breath, she scanned the crowd for a face that was not to be found.

"Oh God," she gasped, the book still clutched to her chest. "When will this nightmare end?"

Chapter 50

Elizabeth was so focused on applying makeup, the knock on her bedroom door startled her. Hearing a cry of protest from Tilley, she looked in her mirror to see the maid holding both hands in the air as the brush she had been holding clattered against the hardwood floor. She was turning toward her maid when another knock pulled her attention back to the door.

"See who it is," she demanded irritably.

"Yes, Mistress," Tilley said as she scooped up the brush and quickly set it on the dressing table.

Opening the door only a crack, the maid greeted the unseen caller before turning to her mistress.

"William says the solicitor is here."

Elizabeth nodded. "We will be down directly."

Tilley relayed the message and returned to finish arranging her mistresses' hair. As the girl worked, Elizabeth looked into the mirror and was shocked by the emptiness she saw in her own eyes.

Something is missing, flashed in her head. *I feel it.*

She was so focused on the thought, she jerked noticeably when Tilley appeared next to her with a dark-gray shawl to complement her black dress. Recovering quickly, she pulled it over her shoulders, and followed her maid from the room.

"What news have you, Mister Kepler?" she asked eagerly as the conservatively dressed visitor snapped his gold pocket watch closed and deftly slipped it into the pocket of his gray vest before nervously adjusting his wire-rimmed spectacles.

The elderly solicitor bowed stiffly before speaking. "I am sorry to be the bearer of distressful news, Madam, but I am informed that Mister Smythe was assaulted in his cell not long after you left him yesterday."

Elizabeth gasped. "Assaulted? Is he seriously hurt?"

Clearing his throat, Mister Kepler again adjusted his glasses. "Unfortunately, I am told he has died from his injuries."

Lifting a hand to her mouth, Elizabeth gaped at the solicitor. "Lord, no. How could this happen?"

"Apparently, one of his cell mates stabbed him with a homemade knife. As is common with the sort who frequent our prisons, none will admit to the crime, nor will they tell the police who..."

He stopped when Tilley burst into tears, uncomfortably watching the maid for a moment before returning his attention to Elizabeth.

"But why..." Emotions stopped her words as she continued to hold a hand over her mouth until she regained control. "What could have set this off?

Mister Kepler shook his head. "People of this sort are prone to random violence, and it takes little effort to send them into a killing frenzy. It is most likely they were upset over his appearance, or the way he looked at them, or..."

He stopped, looking embarrassed, but Elizabeth already knew what he was about to say.

"Or my visit was the cause."

Mister Kepler nervously fiddled with his spectacles again and cleared his throat. "I doubt...that is, I am sure..." Looking at his feet for a moment, he shook his head. "My apologies, Madam, but I am afraid we shall probably never know."

When Tilley continued to sob, Elizabeth guided her to a chair and sat her down. It was a long moment before she again noticed the solicitor agitating on the opposite side of the room, his fingers nervously kneading his hat, his face the picture of discomfort. After Elizabeth returned her attention to Tilley, he cleared his throat once more.

"My apologies for bringing this up at such a difficult time, but will you be responsible for collecting his body for burial?" When Elizabeth continued to watch Tilley without responding, he added, "If so, I could handle the arrangements. It would serve no good purpose for you to return to that dreadful place, especially considering the stress you must be under with yesterday's unfortunate incident."

"Yes," Elizabeth said distractedly, her eyes still on Tilley. "That would be most kind." After a long moment, she turned to the solicitor. "Would it still be possible to bury him in the church graveyard, do you suppose?"

Mister Kepler nodded eagerly. "I can think of no reason why that would not be possible. After all, he was never convicted of a crime. I will speak to the parson as soon as we are finished here and make the arrangements."

"Thank you, Mister Kepler. I am in your debt."

Putting on his hat, the solicitor inched toward the door. "Then if there is nothing more, I will..."

"'Scuse me, Ma'am," William called from the doorway. "There's a Detective Inspector Langdon's here to see ya."

The sight of her new butler's ill-fitting clothes brought Elizabeth a flash of embarrassment. It was all she could do to keep from releasing an exasperated sigh before she nodded.

"Please send him in."

William bowed slightly and was saying, "Yes, Ma'am," when the thin detective slipped past him.

"Thank you for seeing me on such short notice," he announced. "I am of the understanding that you have heard the terrible news."

When neither woman responded, Mister Kepler removed his hat and said, "They have only just been informed. What can we do for you, Detective Inspector?"

"Well," He waved a hand in Tilley's direction. "I'd like another word with your maid, if it's not too much trouble."

"Really, Detective Inspector," Elizabeth protested. "Have you not done enough damage to this household? Is she to be arrested as well?"

"No, Ma'am," he responded. "Just a few more questions, if I may."

When Tilley continued to sob without looking at anyone, Elizabeth said, "Could this wait until another day? As you can see, she has had a terrible shock."

"If it were up to me, I'd be more than happy to oblige, Ma'am, but my superiors want this inquiry concluded today, if at all possible."

Tilley sniffed and blew her nose. "Don't you worry none, Mistress," she said while stuffing her handkerchief back into her apron. "I will speak with the detective inspector."

"Good enough," Langdons sighed gratefully as he motioned for her to move in his direction.

After watching them leave the room, Elizabeth turned to the solicitor. "I really don't understand the attitude of this detective inspector, Mister Kepler. It was a simple accident, nothing more. Jason's death was...such a waste."

"I am in total agreement, Madam, but we must not interfere with his inquiries."

Elizabeth shook her head angrily. "And make my home a prison? It feels as though he is delivering us to the gallows one at a time. Surely there must be a more civil way to perform his duties."

Mister Kepler's anxious stare made it plainly obvious he was uncomfortable with the situation.

"I am sure I do not know, Madam. I have never represented a client accused of murder before now."

Jerking her attention to him, she scowled. "Then you must find someone who has. I fear we may have need of him."

Chapter 51

As soon as our car pulled onto the highway, I started having second thoughts about leaving my aunt's home. If Remmy were looking for me, she would likely assume I was there. Of course, Aunt Susan would tell her where I'd gone, but what if the strange lady were to call and pretend to be Remmy?

Despite my misgivings, I also knew we couldn't go back.

"Dad. We can't go down the coast highway. There are, like, a million places for her to wait for us."

"What can she do?" he asked.

Nodding, Mom turned around. "She's not likely to try to hurt you."

"Maybe not," I mumbled, "but I'm sure she's the one who told me to let Remmy drown while we were in the river. Whatever plans she has for me, it's not likely she'll hesitate to hurt whoever gets in her way."

"You mean, she might attack us?" Mom asked.

The thought so terrified me, all I could do was shrug.

The car slowed as Dad announced, "Then let's give her the good-old runaround."

We turned onto a bridge, and I looked out the window to see we were crossing the Nehalem River. The sight of the flowing water made me shudder.

"Where are we going?"

"We're cutting over to Highway 53. A little further south we'll turn off onto the Miami River Road which parallels the coast highway for ten or fifteen miles before it merges back into it just south of Garibaldi. Few people, other than locals and fishermen, know about this route."

I was feeling depressingly overwhelmed by all that had happened, not the least of which was the nagging sense that Elissa was nearby. I could feel her behind me, her cold eyes boring holes in the back of my head, but though I kept turning around to look, no one was there. It was like waiting for the axe to fall, the anticipation probably being worse than the actual decapitation.

On the other hand, if Elissa did somehow figure out that we were taking this route, it wouldn't be hard for her to follow. The northern part of the Miami River Road is narrow and twisty, with few long straight stretches, and no other routes back to the coast highway. She only had to hang back a half-mile or so and we'd never know she was there.

Getting car sick from the effort of looking out the rear window, I begrudgingly settled into my seat. However, when we reached the southern part of the Miami River Road, where it snakes along the west side of a long, narrow field, I looked back to see a blue sedan.

At the same moment my father asked, "How could she do that?"

"Do what?"

"It's that woman. It has to be."

"What makes you think so?" Mom asked as she turned to look back.

"Who else would try to keep their distance?"

"What do you mean?"

"As soon as I realized there was a car following us, I started varying my speed, and each time I did, she matched it."

"Then let's stop and force her to catch up," I demanded.

Dad jerked his head around to face me. "No way she's going to get her hands on any of us. The woman is seriously demented!"

"I'm calling the police." Mom announced while holding up her cell phone, only to let out an exasperated grunt. "I can't get a signal."

Dad shook his head, his voice a mixture of anger and determination. "We're not far from the highway. You should get coverage there."

I braced myself as the car accelerated and then turned to see the blue car matching our speed. Though the car was some distance behind, I easily made out a single figure.

"It looks like she's alone."

"She could still have a weapon," Dad countered.

The south end of Miami River Road terminates where it intersects Highway 101, and when the stop sign came into view, Mom gasped. "Oh Lord. There are two cars ahead of us."

"We can't stop!"

"Alvin! Don't even think about it."

"As long as we're moving, she can't get a clear shot."

"Honey, you can't be serious."

Hunching his shoulders, Dad gripped the steering wheel with both hands, and announced, "Hang on. We're going to break some laws."

At this point, Highway 101 makes a long, convex turn. As we burst from a tree-lined section of the road, it was obvious that traffic on the highway was heavy, and our chances of just sailing through without being hit were slim.

With only seconds to make a decision, Dad jerked his head left and right to size up oncoming traffic before steering us onto the right shoulder where there was just enough room to zip past the two cars at the stop. As we blew through the stop, horns blared, tires screeched, Mom wailed, and I swore. All the windows on the left side of our car instantly filled with the front end of a huge, oncoming blue-and-white Winnebago. My heart totally stopped as we briefly went airborne, slammed the pavement, and cut a sharp left to avoid a southbound Camry.

The three of us squealed in harmony with our tires as we slid across the roadway, and Dad hit the accelerator in time to avoid the guard rail. I could hardly breathe as we shot up the shoulder past two more cars and then cut across to the oncoming lane to race past a third. We were swerving back into the southbound lane when I pulled my scattered wits together, grabbed the seat back, and looked back to see the blue car pulling to a stop.

"She's stuck at the intersection," I announced as we continued to accelerate.

"Are you nuts?" Mom screamed, her eyes on Dad.

"If I had stopped she could have jumped out and shot us," he gasped. "What should I have done?"

"So you decided to kill us yourself?"

"Where's the police station in Tillamook?"

"We could have died back there!"

"But we didn't," he gasped, eyes on the road. "So where is it?"

Mom stared at him for a long moment before releasing a shuddering breath. "Right next to the bus depot. Second and Laurel, I think."

"Is the Sheriff's office closer?"

Gulping in a breath, she shook her head. "It's south of town, by the airport."

Dad jerked the car into the oncoming lane and raced past another car, eliciting more horn honking and Mom-wailing as northbound traffic pulled to the shoulder to avoid us.

"What has come over you?" she shouted breathlessly.

"Call the Tillamook Police."

"I don't have their number."

There was a moment of tense silence before I said, "Dial 911."

Mom let out a loud sigh and dialed. As she talked, Dad drove like a man possessed, weaving in and out of traffic, sometimes passing on the left, and other times using the shoulder, if it was wide enough. Thoughts of dying in a fiery crash kept my eyes glued on the road ahead, but as we were barreling through the town of Bay City, I turned to look at the line of cars behind us, relieved to see no blue car in the mix.

"They're sending us an escort," Mom finally announced. "We're to go to the Sheriff's office."

"Why there?" Dad asked as the road arced left at the south edge of town.

The sight of flashing blue lights about half-a-mile ahead brought sighs of relief from my parents. Feeling the car slow, I looked back to see a blue car pass a large truck in the row of cars behind us. In the moment it took me to catch my breath, the car turned onto a side road.

"She just pulled off the highway."

"Where?" Dad barked, his eyes jerking to the rearview mirror.

The action caused him to pull the steering wheel slightly to the right, and when our tires hit gravel, the car lurched in that direction.

"Crap!" Dad cried as he cranked on the steering wheel, but overcorrected to send us into a slow-motion one-hundred-and-eighty-degree turn.

As we slid backwards into the ditch, Mom howled a drawn-out, "H-oooo-l-y c-o-wwww", Dad uselessly cranked on the steering wheel, and I held on so tightly my fingers hurt. The car slid off the road, its tires gouging ruts in the soft gravel until we finally came to a stop. For a long moment, the three of us could do nothing but gasp for air until the Sheriff's Deputy's face appeared in Mom's window.

"You folks OK in there?"

Dad jerked a tense nod. "Yeah. Yeah", and we scrambled out.

"What happened here?" the officer asked.

"There was this…" Mom started to explain, her voice several octaves higher than normal, eyes wide with panic. "…she kidnapped my…that blue car was…"

"OK. Let's slow it down, Ma'am," the officer said calmly. "And start from the beginning."

"My son was kidnapped last night," Dad finally gasped. "The kidnapper lost control of her car and ran it into the Nehalem River where my son escaped, but so did she. We were bringing him home when the kidnapper started tailing us. We thought we'd lost her, but she was just catching up when we saw you."

"Could you describe the car?"

When Dad looked at me, I gave as much of a description as I could.

"And you're certain this was the person who abducted you?"

I shook my head. "I couldn't see her face clearly, but it kinda looked like her, and Dad said she was, like, totally tailing us. Who else could it be? It's not like I'm some kind of international spy or anything."

"Did you recognize the car as hers?"

"No," I sighed. "Her car ended up in the river. I've never seen this one before."

The deputy's eyes jerked from me to Dad and then Mom. After taking a look down the highway, he asked, "Did you get a tag number?"

I shrugged. "I think the first three characters were LP2. The next one might be a C or G."

"Oregon plates?"

"Crater Lake, I think."

He pulled out a notebook and scribbled for a moment before looking at Dad again.

"Do you think you can drive safely?"

After swallowing hard, Dad jerked a nod. "If I can get out of this ditch."

The officer eyed him for a moment before nodding as well. "Let's give it a try. Your son and I can push."

It took a while for the traffic to clear enough to attempt it, but with us pushing, and gravel flying, Dad managed to get the car turned around and parked behind the patrol car.

The deputy walked around the car once before announcing, "Doesn't appear to be any damage. If you'll follow me, Sir, I'll take you to headquarters. We can sort this out there."

When Dad nodded, the deputy moved to his patrol car.

Once we were rolling, I felt Elissa's presence again, and turned around to see a blue car pulling out from a side road. Though it was too far back to tell if it was the car that had been following us, my heart started thumping anyway.

Police custody or no, I didn't feel one bit safer.

Chapter 52

Her heart pounding, head spinning, strung out from fatigue and lack of sleep, Remmy climbed onto the bus and stumbled to the back. She collapsed into an aisle seat, her eyes on the front of the bus, holding her breath each time someone started up the stairs, only to release it with a sigh when it wasn't William.

"This isn't over," she muttered after the doors finally closed and the bus started moving.

Releasing a long sigh, she slumped down in her seat, relaxing, and on the verge of falling asleep when a baby squealed. Irritated, she pushed the seat as far back as it would go, pressed her head into the headrest, and stared at the ceiling. When the baby cried out again, Remmy looked over to see a Hispanic woman stuff a bottle into a waiting mouth and rock the little one in her arms.

Closing her eyes, she muttered, "I'll never get to sleep with that urchin screaming."

As the bus rolled over uneven pavement, the woman hummed a tune that Remmy found strange, yet soothing. She thought of Gerry and happier times, and wondered if he would ever speak to her again.

To her surprise, she was floating over an expanse of gravel. Her heart ached when she saw the façade of the old manor house she both loved and hated. Below her, Phillip's body lay on the ground, still and relaxed. He might have been sleeping had it not been for the blood pooling on the paving stones behind his head.

Her attention then turned to the three people next to him. She felt a flash of anger as Jason spoke to the women, his voice so low she could not make out words.

This is it, she thought with a voice that was deeper and gruffer than she expected. *He is going to take over now. She will finally get the younger man she always wanted.*

To her surprise, when Elizabeth and Tilley started moving toward the house, Jason did not follow, and Elizabeth made no effort to encourage him to do so.

I am certain he will follow her. He must have done.

Cook appeared at the corner of the house, drawing Jason's attention to her. Though Remmy still could not hear what was being said, she could see he was showing no interest in going into the house.

If they were lovers, why does he not go to her?

When Jason again turned his attention to Phillip's body, she felt the shock of realization.

I was wrong.

The high-pitched laugh of a baby brought Remmy suddenly awake, surprised to find people standing in the aisle, some anxiously shifting as they waited for the line to start moving. Groggy and disoriented, she looked outside to see the words, "Welcome to Salem, Oregon" on a dilapidated sign.

"God! We're here?"

Shaking her head to clear it, she scrambled up behind the mother and baby, peering around them to see if William had snuck aboard while she slept. Unfortunately, most everyone was facing away from her, so she ducked down to look out a side window, and was relieved to see no one matching his description in the small crowd around the entrance to the bus depot.

As she approached the front of the bus, her breath caught when she spied a police officer standing just outside the terminal entrance, his attention on the people disembarking. As the Hispanic woman moved slowly down the steps, she hesitated at the top, wondering what to do. Someone behind her grunted and she looked back up the aisle to see a large man struggling with his bag as he moved toward her, giving her less than a minute to figure out how to get past the cop.

She looked out again as the Hispanic woman, baby pressed against her chest, walked straight to the officer and pointed at the bus station. The officer shook his head and motioned her inside, but she continued to alternately wave her hand and point. Shaking his head, the officer finally turned away from the bus to open the door and point inside the terminal again.

Hurrying down the steps, Remmy took an immediate left around the front of the bus only to find a high wall blocking her way. Cutting left again, she ran to the alleyway and turned right to find herself at the edge of a small parking lot.

"Now we're on my turf," she growled before sprinting to the street and quickly crossing.

She stumbled while mounting the opposite sidewalk, and it took her several steps to regain her balance before she hurried to the entrance of a bank. Seeing an elevator just inside the door, she smashed the heel of her hand against the call button, and danced on the balls of her feet as she scanned the area to make sure no one was watching. When the elevator doors finally opened, she dashed in, poked the "B" button on the panel, and held her breath until the doors opened again. Still not breathing, she peered into the narrow basement hallway, and only allowed herself a breath when she found it empty. Tripping as she hurried out of the elevator, she grimaced when her shoes squeaked on the polished floor, but after taking another quick look around, she hurried to a nearby bathroom where she barreled in and nearly dove into its first stall.

Struggling to control her heavy breathing, she checked her watch and listened, but could hear only the soft hiss of the air circulation system. However, in less than a minute she heard footsteps in the hall and her heart almost stopped when someone came in. The newcomer sighed as she entered, but Remmy held her breath when the feet stopped in front of her stall. She heard the woman sniffing, and almost gagged on the tension, until the feet began moving again, and the person entered the next stall.

Remmy sat quietly until the woman moved to the sink, and washed her hands. A trickle of sweat ran down the bridge of her nose as she watched the feet stop again in front of her stall for a long moment before the woman hurried out.

"I must smell like a sewer," she muttered. "Now what do I do?"

Leaving the bathroom, she hurried down the hall until she found a door with no name plate. Turning the handle, she found it unlocked, and pushed through to see a vacuum, cleaning supplies, and a large box.

"Maintenance closet," she whispered while closing the door.

The room was tiny, and spare, with no cabinets or back exit. She was thinking this was a bad idea when she spotted a large box at the back. Opening it, she found a brand-new, bright-yellow Shop-Vac.

Grunting loudly, she pulled the unit out and quickly slapped the parts together, not caring if they were in the right place. Grabbing a can of lemon air freshener from a nearby shelf, she sprayed it into the air and onto her clothes. After returning the can to its place, she flicked off the light, and squeezed her small body into the box. As a final touch, she reached up and tossed some rags onto the lid as she closed it.

Feeling claustrophobic in the cramped space, and near to sneezing from the air freshener, she took deep breaths to calm herself and waited. Just as she was thinking the cops might not actually be looking for her, she heard voices outside: a female then a male voice, slowly fading as though they were moving down the hall, but a moment later they grew louder again.

"Someone might be in there," the woman announced as the footsteps stopped just outside the door. "It's just cleaning supplies and such, but we never lock it."

"Please step back, Ma'am," a deep baritone ordered. "I'll look."

The woman muttered something Remmy could not hear as a faint light glowed at the top of her hiding space. She froze at the sound of leather crackling, and imagined the officer leaning through the door to scan the room. Unable to do anything else, she held her breath, closed her eyes, and prayed.

Certain the officer would open the box, she pressed a hand to her mouth to keep from crying out. The terrifying moment seemed to stretch on forever, until she finally heard a long sigh.

"No one in here," the baritone announced as the light went out. "But I understand what you're talking about. There's lots of cleaning stuff in here, but it kinda smells like a sewer too."

"So what do you think, Officer?"

"Whoever it was, it's most likely they were looking for something to steal, and you scared them off. Let's check the security cameras. They'll show us if the person has left the building or not."

Fighting a growing sense of claustrophobia, Remmy listened as the door latch snapped shut and the footsteps grew fainter. A moment later, the twosome passed the room again, the woman chatting up a storm, her voice fading to nothing as they moved away.

Hearing the elevator doors close, she pushed the lid up and gasped in a desperate breath. Her hands shook as she reflexively pulled the front of her damp shirt away from wet skin, and looked around the dark space. Though she could hear no sounds of people outside, she resisted an overpowering urge to bolt from the room, choosing instead to slow her breathing and listen a moment more before finally pushing herself out of the box to rise unsteadily to her feet.

She fumbled in the darkness for a moment until her fingers found the light switch, but before she flipped it on she was momentarily overcome with the overpowering need to get out of there.

"If I can just get past these cops, I'm home free," she muttered while staring at the little bit of light coming from under the room's door.

Finally turning on the light, she grabbed a light-blue smock from a hook on the back of the door, pulled it on, and switched off the light. Holding her breath again, she slowly turned the door knob, pulled the door open, and peered into the empty hallway. Letting out a gasp of relief, she tip-toed to stairs across the hall from the elevator, climbing two steps at a time until she reached the top and peered through a small window in the outside door. Unfortunately, this gave her such a limited view she could see little more than a small space just beyond the door.

"Can't stand around all day," she muttered before pushing through, her eyes scanning the empty entryway before she hurried out the main doors.

Outside, a fine mist cooled her face as she looked around the bank's parking lot, and sucked in a breath at the sight of the police cruiser. It took her a moment to realize there was no one inside, but it still took a great deal of effort to make herself walk past it to the sidewalk.

At the street, she turned left and started jogging toward home.

"Please find me, Gerry," she muttered as she stopped at the next intersection. "I won't hurt you this time."

Chapter 53

"As sure as I'm standing here, Detective Inspector," Tilley argued. "My mistress is a proper lady and would'a never done such as you are suggesting."

Langdons tapped a finger on his chin as he looked around the entryway. "You're certain of this?"

"Well," she said while looking uncertain. "How could they? Jason's room is next to mine, and these floors are as squeaky as a house full a' mice. I'd a heard him moving around in the night, now wouldn't I?"

"Do you sleep well?"

Tilley nodded. "Like a babe, most nights."

Langdons face brightened. "So it is possible that Mister Smythe waited until you were fast asleep before venturing out."

The girl shook her head, but didn't look as certain as before. "Mistress Elizabeth would never allow it."

The detective inspector masked his disappointment with a nod. "I am sure you are right. Thank you, Miss Tilley. Your candor is much appreciated." He motioned toward the drawing room door. "I will trouble you no longer."

The maid gave a quick curtsey. "Good day to you, Sir."

"And you as well," he said absentmindedly as she hurried away, adding to himself as he tapped a finger against the side of his nose, "Maybe I'm looking at this the wrong way 'round."

While moving toward the door, he again scanned the entryway: expensively tiled floor, large potted plant, small side table by the door. It was all so neat and tidy, and yet…

"What am I not seeing?"

He was reaching for the doorknob when William opened it from the outside.

"I say," the detective inspector called. "You're the footman."

Moving in, William jerked a nervous nod. "Butler too, fer the time being, I reckon. That is, until they find a suitable replacement."

"Do you not fancy yourself in the position?"

The young man shook his head. "No disrespect to the mistress, mind, but I'm 'appier in the company of 'orses than people."

"But Jason was, was he?"

"Huh?"

"Comfortable around people, is what I'm asking. He was content with his position?"

"Oh, most certain, 'e were. Pretty much a natural fer it too."

"And how did he get along with the mistress?"

"Well enough, I expect. She never 'ad a cross word to say 'bout 'im, but then, it's not like she'd say as much to the likes of me, now would she?"

The detective inspector glanced at the open door before asking, "Did you ever get the feeling there was something *more* going on between them?"

William looked confused. "More Sir?"

Langdons smiled conspiratorially. "You know, possibly more than should be in a relationship between the mistress of the house and her servant."

The footman scowled. "Jason and the mistress? Ohhhh, I don' know nothin' 'bout that, but I wouldn't a thought so."

"What can you tell me about a gentleman by the name of Colonel Struthers?"

Scowling at the mention of the name, William quickly looked around, as if to make sure they were alone. "The colonel weren't much of a gentleman by my reckoning. Even so, the mistress did seem to take a likin' to 'im."

"In what way?"

"Well, I drives the carriage when she goes to parties, now don't I? More likely than not, if the colonel were also in attendance, 'e'd be the one to escort the mistress to 'er carriage."

"And was your master also in attendance at these times?"

"Oh no. The master bore a strong dislike for that particular gentleman. T'was my feelin' 'e'd as likely shot 'im as look at 'im."

"And during any of these times in which the master was not in attendance, did Colonel Struthers ever get into the carriage with your mistress?"

William jerked a no. "The colonel 'as a certain reputation with the ladies, if you knows what I mean, and Mistress Elizabeth weren't that sort a' lady."

"I see," Langdons said thoughtfully.

"If there's nothin' more, Sir," William said while motioning toward the hallway. "I'm to be playin' me role as butler."

"Yes. Yes. Go right ahead, and thank you."

"A good day to you, Detective Inspector."

"And to you as well."

Langdons watched as William disappeared down the hallway before once more searching the entryway. Just inside the door, he spied a tall woven basket with three umbrellas and a cane. Looking around conspiratorially as his fingers wrapped around the cane, he rotated the shaft until a small golden plaque came into view. Holding it up for a better view, he read the inscription, "Col. MCS", and smiled.

"And what, I wonder, is the colonel's full name?"

Chapter 54

"Gerry," my father protested angrily. "You're not helping."

I shook my head and turned to the Tillamook County Sheriffs Officer. "I'm really sorry about this, Officer McDaniel, but there are, like, too many contradictions in all of this. I just can't say for sure what's going on."

"Was the woman who kidnapped you also the person driving the car that was following you?"

I felt totally foolish as my head shook again. "Who else could it have been?"

"As I told you," Dad added. "Whoever it was, she was definitely tailing us."

Another officer entered and whispered something to McDaniel. When he nodded, the second officer left.

"We just got a report of a car that was stolen from a house just north of Nehalem, and it matches the description you gave. My officers are on the lookout for it."

"So what happens now?" I asked.

McDaniel folded his hands together. "We're sending two patrol cars to the area she was last seen in. It is my guess we'll find the car there, and hopefully get some idea of what she's stolen next."

"So what do we do?" Dad asked.

McDaniel shrugged. "My advice is to stay here until our patrol cars report back, but if you want to return to the Valley, I'll have an officer escort you to the county line."

"Could someone meet us at that point?"

The officer shook his head. "The problem is, you pass through three counties on your way home. That will take a fair amount of coordination to pull off."

"What about the State Police?"

"With all their staffing cuts, they don't have the manpower to take on this task. Truth be known, neither do we, but we have an officer going to Hebo anyway, so he can escort you to that point."

"And then what?"

McDaniel shrugged. "I still advise staying here until we've had a chance to catch this lady."

Without looking at me, Dad said, "Sounds good to me."

"No!" I protested. "Remmy's in danger. We have to get home and help her."

It was Dad's turn to do some head shaking. "I have to protect you and your mother, and driving around with some crazy woman on the loose isn't the way to do it."

"We don't know that she'll try to hurt any of us. Remember? Remmy had the gun."

"Maybe she took it away from her just before you got into the car."

I looked at my hands, trying to get a visual picture of that night, but the boundaries between what happened and what I've since imagined were starting to blur.

"We need to get back to Salem, and soon."

Officer McDaniel held up a hand, his index finger extended.

"For starters, from what you've told me, it's possible she has your friend."

All my muscles went taut as I gave my head a sharp shake. "I didn't get the sense that…I…it wasn't…" Feeling overwhelmingly frustrated, I looked from Officer McDaniel to my father and back and fought down my desire to scream. "I'd have known if she were in the car."

The officer's eyebrows shot up. "How would you have known?"

Out of the corner of my eye, I saw Mom move close to Dad and take his hand. I knew they were going to think me a dumb kid, but at this point, I didn't care.

"Ever since I met Remmy, I've had this uncanny sixth sense of knowing when she was close by. I could be in a room, like totally not looking at the door, and I'd know the second she came through it."

There was a long pause as the adults looked from me to each other and back.

"A sixth sense?" Officer McDaniel more said than asked.

I nodded emphatically. "It has never failed."

"This happen with anyone else?"

His question made me pause, not because I didn't have an answer, but because I hadn't made the connection before now. When I thought back on it, I had felt a strange presence while walking down Aunt Susan's driveway in the dark, and hadn't realized until just now that it wasn't one person, but two. I already knew I could sense Elissa's presence, but until now hadn't realized that it was almost the same feeling I had when connecting with Remmy. There was more between these two than I had realized.

Strange as this may sound, I now knew I needed to find Remmy as soon as possible.

"Yeah," I answered hesitantly. "Just one other."

"Who?"

"The woman who kidnapped us."

Chapter 55

"Holy crap," Remmy exclaimed as she rounded the corner to find two police cars in front of her home. "Holy double crap!"

Barely able to breathe, she scrambled across a yard to hide behind a large bush, stopping only when she was sure they could not see her. An officer was at the front door while two others milled around their vehicles. A fourth was still in his car, concentrating on a computer attached to his dash.

She could see her parents in the doorway, her father appearing confused as he spoke with the officer while her mother rubbed her arms and looked anxious.

Remmy rolled her eyes. "There goes my chance to, like, break this to them gently."

Her father disappeared inside the house, but after only a moment, reappeared with a piece of paper

"Oh this just gets better and better," she mumbled as he handed the item to the officer. "Now they've got my picture."

Up to this point, Remmy could not hear what they were saying, though she had a good idea. Then her mother held up both hands. Only part of her statement made it to Remmy's ears, but what she heard was,

"She's a good…never done anything like…please bring our daughter home…"

As the officer nodded noncommittally, Remmy heard a door open behind her.

"I wonder why the cops are at the Reeds," a woman was saying as two people moved onto the front porch of the house she was hiding next to.

"Hope it's not their daughter," a man added. "She always seemed like such a nice girl."

"Pregnant?"

"That wouldn't bring the cops to their house."

"Drugs?" the woman asked with a disapproving tone.

"It happens to the nicest people."

Resisting the urge to jump up and tell them to go to Hell, Remmy kept her head down and slipped to the side of the house. When she was sure she was out of their line of sight, she straightened and ran to the back yard.

"Stupid jerks," she growled before scaling their back fence. Her feet were just sinking into spongy bark mulch when she heard a low growl, and froze.

Turning slowly, she saw a chocolate lab glaring at her, his teeth bared.

"Whoa there, boy," she said softly. "I'm totally not going to hurt anyone."

The dog barked once and moved several steps closer.

"That's a good boy," she said nervously. "Why don't you, like, sit down and…"

She stopped when the dog's butt dropped to the ground and his tongue lolled out one side of his mouth. Releasing a huge sigh, Remmy leaned against the fence for a moment before pushing off and moving toward the house. To her surprise, the dog quietly followed on her left side, rushing ahead as she approached a side gate as though he planned to escort her out.

"No, boy," she insisted as she flipped up the gate's latch. "Stay here."

Though the dog obediently sat, he rose again when she moved through the gate. As soon as the latch rattled into place, the lab started barking as though protesting the apparent betrayal.

Afraid someone might look out a window and see her, she sprinted to the street, and looked both ways before dashing across. She was stepping onto the opposite sidewalk when the black nose of a patrol car appeared at the far end of the block. Ducking her head, she ran down a nearby alley, and stopped behind a cluster of garbage cans to watch the patrol car move slowly past. Her breath coming in gasps, she was struggling to decide what to do when she heard a car door opening.

"Go around to the other side," a woman was saying just before the door slammed.

Sprinting further down the alley, Remmy cut through a hedge on her right. The yard was littered with a mixture of children's toys, broken furniture, discarded clothing, and old car parts. She sprinted through the yard, all the while scanning the space for a place to hide, but in her distracted state, her toe snagged something partially buried in the ground and she was vaulted onto a deflated kiddies' pool piled high with plastic toys. Stifling a scream as the toys rattled across the lawn, she slid through a slimy layer of black dirt and mold that coated her hands and knees.

Freezing in place, Remmy listened until the officer's footsteps stopped opposite her location. With a grunt, she scrambled up and raced down the right side of the house to find the rusty shell of a car blocking her path. The sound of the officer pushing through the hedge left her no choice but to squeeze her thin frame between the car and the fence.

It was a tight fit, but once clear, she looked back to see the officer coming around the corner of the house.

"Stop!"

Though she wanted to obey, something she could not explain kept her running. At the sidewalk, she looked back to see the officer trying to get past the derelict, but the space was too narrow for her stockier body.

"Suspect is heading for the street."

Remmy started to turn left, but stopped when she heard,

"She's headed your way. My way is blocked. I'm going around…"

The voice faded as the woman vanished from sight, and knowing where she was headed, Remmy did a quick one-eighty, and ran as fast as her legs would go. However exhaustion was draining her strength, and it was all she could do to keep up the pace. As she neared the end of the block, the sound of the police cruiser cutting around the corner gave her a boost of adrenaline that carried her across the street and into a nearby alley. Gasping for air, she stumbled and caught herself, the sound of the accelerating cruiser making her desperate to find a place to hide.

Halfway down the alley, she spied a dense tangle of brush behind an apparently deserted house. Diving into the mass of weeds and vines, she fought her way to the middle and squatted, gulping in air as she struggled to slow her breathing.

Hearing the radio again, she pulled herself into a fetal position, closed her eyes, and pressed her forehead against her knees. Her heart pounding, lungs aching, she hugged her legs and listened.

Her breath caught when feet crunched gravel a few feet from where she sat. A slow, hushed, "I'm sure I saw…", interrupted by a garbled voice on the radio, and then the woman replied, "Nope. Nobody here."

The radio squawked again, and the officer responded, "Yeah. I'll meet you at the end of the alley."

As the footsteps grew fainter, Remmy leaned back and gasped in a desperate breath. When she finally opened her eyes, she discovered a large white-and-black-striped spider crawling up her arm. With a calmness that surprised her, she flicked the arachnid off and turned to where the officer had been.

A slamming car door made her suck in another breath, but she held her position until she could no longer stand the chilling wetness soaking into her pants. Her entire body shaking, she tried to stand, but the dense undergrowth crowded in to keep her hunched over. She took a tentative step on wobbly legs and struggled to make a path in the snagging vegetation. The effort kept her off balanced, and when her foot snagged a root, she staggered through the thicket, fighting vines grabbing her clothes, branches snagging hair, and cobwebs blanketing her face. Desperate to free herself, she lunged forward, tripped, and fell sideways into the prickly vegetation to cry out when a thorn stabbed her cheek and was just as quickly ripped out.

"Damn," she swore, her eyes closed as she listened for a sign that the officers had heard her.

When it was clear they had not, she moved to the edge of the brush and peered into the alley. Seeing no one, she started to step out, but was stopped by a feeling she didn't quite understand.

I didn't hear them drive off. Where are they?

It suddenly occurred to her that she wasn't sure if it was her or Phillip asking the question.

Could he be taking over my body? Will he hurt Gerry again?

She took a deep breath and tried to push the thoughts away, but that only increased her anxiety.

"You're not going to work this out standing here," she chastised.

Doing a quick about face, she moved back through the brush to the edge of a small yard filled with a waist-high mass of water-soaked weeds. The dark house was obviously empty: its roof sagged, peeling paint hung from decaying walls, and the windows were shattered cavities. Wanting to be anywhere else but here, she took one last look toward the alley, let out a sigh, and continued into the yard. The weeds splashed wet and cold against her pants as she moved to the side of the house and slipped past an overgrown rhododendron. Dropping to hands and knees, she scrambled to the remains of a wooden fence, and peered around it to see the back end of an idling patrol car.

"I'm so totally not cut out for this shit," she gasped angrily while returning to the back of the house.

The rear door had been stripped of all hardware except rusty hinges that gave a protesting squeak when she pushed through to find herself on a small porch reeking of mold and mildew. Too tense to even breathe, she pulled the door closed and tippy toed on squishy floorboards through the narrow remains of a gutted kitchen to the small front room. The smell of decay grew stronger as her shoes crunched debris on naked wood. Crossing the living room, she slowly approached the front window to push the remains of a rotting bed sheet aside, and shook her head at the sight of the police car parked at the curb.

Sucking in a deep breath, she looked around the room.

"What a lovely place to pass the time," she muttered while scrunching up her nose and peering into a closet-of-a-bathroom stripped of its fixtures. "And to think, my folks were going to, like, take me to Hawaii after Christmas." A laugh/sob erupted from her. "What the hell was I thinking?"

The sound of an accelerating car drew her back to the window to see the cruiser was gone.

"What the hell *was* I thinking?"

Chapter 56

Leaning against the ornate mantle of his fireplace, the swarthy, sandy-haired Colonel Struthers clipped the end of his unlit cigar and stared haughtily down his nose at the detective inspector standing just inside the entryway of his parlor.

"What was I doing where?"

"At Montgomery Manor?" Moving closer, Detective Inspector Langdons held up the walking stick. "I found this in their umbrella basket."

Pushing away from the mantle, Struthers took the cane, gave it a cursory glance, and laughed.

"So that is where the blessed thing had got to."

"You're saying this here stick is your property?"

Struthers nodded. "Most definitely, but to be clear, Detective Inspector, I own a number of these, and have the regrettable habit of misplacing them."

"And when were you last at Montgomery Manor?"

The colonel's eyes went wide, but his smile implied a different story.

"I have never been," he answered. "The "lord" of that particular manor would fill my nethers with buckshot should I dare to set foot on the premises."

"You did not get on with Mister Montgomery?"

When Detective Inspector Langdons held out a hand, the colonel returned the cane and then waved his own hand with a flourish.

"He was beastly to his lovely wife, and I would have none of it."

"And you told him as much?"

"To his bloody face!" Struthers declared while turning away. "He did not take it well, I must say. Tried to smash in my noggin with his own walking stick. Had it not been for his wife's presence, I would have given him a good thrashing and been done with it."

"And when did this confrontation take place?"

Struthers let his eyes drift toward the ceiling and tapped his chin several times.

"Yes," he announced finally as he looked at the detective inspector again. "I believe it was Bonfire Day, the year before last. We were both attending a party at…some place or other, I cannot remember. The old beast became frightfully jealous over the attention his wife was paying me. He tried to start a fight, but when I refused to take the bait, the toad banished me from his estate forever."

Moving to an overstuffed chair, he sat without indicating for the detective inspector to join him and again waved a hand dismissively. "Rather an overdramatic waste of effort, I should think. I have not set a toe on the blighter's property, either before or since."

Langdons held up the walking stick. "Then why was your cane in their umbrella basket?"

Struthers shrugged indifferently, but the detective inspector thought he saw nervousness in his face.

"Oh that. It is rather simple, really. I must have dropped it at some time whilst entertaining Mistress Elizabeth in her carriage. Though I must say, she is *not* an easy woman to chum up to, if you know what I mean."

"So the two of you were not close?"

A hint of mischief shone in Struthers' eyes. "What are you implying, Detective Inspector? Has someone said that Eliza…Missus Montgomery and I were -- dare I say -- intimate?" He barked a laugh. "Then you are being led down the proverbial primrose path. You should not place so much importance on the idle prattle of commoners."

"Do you have reason to believe a member of the lady's staff is unhappy?"

Struthers' mouth opened as his head snapped back, but instead of speaking, he quickly lowered his chin, and glared at his visitor.

"You are putting words into my mouth, Detective Inspector," he said while looking at his fingertips. "I said no such thing."

"But you implied it."

"I'm sure I did not." Dramatically pushing himself from the chair, he hurried to the door, yanked it open, and waved the detective inspector out. "And if you have nothing to convey other than idle gossip, I have a busy day and am eager to get started."

Langdons thought of protesting, but changed his mind and moved to the door.

"Thank you for your time, Colonel. I'm sure we shall speak again."

Struthers did nothing more than nod in response before closing the door.

After leaving the apartment building, Langdons turned back to look at the Colonel's modest accommodations. Though the area in front of the building was clean, the brick siding looked shabby, window frames were in need of painting, and the concrete stairs worn.

"Marrying Mistress Montgomery would surely improve his situation," he muttered while continuing on to his carriage. He stopped at the vehicle's door, and turned again to see the colonel's face in a window. "I wonder what his busy day entails."

Chapter 57

"I can't believe I let you talk me into this," my father growled as we followed the Tillamook County Sheriff patrol car into Hebo.

"We can't just sit around and do nothing."

Mom shifted in her seat to look at me. "How do you plan to help Remmy, assuming she managed to make it back home?"

I shrugged. "She'll be in Salem before we get there."

"How can that be?" Dad asked incredulously.

Looking out the window, I tried to clear my mind and make sense of the mess of confusing emotions; distorted memories, both past and present; and angst over what was going on right now.

"Can't say. I just know that woman doesn't have her."

"How is it you are so certain?"

"It just came to me, but, like, it's totally real. I'm certain of it."

"You'll stake your life on a…" Dad abruptly stopped speaking, his eyes boring into me via the rearview mirror. I did my best to stare back for a long moment before he asked, "Any idea of where we'll find her?"

Sitting back in the seat, I took a deep breath and let it hiss through my teeth. "She'll try to go home."

"Try?"

"Dad!" I protested. "I told the cops where she lives. They're so going to be there waiting for her."

"So where does that leave us?"

I felt my head shake as I racked my brain for an answer.

"Let's go by her place and see where it leads."

Dad looked at Mom, and after a moment, she shrugged.

"No, we're going home," he finally announced. "The police can handle it."

"What are they going to do?" I asked angrily. "You know they'll just think I'm a crazy kid, like the Tillamook cops did."

Dad stabbed a finger at the patrol car ahead of us. "They took us seriously enough to provide an escort."

"And are totally thrilled to be rid of us."

Turning in his seat, Dad glared at me, but before he could speak, Mom put a hand on his arm.

"Alvin, please. Let's not run off the road again."

Facing forward again, he waved a hand. "We're going home, and that's final."

"But I…"

"No 'buts' about it, Son. The professionals can deal with this."

I was about to argue when we slowed at Hebo to turn left onto Highway 22. As we waited for an oncoming log truck to pass, I was struck with the feeling that Elissa was close by, and reflexively jerked around. There were no vehicles behind us, and as we turned, I tried to look into each of the many cars parked along the highway, but they were just a blur.

"I don't want to argue about this anymore," Dad announced.

"Uh, no," I agreed distractedly before settling back in the seat. "What?"

Even though there was no car behind us, the sensation was strong, but I had no idea how this thing worked. She could be in our trunk, or a mile away.

"I thought I saw something," I lied. "Guess I was wrong."

Dad sighed, "Good thing."

"Yeah," I muttered under my breath. "Or not."

Then it hit me. If I could sense her presence, she would also know where I was.

Oh God, I thought while again turning in my seat to look at the road behind us. *There's no way I can hide from her.*

But if that were true, Remmy couldn't hide either.

"Dad, I…"

"What?" he interrupted angrily.

I intended to tell him that Elissa was nearby, but realized it would serve no purpose except to distract him, and the last time I did that we ended up in the ditch.

"Sorry. Nothing."

"What do you mean, nothing?"

I shook my head. "I just want to get home."

Snorting angrily, he stabbed a finger at the patrol car. "I'm as eager to sort this out as you are, Son, but there's a cop in front of me. What can I do?"

"Yeah. Right," I acknowledged while straining to stop myself from looking back for the car I was sure I wouldn't see.

And why is it I feel so much like a Judas Goat leading her to Remmy?

Chapter 58

Squatting in the small, dilapidated living room, her back against soggy sheetrock, Remmy felt tears trickling down her cheeks as she pulled the thin cloth of the stolen smock across her chest and shivered.

"Wish I hadn't dumped my jacket," she complained just before something small scurried across the floor in another room. "Crap! I so won't be sleeping here tonight."

The sound of another creature brought her to her feet and when a larger dark shape briefly peered out of a hole in the opposite wall, she pushed herself up, rushed to the front door, and yanked on the knob. Swollen with moisture and rot, the door resisted, but claustrophobic fear gave her a surge of energy. When she yanked again, the door shuddered partway open and stuck.

Squeezing through the narrow opening, she rushed onto the porch, and was immediately thrown off balance when her feet slipped on its slimy surface. Shifting her weight to compensate, she heard a loud crack and felt the floor droop beneath her. Stumbling sideways, she took two exaggerated steps toward the stairs, the entire porch protesting as she bounced over its spongy, rotting surface.

Her reflexes slowed by fatigue and hunger, she thumped down the steps, her left foot coming down hard on the crumbling sidewalk. She squealed when the foot rolled and pain shot up her leg.

The throbbing ankle brought a clarity and purpose as she gasped in a sharp breath, and quickly shifted her weight to the other foot. After taking several one-legged hops, she tried putting pressure on the injured ankle, and was unprepared for the sharp pain. Crying out, she shifted her balance back to her good foot, only to have it come down on the edge of the concrete and tip her forward into the yard.

"Yaaaa," she cried as she crashed onto a sodden mass of dead grass and weeds.

Reacting instinctively when the chilling water touched her skin, she rolled over and started to rise, but the sight of a car turning onto the street forced her back to hands and knees. Moving on instinct, she scrambled to the dying remains of a low hedge, dropped to her belly, and held her breath. The car passed slowly, its radio blaring a song in Spanish through an open passenger window.

Cold moisture chilled her skin as she lay at the base of the hedge, afraid to even look for fear they might see her. Her eyes tightly closed she listened until the sound of the music began to fade then desperately sucked in air, opened her eyes, and watched the car turn into a driveway at the end of the street.

Rising slowly to her good foot, she waited until the car was out of sight before tentatively putting pressure on the sprained one. At first, it hurt too much to take any weight, but after briefly flexing the ankle, she managed to take one timid step then another.

"I've got to get to Jasmina's," she groaned while hobbling to the street.

At the sidewalk, she stopped, her mind blank as she looked both ways for the police. The light dimmed, and the sudden change drew her attention to a black cloud covering the sun, its shadow turning the world around her dark gray. She could also see the feathery underbelly of the cloud as rain fell from it.

"Shit!" she protested while limping to the end of the block and anxiously looking around. Seeing the coast was clear, she turned left and hurried as fast as her aching ankle would allow, but could not resist repeatedly looking back to see if she was being followed.

She had barely walked a block before raindrops pelted her skin. A minute later, the few became a deluge. Her desire to run, was restrained by the pain. Whoever, as she continued on, the ankle warmed up and allowed her to set a faster and faster pace until she was finally able to jog.

Wiping water from her face, she took a deep breath and pushed on, but halfway to her destination, she stumbled, and did a slow-motion crash into a nearby telephone pole. Leaning on it for support, she sucked in desperate gulps as rain poured from the sky, soaking her with water so cold that even the exertion did nothing to stop her shivering.

Every bit of her wanted to sink to the ground and give up, but something else, something deep and primal forced her to keep going.

"Almost there," she gasped while slogging up the sidewalk, each step more difficult than the one before. "Jasmina must know."

Reaching the imposing rise in the road that led to Jasmina's house, she hesitated briefly, her tears mixing with rain as she shook her head and trudged on, putting one foot in front of the other, step after agonizing step until she lost track of time. She continued to slog on, keeping her head down until the sidewalk ran out and she looked up to see her destination glowing white, even in the pouring rain.

Spots dotted her vision as she struggled to focus on the house, no longer worrying about the police as she stumbled across the street and staggered toward the back.

Slowly climbing Jasmina's steep driveway, she mounted the steps to the small back porch, but her finger shook so badly it took two tries to ring the doorbell. When no one came, she pressed her forehead against the doorframe and rang again. Still getting no response, she peered through the door's window to see a dark empty hallway.

"Jasmina," she cried, her fists pounding the door. "Please!"

When the hallway remained empty, she sagged against the door for a moment before moving unsteadily to the garage, the sound of her heavy breathing totally masking the world around her. Pushing open the garage's back door, she gasped a desperate sob upon seeing the empty space where Jasmina's car should have been.

Her legs gave out, forcing her to grab the door's frame for support while she looked once more at the house, its dark windows echoing the vast emptiness at the center of her being.

Unable to stand any longer, she pressed her back against the frame and slowly slid to a squat.

After her forehead thumped against her knees, she sobbed, "Oh God. Someone please help me."

When her eyes closed, she saw burning buildings, shadowy figures dancing in the dark, and the face of a beautiful woman. Her diaphragm spasmed uncontrollably as she opened her eyes, rolled onto her side, and curled into a shivering ball in the open doorway.

"Help!"

Chapter 59

Rain pounded the roof of his carriage as Detective Inspector Langdons sat in dry comfort and watched water bounce off his sergeant's helmet while his subordinate peered over the hedge blocking Langdons own view of the apartments beyond. Within a minute, he saw the sergeant shrug and turn, the overweight man's boots splashing through puddles as he slogged back to the carriage.

"Beggin' yer pardon, Detective Inspector, Sir, but the lane is clear. What exactly is it I'm supposed to be keepin' an eye out fer."

"If my opinion is worth anything, we may soon catch a murderer trying to confer with his partner in crime."

"And who might that be, Sir?"

"A gentleman known as Colonel Struthers lives in those apartments. Do you know him?"

Hunching his shoulders against the driving rain, the sergeant nodded uncertainly.

"Yes, Sir, but from what I 'ear of this person, 'e ain't the murderin' type."

Langdons nodded thoughtfully. "Just you wait, Sergeant. We may soon learn that all is not as it seems."

The sergeant looked from his superior to the hedge and back.

"So you say, Sir," he said uncertainly. "So you say."

The detective inspector tapped his cane against the carriage door. "So I *do* say, Sergeant. Now hurry on back and let me know when his carriage approaches."

"Yessir, Detective Inspector, Sir. I'll do just that."

While watching the sergeant plod back to the hedge, Langdons shook his head. "It's a wonder we keep the peace with slow-witted dolts the likes of him pounding our beats."

Looking at his feet, he had just started tapping the tip of his cane on the carriage floor when he heard the sergeant calling,

"Detective Inspector, Sir! 'e's just 'ailed a cab and it's a comin' down the lane."

Opening the carriage door, Langdons waved the sergeant in while listening to the vehicle rattle over cobblestones.

Before the gasping sergeant had completely pulled himself in, Langdons tapped his cane on the roof.

"Follow them, but not too closely," he shouted. "After all, we already know where they are going."

The carriage jerked when the horses responded to the snap of their reins, knocking the sergeant off balance. Langdons threw up his hands to stop his subordinate from falling on him, sneering as the man collapsed onto the seat opposite before shaking rain from his helmet and using his free hand to wipe water from his coat.

"Don't get too settled in, Sergeant," Langdons said while wiping drops of water from his face. "We will have him soon enough."

"Yes, Sir," the sergeant responded glumly as he pulled the helmet back onto his round head. "I reckon so, Sir."

When they turned the last corner before the Montgomery estate, Langdons leaned out the window and smiled as he watched Struthers' carriage turn and enter.

"As I suspected," he gloated. "Our pigeon has come home to roost."

Chapter 60

"Turn left up here," I demanded, my body straining against the seatbelt as I stabbed a finger at the upcoming street.

I could see Dad's head shaking. "No, we're going…"

"Dad, you have to listen to me," I insisted. "Remmy's at her aunt's house and she's in trouble."

"And how could you know…" Dad stopped abruptly and stared at me in the mirror for a long moment before shaking his head. "Oh, yeah. That psychic connection thing."

"Please! I'm *not* making this up. I don't know how it works, but it's totally real."

"That doesn't make it true."

"It does!" I argued, my voice cracking as tears ran down my cheek. "You gotta believe me."

"Listen, Son…"

"Let's give it a try," Mom interrupted, her turnaround so surprising that Dad nearly stopped to car to gawk at her.

"You're saying you believe in this psychic stuff?"

Her head shook as she turned to give me a stern, almost accusing look. "It will only take a moment, and then he will know it's only his imagination."

I jerked my attention from one parent to the other until Dad's shoulders sagged and he nodded. "OK, but we're just going to drive past."

"That's all I ask," I said while falling back into my seat, already certain of what I would do if he didn't stop.

Remmy! Please be there.

When we hit the steep rise leading to Jasmina's house, the car slowed, its straining engine seeming to complain as Dad pressed on the gas pedal.

"It's right up here, on the right," I said as we approached the house.

"I see it," Dad snapped angrily.

My hand was on the door release as the car slowed and when it was obvious he really wasn't going to stop, I pushed with all my might.

"Gerry?" my parents cried simultaneously as I shot out the door.

I hit the ground running, but heavy rain splashed my face, nearly blinding me. My toe snagged the edge of the sidewalk, throwing me off balance, and allowing me only two exaggerated steps before I was somersaulting on wet grass. My body was so pumped up with adrenaline, I was quickly on my feet and sprinting toward the house.

At the front door, I both rattled the brass knocker, and rang the doorbell. My senses were on fire, heart thumping, and legs pumping. When no one appeared, I hammered the knocker again, my terrified brain so filled with conflicting thoughts it took me a minute to realize Dad was speaking.

"...there isn't even anyone at home."

"No," I protested, my finger stabbing the doorbell again. "She's here and she's in danger. I know it!"

"Well, we're not going to kick the door in just to prove..."

Rapping the knocker one more time, I ran to a nearby window to peer into a dark and empty living room.

"Remmy!" I screamed as I started running toward the back.

"Where are you going?" Dad shouted after me, but I couldn't stop to answer.

Turning sharply at the corner of the house, I slipped on wet grass, dropped to one knee, and bounced up. It was then I saw a light-blue shape lying next to the garage and my heart nearly exploded.

"Son of a...DAD!"

Panic stopped my breathing as I sprinted across the grass, dropping to my knees only inches from my friend, in tears and uncertain as to what I should do. Her face was deathly pale, and she was shivering so hard her hands wobbled when she held them out to me. I grabbed them and tried to pull her up, but she was like a ton of dead weight.

I heard Mom cry, "Oh my Lord", but could only look at Remmy's face and wonder how I had failed her.

Not this time!

Stripping off my coat, I draped it over her, desperation freezing my mind, her eyes all I could see as my parent's voices were lost in the roaring noise in my head. I saw her lips moving, and leaned closer to hear, but instead of speaking, she grabbed my shirt with shaking hands and pulled me down so quickly I had to brace myself to keep from falling on top of her.

When our faces were close enough for our noses to touch, she blurted something unintelligible.

"What? What did you say?"

"I'm sorry," she sobbed through chattering teeth. "You have to believe me. I never meant to hurt you."

"Hurt me? How?"

A shudder went through her body. "I threw the wrench through your window."

"You? Why?"

"I knew Elissa wanted to kidnap you, so I brought the wrench to hit her." She gasped in a breath, tears streaming down her face. "When she took off and the lights came on in your house, I threw it at the window to convince you she was dangerous."

Putting her hands over her face, she released a loud sob and peeked through her fingers. "I didn't know you would be cut up like that. You have to believe me!"

"I...b...believe you," I stammered, tears streaming down my nose to plop onto hers.

Not seeming to notice, she lifted a shaking hand and pressed it against my cheek. "I love you, Gerry Patterson."

"I love you too," I said, but the moment was broken by that strange sensation of another presence nearby.

Still holding Remmy, I looked up to see a stranger, who at first looked like a street person.

"Who...?" was all I could blurt out before he moved in and gently pushed me aside to place his own jacket over her.

Unlike Elissa, this man's eyes were soft and dark. Though I'd never seen him before, I suddenly felt calmed by his presence. Remmy, on the other hand, barked a cry of alarm.

"My name is William, and I'm not here to hurt anyone," he said calmly. I felt Remmy squeeze my hand as he added, "We're just looking for a chance at freedom."

"We?" I asked as Elissa appeared at the bottom of the driveway. "What's she doing here?"

"Elissa used to be Jason," William explained as a chubby, nervous woman appeared next to him. "And the other is Matilda, who you would know as Tilley."

As the two women walked up the drive, their bodies started to glow, and I saw the ghostly image of a man overlay Elissa's. He was shorter, and squat, though not fat, and carried himself with an air of proud, but not arrogant dignity. Though the overweight woman also glowed, she didn't seem to change much at all.

I suddenly felt a strange kind of energy course through me, and held up my own hands to see they were also superimposed with a ghostly pair: small and delicate, with slender fingers. I could make out lace cuffs and puffy sleeves, and when I made a fist, the image did too.

Remmy coughed, and I looked down to see a face that made me want to pull back, but I couldn't move. I'd not had time to deal with the fact that she had been my abusive husband, and a part of me wanted to jump up and run from this ghostly person. Thankfully, the other part -- the more present part of me -- would not let her go.

Blinking twice, I once again turned my attention to the approaching apparitions hoping this might somehow be a hallucination, but Remmy's squeak of alarm made me realize it wasn't.

"What the hell?" my father cried.

I turned to see my parents looking from one newcomer to the other, their mouths open, eyes wide.

"The time has arrived," William said calmly. "The two of you complete the circle."

Remmy squeezed my hand so tightly it hurt, making me look down to see both of her faces awash with panic.

"They're going to kill us!"

Chapter 61

"What sort of rubbish have you dragged me into," Colonel Struthers announced angrily as he barged into Elizabeth's drawing room with William stumbling along behind.

When Struthers stopped, the butler moved up to grab his arm, but stopped suddenly as though he realized what a breach of protocol that would be.

Taking a step back, he shifted uncomfortably in his ill-fitting clothes and bowed toward Elizabeth.

"Sorry, Ma'am," William pleaded, "but 'e wouldn't wait fer me ta…"

Elizabeth held up a hand to stop him, and tried to put some warmth into her smile. "Thank you, William. That will be all."

His concern obvious, William jerked his eyes from her to the colonel and back before performing a clumsy bow and moving to the doorway.

Pulling it partway closed, he looked back. "I'll be just out 'ere if ya 'ave need of me, Ma'am."

When William did not move, Elizabeth said, "Please have Tilley bring tea."

He took one more look at the colonel before nodding. "Yes, Ma'am."

Struthers feigned indifference toward the butler, but still waited until the latch clicked into place before speaking.

"What in the blazes kind of butler is that?"

The insensitive question reminding her of her recent loss, Elizabeth turned away briefly to regain her composure before motioning for him to sit. Without waiting for him to do so, she moved to the settee and sat.

"Our regular butler was killed recently whilst being unjustly detained."

Struthers gave the offered chair a cursory look but remained standing. "I am told he murdered your husband."

Finding the intrusion increasingly loathsome, Elizabeth looked away again as she stifled an equally inappropriate rebuttal. She struggled to keep her face neutral when she finally turned back to face the colonel.

"My husband's death was a terrible accident."

"I was recently visited by a detective inspector who takes a different view," Struthers stated angrily with a flick of his hand as he moved to the fireplace and overdramatically jerked around to face her. "He is also of the absurd impression that we are co-conspirators. Can you imagine the implications should such an accusation be made public? I shall be ruined."

Rising from her seat, Elizabeth moved to the window, hoping to diffuse her growing anger by finding something pleasant to look at outside. To her dismay, she instead saw the detective inspector's black police carriage pulling to a stop. As he and his sergeant erupted from the vehicle, she turned back to Struthers.

"And you sought to prove his theory by dashing over here to...do what, exactly?"

"Prove his...? What are you...?"

He stopped at the sound of insistent voices echoing in the entryway, and was turning in that direction when the door burst open and the two policemen rushed into the room.

"Sorry again, Ma'am,' William called from behind them. "But they wouldn't..."

"Well, well, well, Colonel," Langdons interrupted, his eyes on the pair in front of him. "I can't say it is a surprise to find you here."

Looking confused for only a moment, Struthers resumed his usual aloof demeanor and glared at the newcomers. It was only Elizabeth who noticed William still standing in the doorway, looking very much, despite his new clothes, like a farm hand as he scowled at the three men invading his mistresses' sitting room.

"I certainly do not know what you are implying, Sir," Struthers protested as Elizabeth watched her footman give his head a sharp shake and quietly close the door.

Unaware of what was going on behind him, the detective inspector also shook his head. "It struck me as odd that of all the people I have spoken to about this matter, only you, a man who insists he has never once set foot in this house, comes here straight away."

The colonel snorted derisively. "Your accusations were alarming to me, Detective Inspector. I wanted to find out why you would think me involved in this unfortunate matter." Walking quickly to the fireplace, Struthers turned back and glared at the policeman "Let me assure you, Detective Inspector, if I hear even a hint of these unjustified accusations from anyone, I will most certainly sue for liable."

Giving his narrow shoulders an exaggerated shrug, Langdons moved up to the colonel. "Be that as it may, Sir, but I have a duty to perform. I must ask you to accompany me to the station for further questioning."

Struthers' back stiffened, his face red. "I will do no such thing."

"You will, Sir, as will Mistress…"

"NO!"

They turned to see William standing in the room's doorway, nervously gripping a large, double-barreled shotgun. Shocked at the sight of the weapon, Elizabeth gasped as Langdon's sergeant cried, "Lord almighty!" and backpedaled to the nearest window.

"What in heaven's name are you doing, Lad?" Langdons demanded.

William grimaced as he pulled back both hammers, and aimed the weapon. "You've no right to accuse our mistress of such things."

Holding up a hand, the detective inspector took a step sideways so his body half covered the colonel's. "Be a good lad and put that down."

"William," Elizabeth pleaded. "Please listen to the detective inspector and..."

Anger, pleading, and frustration showed on the lad's face for an instant before he briefly dipped his head. When he looked at her again, his cheeks were flush, mouth tight, and eyes squinting.

"They have no *right*…"

As he placed emphasis on the last word, the gun exploded.

Chapter 62

"What do you mean, 'complete the circle'?" my father asked.

William looked at him briefly before turning to me. "Do you remember the poem? It said at least five of us are necessary for this to work."

My gut cramped as I visualized the piece of parchment with a poem written on it.

Death and hope are a curious mix,
Yet together shall they play
A perplexing role in our torn life
Over which we have no say.

"Are you Death? Do we have to die?"

Elissa shook her head. "Death is only a transition from one physical form to another. However, if we don't do this…"

"What is it you plan to do?" Dad interrupted.

"We want to go home, you idiot," Tilley snarled.

"How will you accomplish this?" I asked while pulling the shivering Remmy into a sitting position, and hugging her close.

William looked at Tilley. "We've summoned a friend of ours. He's joined with someone you know very well."

"Who?" my mother asked anxiously. "The Devil?"

Tilley barked a derisive laugh. "You don't understand any of this, do you? There is no such thing as…"

Screeching tires drew our attention to the street as a car bounced up the driveway. I thought the driver was going to run over the threesome, but she stopped abruptly, ratcheted on the brake, and pushed the door open. To my utter astonishment, Jasmina jumped out and ran toward us, her attention jumping from Elissa to me.

"Oh good. I'm not too late."

Chapter 63

A stunned Elizabeth gaped at the wide-eyed, open-mouthed William as the smoking shotgun slipped from his fingers. The distant, echoing sound of the weapon striking the floor startled her, and she turned to see Colonel Struthers slumping into a sitting position, his back against the settee, a gory hole in his chest, and life fading from his eyes.

Beside him, Detective Inspector Langdons stood with his back to her, his hands gripping his right side, just below the ribs. As the Colonel rattled his dying breath, the detective inspector turned his head to give her a look of total surprise. Her attention was drawn to blood pooling around his right shoe, but when she again looked at his pale face, he released an anguished cry and toppled over like an uprooted tree.

"Merciful heavens," the sergeant moaned, his mouth open, eyes bulging, attention jumping from William to the bloody corpses and back several times before the policeman slapped both hands over his mouth and sprinted from the room.

Her mind reeling, Elizabeth stared at the scene as though she had just been transported to an alien world. She had lived for years with the ugliness of her husband's disfigurement, and the violence of his abuse, but it had not prepared her for something like this. She was staring without comprehension at the carnage until a sobbing William pulled her attention to him as he dropped to a squat, hands over his face.

"You poor, simple fool," was all she could think to say, but his lack of response made it clear he could not hear her.

Tilley's footsteps in the hall drew her attentiion to the doorway. Resisting the numbness taking over her body, she slowly lifted a hand, intending to warn the high-strung girl to stay out of the room, but could not make her lips move.

"Mistress, what was that noise I just…Oh Lord!"

Her mouth opening in a silent scream, she released the tea tray and held both hands out, as though trying to push away the ugliness in front of her. The sound of china crashing to the floor was distant as Elizabeth watched Tilley retreat several steps before her head lolled back and she collapsed to the floor in a dead faint.

Hearing the sergeant retching outside her front door, Elizabeth jerked her attention from the sobbing William, to the prostrate Tilley, to the corpses lying only a few feet away, and finally to the blood splattered on her dress.

Feeling dizzy, she hurried to a nearby chair and plopped down into it, her eyes closed.

"Can it honestly get any worse that this?"

Chapter 64

Jasmina's red curls bounced as she jerked her attention from one person to another before settling on Elissa.

"You know who we are, don't you?" Elissa asked.

Jasmina nodded. "But I'm curious. How is it you are aware of who you are in this life, and weren't in the previous ones?"

Elissa shrugged. "I'm not sure. When I was a child I had fantastic dreams that were so vivid they felt like memories. As a teenager, I used the Internet to learn that the people I dreamed about were actually real." Her head shook as she pointed at me. "I even managed to find a copy of a newspaper article about Phillip's death, but was so enraged by the inaccuracies, I tore it up."

"But how did you find the others?"

"It began with William. I was in a crowded mall, and felt myself drawn to a street urchin having a heated argument with someone. When I approached him from behind, he suddenly stopped talking and turned to face me. We instantly knew each other, and not long after that, started looking for the others."

Feeling utterly dumbfounded, I looked at Jasmina, asking, "How did you know about them?"

Her expression was questioning as she motioned to Elissa whose eyes moved slowly from her to me. "I think she...or rather, he called me."

"You're one of them?"

While smiling hesitantly, Elissa shook her head. "Jasmina is different than the rest of us, and from you. She may be able to provide the connection we need."

"Connection?" my mother asked anxiously. "Are we talking about some kind of séance?"

His head shaking, William stepped forward, pointing at Jasmina. "You might think of her as half-born."

My parents shook their heads in perfect unison, but it was my dad who spoke. "Half...*born*? What the hell does that mean, or do I even want to know?"

"God in Heaven," Mom gasped. "You don't honestly expect us to believe you are some kind of vampire, do you?"

"That's just a myth," Tilley laughed while pointing at her bared teeth. "Thee. No blood-thucking fangth."

Elissa stepped up beside William, her eyes on Jasmina.

"This woman's soul resides partly in your world and partly in what you refer to as the spirit world. She can see what remains of the essence of those who have previously occupied corporeal bodies."

From my parent's expressions, I suspect they would have been less confused if she had been explaining Einstein's Theory of Relativity...in German.

"You're ghosts?" Dad asked.

William shook his head. "That is only what you might think of when you see us intersecting your plane of consciousness outside of a corporeal body. We're really..."

He stopped when Elissa put a hand on his shoulder. "It does no good to explain."

"They deserve to know."

"Maybe, but there's no chance they'll understand..."

The last word came out garbled and raspy. Oddly enough, I understood what she was talking about, though I couldn't possibly put it in human terms. From Remmy's surprised expression, it seemed that she did too.

"We'll never understand what?" my father asked.

Elissa pointed a finger at herself. "Our existence is so far removed from yours there isn't even a concept for it in your language."

William shrugged. "It doesn't matter if you understand. What you need to know is that a rift, of sorts, opened between our two universes many generations ago. We came through that rift, but it closed before we could get back, trapping us here."

"What kind of rift?"

Elissa looked at the others before shaking her head. "It is difficult to explain, but in essence, think of it as a tear in space-time."

"Except," William added. "It's not about space or time, but…"

The grating sound tore at our ears as Elissa shook her head. "As we said, it is a concept that you cannot even begin to imagine, let alone articulate."

William nodded. "We have been *stuck* on your world for a very long time, but we have sensed that the rift is opening again and we might be able to get back."

"But why didn't I know about you before now?" I asked.

"I'm not sure," William answered. "We know that in previous lifetimes, our ethereal essence was submissive to the human spirit, as it currently is with you two. For some reason, it is different for us this time, and once that happened, we began to find others like ourselves."

"You say you have a way to get back," Dad stated. "How?"

"It won't be easy, but first we need to…" He paused and tapped his fingers together. "We need to shed our corporeal forms in order to return to our own existence."

"Oh my God!"

Jasmina's cry made us all turn to look at her as William shook his head and said, "There really is no…"

He stopped when Elissa put a hand on his arm. "She's starting to understand."

"What?" my father asked anxiously.

Jasmina turned to Elissa. "You can't be serious."

Elissa shrugged her thin shoulders and looked at William who jerked a nod.

Facing Jasmina again, she said, "William is right. There is no other way."

My gut cramped so sharply I felt myself being pulled forward. Though I already knew the answer, I had to ask.

"What do you mean?"

"Our souls must be freed at the same time so that we can use our combined energy to pass through what is left of the rift."

Dad barked a humorless laugh. "I don't like the sound of that."

Looking flustered, Elissa first turned to William who shrugged and shook his head. She finally gave the wide-eyed Jasmina a questioning look. As Remmy wrapped her arms around my neck, her aunt gulped in a deep breath, faced us, and opened her mouth to speak, but when nothing came out, she shook her head.

Turning to Elissa again, she said, "Surely there is another way."

After William and Elissa shook their heads in unison, she turned to look at Remmy and me.

"We all have to die."

Remmy whimpered and tightened her grip. Stunned, I blinked rapidly for a moment, but rather than being terrorized by her statement, I felt a confusing sense of loss, frustration, and even more surprising, relief.

"Yeah," I said distractedly as a dark memory seemed to come out of nowhere. "I've been there before."

Chapter 65

Feeling completely lost, Elizabeth stumbled down the long passage. Her hands were bound tightly in front of her and attached to a wide belt at her waist. Additional ropes bound her elbows tight to her side, keeping her from using them to strike out.

While a priest droned on behind her, her toe snagged something in the floor that sent her pitching forward. Two female wardresses in black suits caught her by the arms and guided her through the narrow door to the small platform referred to by the other prisoners as the "Cold Meat Shed".

She felt herself resisting at the sight of the small, sparse execution shed, walled in on three sides and open to a courtyard on the fourth. Keeping her head down, she looked out at a small cluster of people about fifteen feet below. They seemed excited at the sight of her, and before she could look away, a series of bright flashes left black spots in her vision. When she looked up, the only thing illuminated by the dim overcast glow on this drizzly morning was a single loop of rope hanging from a freshly whitewashed beam.

The sight took her breath away, and she hardly felt the matrons trying to push her forward, or heard them urging her on because all of her energy went into resisting. She was starting to make progress when a soft, but insistent male voice announced,

"I'll take her."

Strong fingers gripped her right arm, making her head jerk around to see a man's dark eyes as his free hand pressed into the small of her back.

"Come along now, Miss. It won't do no good to cause trouble."

She tried to retreat one final time before being forcibly ushered to the middle of the room. At this point, she nearly lost her balance because the floor moved slightly under her weight, and shifted again when she came to a stop.

Her chest tightening, she struggled to remember what brought her to this desolate place. She visualized William holding the long, double-barreled shotgun, and then two nearly simultaneous explosions. She was certain the stupid boy never dreamed of killing anyone, but his clumsiness cost them all dearly.

Unfortunately, the constable left him alone in the library, its walls festooned with the heads of Phillip's many hunting conquests before he went off to war. Though the alcohol and two other shotguns had been removed, the officer failed to see a loaded pistol under a stuffed lion's head. Poor William had used it to take his own life, and saved the crown the cost of a trial.

Of course, had the simple boy only killed one person, or had they been commoners, it might have ended there, but the outcry was too great. Not only had a policeman died, but Colonel Struthers was the second son of a duke. The public and the police wanted someone punished and she was the only one remaining.

As people moved around her in the Cold Meat Shed, her mind flashed to her very public trial, the gallery filled mostly with common people, thrilled with the aspect of someone from the upper class being in the dock, and very vocal about their desire for a conviction.

Her clueless solicitor had foolishly encouraged her to wear her finest dress in the hopes the jury would see her as a helpless woman, a victim of her abusive husband, but otherwise unable to harm a soul. Instead of helping her case, the ploy played right into the prosecution's argument.

Detective Inspector Langdons' notes were produced showing that he suspected her of seducing both Colonel Struthers and her butler and conspiring with them to murder her husband. The prosecutor convincingly argued that such a beautiful woman could also have used her womanly whiles to convince the poor, stupid William to murder the detective inspector and her remaining co-conspirator in cold blood. The way he put it, there was "no immoral pit she would not descend into to be free of her abusive husband."

By the time her solicitor stood to present her defense, the jury had already reached their verdict.

The large, modestly dressed warden stepped in front of her, drawing her attention from the rope to his stern face, but instead of hearing what he was saying, she recalled the words of the judge,

"Elizabeth Montgomery, you stand convicted of the horrid and unnatural crime of murdering Phillip Montgomery, your husband. This Court doth adjudge that you be taken back to the place from whence you came, and there to be fed on bread and water till Wednesday next, when you are to be taken to the common place of execution, and there hanged by the neck until you are dead; and may God Almighty have mercy on your soul."

She suddenly realized the warden was still speaking, but only his last words filtered into her consciousness. "…one last chance to confess your crime. Would you like to do so?"

Struck by the absurdity of his statement, she stared at him for a long moment before jerking a no. His expression did not change as he nodded and quickly stepped aside. She tried to watch him walk away, but was stopped when a white bag was pulled over her head. The covering muffled the sounds around her, and when the priest started chanting again, his words were hollow, distant, and barely audible against her heavy breathing and the thumping of her heart.

She wanted to cry out, "I am innocent!", but held her tongue. She had said it so many times even she began to wonder if it were true.

You should not have let him die so soon. We will have to try again in a different time.

The thought made no sense, and she shook her head to clear it.

I did not kill him.

It does not matter. He was killed and we must start again.

How can I…

Her thought was interrupted when a noose was lowered over her head, but it was the pressure of the extra loop of rope pressing lightly against her spine that caused her to gasp in a breath. Though the priest was speaking louder now, she still could not make out the words, mostly because her panicked breathing roared in her ears. Struggling for something to grab onto, she turned toward the sound and strained to hear.

"…in the name of the Father, Son, and Holy Ghost, I deliver you to God. May He have mercy on your eternal soul."

Do I have a soul? Is there really a heaven?

"I give you one last chance, my child, to confess your sins before you stand in judgment in the presence of God," the priest said.

She took in a deep breath and briefly considered giving him what he wanted. After all, there were many times she had wished Phillip would die and leave her in peace.

What will that accomplish? I will still hang.

"I am very sorry, Reverend," she heard herself saying, "but I will not confess to a crime I did not commit."

Hearing the priest's footsteps as he moved away, she suddenly realized that this was the final step. The thought stripped air from her lungs, and while she wanted to cry out, she could not generate enough wind to make a sound. Her struggle to breathe was stopped by a sound much like a door latch rattling into place.

This is it, she thought as something thumped loudly.

She felt herself falling, and her thoughts flashed back to the day she tumbled off the roof. She tried to look up to see Phillip's head against the gray sky, to shout out her hatred for him, to rail against…

Chapter 66

"Die?"

Just emerging from the memory of the end of my former life, I couldn't register who spoke. I was still in a squat, my arms around Remmy, head spinning, stomach churning, and struggling with the sense of falling. A strange sensation made my head jerk up and rocked me back on my heels, pulling Remmy with me. She gripped me tighter until I regained my balance and looked up at Elissa, but my vision was blocked because my father had moved between us.

"Over my dead body," he stated adamantly.

Blindsiding me, Mom wrapped her arms around my neck, and nearly knocked both of us over.

I extracted myself from the strangle holds of both women and stood. "Why do we have to die?"

William looked at Elissa who shrugged. "You just do."

"Not good enough," Mom argued as she rose beside me.

"There's no other way. The soul cannot be extracted while he lives."

In the name of the Father, Son, and the Holy Ghost, I deliver you to God. May He have mercy on your eternal...

"I totally don't want my soul extracted," I heard myself saying as I tried to get a grip on what was happening.

"We must," Elissa protested.

"He doesn't know what you're talking about," Jasmina insisted loudly while holding one hand in the air. "I'm not sure you do either."

Elissa looked from Jasmina to her companions and back. "What do you mean?"

Closing her eyes, Jasmina stumbled back a step, and almost fell on the steep incline of her driveway. As she recovered, her attention locked on Elissa.

"I was wrong about you," she said before looking at the others, one at a time. "I was wrong about all of you."

"Wrong? What do you mean?"

I was surprised to see Jasmina's head shaking as she looked from me to Remmy.

"Your body is housing two souls, not one."

"Two?" my mother asked anxiously. "What do you mean?"

Jasmina's head shook slowly. "I've never seen anything like this before."

"Like what?" I asked nervously.

"I'm sensing something totally foreign in you. Like it's not even from this universe."

"Good or evil something?" Dad asked.

Shaking her head again, Jasmina closed her eyes and clasped her hands together. "It feels ominous, but for some reason, not threatening…at least to humanity.

Dad gave me a puzzled look. "Humanity? What is she talking about?"

Elissa held up both hands, palms out. "We are not a danger to your species."

I felt my own head shaking. "You want to kill me. That's a pretty big threat in my way of seeing things."

William strode forward so quickly I took a step back, afraid he was going to attack me.

"Listen," he said. "We'd rather not harm you, but we have no choice. We must die together or we will not make it across the void."

"The void?"

When both William and Elissa remained silent, the heavyset Tilley stepped forward, the blemishes on her face becoming more apparent as her face flushed.

"Look, stupid little human. It's really simple. Since we're the ones in control, you die." She turned toward Elissa. "Stop wasting time with these puny creatures and let's get on with it."

"And what if we don't want to cooperate?" I asked defiantly.

"Not a problem," Tilley snarled as she reached into her huge purse and pulled out a gun. "Cooperation not required."

"Now, Tilley," William said anxiously. "Let's not get ahead of…"

"Shut it. Will ya?" she protested. "How many times do I have to get saddled with that gawd-awful name? I want this to be over!"

"Yes, but if you kill him too soon, he'll be gone before we can join…"

Stepping closer to me, she pointed the weapon at my face.

"Them first, then you two, and finally me," Tilley shouted. "Five is all we need, so that ought to do it, right?"

I didn't know if they replied because my attention was on her angry, contorted face as she closed one eye and sighted down the weapon's short barrel.

Before I could even gasp, she let out a cry and vanished from sight. Stumbling back a step, I looked down to see her sprawled on the ground with Dad on top of her. I was still trying to think of what to do when Mom moved in, planted a foot on the woman's wrist and yanked the pistol from her grip.

While Tilley howled in frustration, my mother did a quick spin, and straightened to face the remaining two.

"Ok…uh…hold it…*right* there," she said haltingly, the gun shaking in her hands.

"No!" Tilley screamed and struggled in vain to throw my father off.

Mom was still watching Elissa and William when Tilley grabbed her ankle. Caught totally off guard by the action, she jerked her hands down to regain her balance and the weapon went off.

Mom screamed, Tilley howled, and Dad bellowed as shards of concrete stung exposed skin. Moving more quickly than I would have thought possible, Tilley released Mom's ankle, flipped my shocked father onto his back, and was on her feet, ready to charge. However, my mother had been a cheerleader in her distant past, and despite the spanning years, she recovered quickly.

"Not good enough, *bitch*," Mom snarled, her now-steady hands gripping the weapon. "Back off!"

Tilley froze for a moment before backpedaling to where her companions stood.

"Good job, Till," William said sarcastically as he watched her pluck a sliver of concrete from her cheek.

"Shut it, pig!"

Rolling his eyes, William shook his head. "Let's get this done. I am so tired of these putrid bodies."

"I don't care what you do," my mother growled as she jerked the pistol's aim from one person to another, "as long as it doesn't involve killing my son."

"Hold it!" Jasmina cried, her hands waving above her head. "I believe there's another way."

Mom kept her eyes on the threesome as they turned toward Jasmina.

"OK. This is how I see it. There are two spirits in each body, and all you need to do is release the one who doesn't belong here."

"But there's no way to free just one," Elissa argued. "It has to be both."

"What if it doesn't?"

Elissa looked at her companions and shrugged. "Nobody's ever found a way. That's why we've been trapped here for so long. There were originally hundreds of us, but as time passed, many have either lost their connection to humans, or just given up and vanished into the void."

Tilley took a quick step forward, her cheeks flush with anger. "We've been working all this time to get back home. I'm not interested in trying something new. Will somebody please kill these people?"

Jasmina shook her head. "You can sense the presence of your kind among our people, can't you?"

A scowling Tilley glanced at Elissa before answering, "Yeah...so?"

"Then you must have an ethereal energy different from ours. I have second sight and can help you focus that energy to extract all five of you at the same time."

"How?"

Closing her eyes, Jasmina placed her hands flat against her chest and took a deep breath. She held the pose for a moment before opening her eyes and looking at Elissa.

"You said I was half in this world and half out," Jasmina said as an uncertain Elissa jerked a nod. "Then you know I'm telling the truth."

After glancing at my pistol-packing mother, Elissa turned to her companions.

"What do you think?"

William nodded immediately, but Tilley shook her head. When she opened her mouth, a short spurt of static burst out.

Elissa nodded and turned back to Jasmina. "I suspect you didn't understand that. In your terms, she's afraid this is a trick."

Jasmina nodded toward my mother. "We hold all the cards. We don't need to trick you."

"Wait," I cried as a sudden realization hit me. "I'm sensing another presence."

When all eyes turned to me, I reached down and pulled Remmy to her feet, happy to see that though she was moving slowly, she was no longer shaking.

Jasmina smiled. "That would be Colonel Struthers."

Elissa's eyes went wide. "How would you know about him?"

"Like you, he felt drawn here," Jasmina explained as Remmy's body sagged against mine. "He knows who you are, and wants to join you."

Her eyes moving from my parents to Jasmina, Elissa asked, "Which of you has him?"

"That would be me," Jasmina announced. When everyone turned toward her, she smiled sheepishly. "So you see, I also have an incentive to make sure this works."

Chapter 67

After I guided Remmy into Jasmina's office, her aunt unfolded a blanket and helped me wrap it around her.

"Put her on the couch," she announced. "We need her in the circle for this to work."

After gently setting my girlfriend down, I turned to Jasmina. "If you had the colonel's essence in you, why didn't you tell me the first time we met?"

"Because we weren't joined at that time."

"What?"

She shook her head. "I tried to explain when you called from Nehalem, but you hung up on me." Sitting next to us, she took one of Remmy's hands in hers, but looked at me.

"When I connected to you the first time, I sensed a kindred soul: someone who could also connect with the spirits. As I said earlier, my mistake was in not recognizing that you and Remmy both had two souls in you. I didn't fully realize what was going on until after I went to a book reading downtown."

Laughing softly, she rose from the couch and started arranging other chairs into a semicircle in front of the couch.

"You can imagine my surprise when I found the Colonel in the body of a street person. The poor fellow thought he was mad because he had been hearing voices for some time, and most recently, the colonel insisted that he come to Salem, where I found him. However, when I touched his forehead, the colonel's spirit jumped to me."

"And this homeless person is still alive?"

Jasmina laughed again. "Alive, sane, and with a little help from me, and the Union Gospel Mission, on a bus that will take him home."

"So what do we do now?"

"It is my belief that these spirits need to be together so they can escape into the rift they've been talking about. If that is true, we only need to provide the catalyst to make that happen and they should be able to take it from there."

"What's the catalyst?"

Her smile was uncertain. "Me."

Her discomfort transferred immediately to me.

"I don't know. This all seems very…"

I stopped when Remmy put a hand on my arm. "She can do it."

"Yeah, but how do you know they won't try to, like, suck us into their world as well."

"I don't think so," Jasmina countered. "They want to be free of us just as much as we want them gone."

"I certainly hope so."

"How is this going to work?" Elissa demanded as she entered the room.

Jasmina waved a hand at the chairs. "Everyone sit."

"Oh gawd," Tilley complained as she plopped into a chair. "This isn't going to be another one of those silly séances, is it? We've already tried that, and it's plain shit-on-a-stick useless."

Jasmina shook her head. "This is definitely not a séance."

Elissa put a hand on her colleague's shoulder, but her eyes were on Jasmina. "Do you really think you know how to get us home?"

Shrugging, Jasmina motioned toward the chairs. "I can't guarantee it will get you there, but at least it will get you on your way without killing your hosts."

"I don't care who dies," Tilley whined. "I just want out of here."

Looking at her, Jasmina shook her head. "But your original plan won't work."

Tilley's eyes shrank to narrow slits. "How would you know?"

Jasmina nodded toward Elissa. "As you said, I'm only half here. Once I started looking at things from that perspective, I realized what happened to those who went before you."

Tilley shifted her bulk in the chair and gave Elissa a questioning look. "You said they made it home." She turned to Jasmina. "They got home just like we will."

Remmy's aunt shook her head. "Some may have, but only if they could properly focus their energy. Otherwise, they were too slow to outrun the *Tsabbat.*"

"*Tsabbat?*" my mother asked.

"It is a being that lives in the dark space between our universes. Think of it as a predator, feeding on the souls of those who venture into the void."

Tilley jumped up, knocking her chair over as she rose. "No! That's not true. It can't be!" She turned to Elissa. "Tell this fool they all made it."

Elissa shook her head. "I hope they did, but while we are in these bodies, we can't see beyond this world. Her guess is as good as mine."

"I'm not guessing," Jasmina insisted. "All my life, I've had this reoccurring nightmare of moaning souls being encircled by a black cloud. I would try to reach out to them, but their cries grew fainter and fainter as they slipped away from me into the darkness. I always woke up crying and unimaginably cold. Now I know why."

Letting out a long sigh, Elissa slumped into a chair, her eyes closed, chin on her chest. Tilley's eyes jerked from her comrade to Jasmina and back.

"Then we're doomed?"

Jasmina shook her head. "Not if you do as I tell you."

"Why should we listen to you?" Tilley cried.

William held up a hand, palm toward her. "Maybe she's on to something here. We can at least hear what she has to say." When Tilley scowled at him, he nodded at my mother and sighed. "It's not like we have a choice."

Tilley turned toward Mom to see her grip tighten on the pistol. "You're going to get us all killed!"

Mom shook her head. "That's not my concern right now. Shut up and listen."

Spittle dripping from the edge of her mouth, Tilley yanked her chair back up and plopped her wide butt onto it.

Looking at Jasmina, she grumbled, "I don't care what you do. Just get me out of this grotesque body."

Chapter 68

Elizabeth felt herself falling in a blackness darker than she could ever have imagined. An expanse of coldness tugged at her, not strong, but constant, pulling her former human shape into an indistinct blob. She tried to resist, to keep her womanly shape, the last vestige of her humanity, the only…

Her thoughts stopped when she realized there was something else intertwined in her being, another separate and distinct soul that had been with her for so long she thought of it as a part of herself. She tried to focus on the *other*, whose thoughts so overlapped hers she hardly knew which were hers and which belonged to *it*.

She was still puzzling over this new discovery when she became aware of five tiny points of light revolving around her. The sight should have surprised her, but for reasons she could not yet explain, it didn't. Some of them had been out here longer, and their orbits were wide and elliptical. Other, more recent like herself, moved faster and kept more circular orbits. Ancient memories told her that it would have been better if they all left Earth at the same time, but that hadn't happened, so she would do the best she could.

She tried calling to the lights, but had no voice. Even so, she felt they belonged to her, and she to them. Focusing her thoughts, she sensed in each a presence that responded eagerly to her touch, spilling their own emotions into her consciousness, spreading a feeling of happiness she had long forgotten even existed.

However, her mood turned sour when she sensed something else in the darkness. Unlike her points of light, or the *other*, this being felt like an infinitely cold, incredibly dark, totally unsympathetic predator. To her dismay, this new force pulled at the weakest of her companions, stretching out their orbits until she feared the outer ones would soon break away and be lost to her.

Her companions sensed it as well, making them anxious and confused.

What is happening?

It is the Tsabbat, the *other* announced, its demeanor angry, even desperate. *We must find some place to go, and it has to be now.*

Go where?

Anywhere but here.

Though the *Tsabbat* pulled one end of her comrade's ellipse further away, she noticed the other end of the orbit was passing closer to her, and when that happened, she felt its strength combining with hers.

At that instant, she knew what she must do.

The five orbits varied in speed: the outer ones slow and elliptical, the inner ones much faster, more circular. She watched each orbit until she could see they were all going to be close at the same time. As the moment approached, she mentally touched them, drawing on their strength and focusing it on one point in the blackness. When that produced nothing, she scanned the dark space until she felt a presence, but the energy was wrong. Searching further, she found yet another more attractive presence.

"Home!"

Though their combined energy was barely enough to make the jump, she started to move toward it anyway, but they moved too slowly, and before they were halfway across, the *Tsabbat* pulled at the outer companion, disturbing its orbit and throwing the group off balance. She cried out in frustration when the confusion reduced their momentum until there wasn't enough to make the jump.

She tried to gather energy for another try, but as she did, two of the others started to waver.

The Tsabbat is powerful. It will take us home, they cried.

She knew it was a lie, they all did. The *Tsabbat* would only suck away their energy and leave them to float forever in the cold void.

One more try, she pleaded. *We can make it, I promise!*

Knowing the *Tsabbat* would try to block them again, she moved toward home while searching the void for another way to go. One by one, she found and rejected points of entry because those realities had no sentient life. From past experience, she knew they needed physical bodies to protect their souls from the *Tsabbat* until they could organize another attempt.

She finally locked on one with the mental energies she was looking for. There was life beyond that portal. Her excitement quickly faded when she realized it was the place she had just come from.

Earth, she sighed.

She did not want to go back there again, but two of her bright lights were growing terribly weak, their orbits stretching more and more. If they tried to get past the *Tsabbat* now, it would intercept and destroy them. Fear nearly overwhelmed her as she watched the different orbits. When the balance was right, she quickly changed direction, putting all their remaining energy into creating a tunnel in the blackness. Tendrils of black shot out from the *Tsabbat*, and moved quickly to encircle them, but before they could, the tunnel fully opened and bright light flooded out, its intensity blowing away the tendrils of darkness.

Follow me, she thought, but it was unnecessary. While the bright light kept their enemy at bay, it also pulled them toward it. As they accelerated into the tunnel, she felt a distinct dichotomy: the *other* inside her definitely wanted to return, she did not. She had no real sense of the pace of her movement until she reached the end of the tunnel where everything became a blur.

The next instant brought total darkness. That is, until an Adidas tennis shoe hit her in the back of the head.

Chapter 69

I awoke with a start, rubbing the back of my head, and feeling shocked because I'd fallen asleep while the others were arguing over our fate. Remmy was also asleep, but she stirred when I looked up to see everyone else was standing, and Elissa was talking.

"...speak for the rest of us, but will this work?"

Jasmina shrugged. "If we work together, it might. The last time you tried, your combined energies were too weak and the *Tsabbat* blocked you. My plan is to..."

"Your plan?" Tilley cried. "Who put you in charge?"

Elissa held up a hand to silence Tilley, but I was shocked by a sudden realization my recent dream had brought forward.

The Tsabbat didn't try to kill us. It made us go back here.

"Listen," I said, but Elissa interrupted.

"She has a point. Why should we trust you?"

Though anxious to speak, my brain was filled with too many conflicting thoughts, and I couldn't get my mouth to work. I looked up to see Jasmina motioning for William and the others to sit and then she settled in next to Remmy. I tried to swallow the frog in my throat, but before I could speak again, a groan from Remmy pulled my attention to her. The sight of her pale face and shaking hands, feeling her body leaning heavily against me, brought on a sense of panic.

"We totally need to do something soon," I croaked. "Remmy needs a doctor."

She groaned again and snuggled into my side, but the sound of someone snorting made me look up to see Tilley glaring at me.

"They're the crux of all of our troubles," she snarled. "We've been circling them like planets around a dead sun. We'd have made it home last time if she hadn't pulled us off course."

"We wouldn't have made it," I protested. "The *Tsabbat* was about to..."

"You come back to them for a reason," Jasmina interrupted, her focus on Tilley. "They may be the key to your escape."

"How?"

"I'm not sure, but I feel it in my bones."

"What do I care about your feelings," Tilley snarled as she rose with her hands outstretched as though to strangle Jasmina. "I'm trying to get away from these damned bones!"

"That's far enough," my mother shouted, her pistol at the ready.

I was surprised to see how steady the weapon was, and the sight gave me a weird sense of pride.

My mom: a pistol-packin' momma. Who'd a thought?

Tilley lowered her hands. "We…don't…need them," she said slowly, emphatically. "They're the reason we can't get out."

"How do you know," Mom asked.

"Because ever since I was that stupid maid, they've been at the center of one kind of disaster or other."

"How many lives have you lived since then?"

"Two," Tilley snapped. "I was twenty-three when Mistress Elizabeth was hung, and lived on to fifty-one years of age. In the next life, I was flying from Germany in an airship. I didn't know why at the time, but I sensed her presence when she boarded."

"An airship?" Dad asked. "What year was that?"

"Nineteen-thirty-one. I was eleven, and the airship was called the Hindenburg."

"Oh Lord," Mom exclaimed. "You poor dear."

"But that means you had another life between then and now," I observed.

Tilley shook her head. "I don't want to talk about it."

I felt my head shake as well, and was surprised to find myself saying, "That's because you were the cause of that little disaster."

"I hate you!"

"But you all need me to make this work," I stated, trying to act more certain than I felt. "Right, Jasmina?"

Jasmina's eyes were wide as she nodded. "We need both of you, or we'll be stuck here forever."

"Or risk being left in the void," Elissa added.

"Correct."

"So what are we going to do?" Tilley asked anxiously.

Standing, Elissa walked behind the circled chairs, only stopping when Mom pointed the gun at her.

Not looking particularly concerned, Elissa stared at her for a moment before turning toward Jasmina.

"You seem to be our only hope."

"Remember," Jasmina said while nodding. "The soul in me is also one of you."

"Are there others we'll be leaving behind?"

To my surprise, Remmy stirred and looked up at Elissa. "There have to be."

Jasmina put a hand on her arm. "Have you sensed others of our kind during this lifetime?"

Remmy hesitated before nodding. "When I first met Gerry, I thought it was just, you know, love that made him so special. It wasn't until he started telling me about his daydreams that I, like, knew there was more to it than that. Not long after that happened I started hearing voices." She sat up and looked at the others. "Your voices, and others, speaking to me in a way that really freaked me out."

"How did you know we were among the voices?" Elissa asked.

Remmy shook her head. "I didn't until today. Before that, I thought I was, like, totally crazy. It got even worse when I started recalling the memories of my past lives."

William jerked to his feet. "You died too soon and messed up our timing. If you hadn't been so weak, we'd be home now."

Jasmina shook her head. "You should thank her for that. If you had tried earlier, you might all be dead now."

"How can you know that?"

Suddenly remembering the dream I just had, I kissed Remmy's forehead and shook my head. "I remember now. Because Remmy and Jason's energy levels were so low, we lacked the momentum to escape. The *Tsabbat* was catching up with us, and if I hadn't decided to come back here, we'd have been split up and thrown into the void."

"Says you," Tilley said bitterly.

"You know he's telling the truth," Jasmina argued. "He has as much to lose as you."

Elissa jerked her attention from me to Jasmina and back several times before nodding. "I thought that was just a nightmare."

Rising, Jasmina moved to Elissa and extended a hand. "We have to do this together. If our energy is not properly focused, we won't be able to move fast enough and will fail."

Taking the offered hand, Elissa held it for a long moment, her eyes searching Jasmina's face. For her part, Remmy's aunt kept her gaze steady, face neutral. They seemed to be communicating, but I had no idea how.

Finally nodding, Elissa released the hand. "You're in charge. What's next?"

"Everybody sit," Jasmina announced as she returned to her place on the couch. "When you're ready, take the hand of the person on each side of you."

Everyone sat but my parents who looked like they just realized they had crashed the wrong party.

Jasmina smiled at them. "We need your help too."

"What can *we* do?" Mom asked anxiously.

"Join the circle. You'll act as an anchor for those who wish to stay here."

Still looking unsure, my parents gave each other questioning looks before pulling two more chairs into the semicircle, but when they started to settle in next to each other, Jasmina motioned my father back.

"To give us better balance, you sit between Elissa and William."

Looking hesitant, Dad turned first to my mother then to me. Trying my best to smile, I nodded, but he still hesitated a moment before moving his chair to the designated spot. Mom quickly settled in between me and Tilley.

"This will be a new and possibly disturbing experience for us all, but it is vitally important that you maintain physical contact with your neighbors at all times. If you break the circle, there's no telling what will happen."

Holding Remmy's hand on one side, and my mother's on the other, I closed my eyes and waited for Jasmina to start, expecting some kind of ritual chanting, but as the circle completed, a surge of energy raced in through my right hand and out my left. I started to pull away, but Remmy gripped me tightly.

"I hope we're, like, still together after this is over," she whispered.

Before I could respond, Mom's hand jerked sharply and I opened my eyes to see Tilley reaching for the gun in her lap. Though Mom could have grabbed for the gun as well, she grabbed Tilley's arm as something ghostlike began to race around the circle defined by our connected bodies.

"Tilley! No!" Elissa cried as the woman rose with the pistol in her left hand.

Since Mom was holding Tilley's left arm, and William gripped her other hand, the ghostly flow of energy continued, producing an ever-increasing menagerie of sounds, and brightly colored streaks of light. Tillie's mouth was moving, but the noise blotted out what she was saying as she fought her neighbor's efforts to keep her from using the weapon.

I was jerked out of my fixation on Tilley when the room around us vanished, and I could see nothing but translucent images of ourselves still forming a circle created by our hand-to-hand contact. Tilley no longer held the gun, and our bodies were slowly melting into the stream of energy.

I started to panic, but quickly realized that not all of what we were was dissolving. Eight forms that looked very much like the humans we were, rose higher and higher until we were floating above the energy stream.

As I watched in stunned silence, bright colors wove in and out of the spinning stream, and the roar differentiated into buzzing, scraping, tearing sounds that seemed to alternate as though the beings were speaking to each other.

The spinning stream floated in place briefly before moving away, but when it was no longer under our feet, it seemed to hesitate.

I was beginning to wonder what would happen next when my head filled with a disembodied, "Thank you."

And the stream vanished.

Chapter 70

Tilley! No!

He watched as his mother fought with the silly girl, and was only mildly surprised when they started dematerializing, or so it appeared. He could see right through everyone in the room...and come to think of it, even the room's walls, and the house next door, and the one beyond that, and...

The strange energy coursing through his body surged, and he looked up to see himself rising out of his own body. Ethereal shapes were coming from everyone except his parents. Except they were not his parents anymore, because he was no longer Gerry, but just the essence of the spirit who once shared his body.

"It's working!" he exclaimed to anyone and no one. "We're going to make it."

Noises around him made it clear the others were also cheering and talking, but none seemed to be paying attention to the beings below them.

"We have to go," he announced.

It took him a moment to remember how to move in their ethereal state, but when they were finally moving away from the humans, Elissa's essence cried out,

"We should thank them."

The Gerry essence had the sense of his head shaking, even though he no longer had one.

"How?"

She started spinning faster than the others, her rate reaching the frequency of psychic energy.

"Do it now."

Focusing his thoughts, he aimed them at the group floating above them.

"Thank you."

While the humans flashed a look of surprise, he started moving toward the rift. The Gerry essence had planned to move slowly into the no-man's land his people referred to as the Interval, but the extra energy generated by Elissa's motion shot them through it like a cannon ball.

He exploded into a pitch-black darkness, a place so unbearably cold he was briefly disoriented. It was so dark he could not tell if he was dreaming or awake. For a tense, stretched-out instant, he was nearly overcome with a deep, aching emptiness that made him want to cry out, but before he could figure out how to utter a sound, he sensed one of the others then another, and another. A feeling of hope held back the despair as he brought each of them back into his influence and held them close.

However, the reunion was not without stress. As with him, the rapid transition from Jasmina's office to the Interval had been disorienting for his companions. In addition, they each felt the sudden loss of the soul they had been intertwined with for so many lifetimes. Even Tilley, who wanted nothing more than to escape from the Earthling's universe, seemed unsure as to what to do.

Unfortunately, the reunion with his comrades did not reduce the Gerry essence's feelings of angst. He knew they had to move quickly. The *Tsabbat* would surely sense their arrival and come for them. They needed somewhere to go, and any delay threatened failure.

Not this time!

His mind now focused, the Gerry essence nervously probed the Interval for their home. His first contact was with the earth-space they had come from, which increased his stress because he thought they were moving away from it. He continued probing the dark space for an alternative when another presence reached his consciousness, bringing a coldness that went beyond temperature. This creature was not only devoid of light, it lacked even the hint of a compassionate soul.

The Tsabbat!

Sensing the newcomer was approaching on his right, he turned left, and desperately probed for a new point of contact, rejecting each in turn because they lacked a sentient being they could connect with. Unfortunately, in the pitch-black darkness of the Interval, he had no idea of how fast they were travelling. When they started moving away from the *Tsabbat*, it hurried to cut them off. However it was propelling itself, it was faster than the Gerry essence thought it would be.

It may get us, but I'm not settling this time.

He probed again and was relieved to feel a sudden wholesomeness that was already a part of his being: a sense of belonging not felt in a very long time.

"I've got it," he exclaimed. "Focus with me."

"Are you sure?" the William essence asked.

"Yes," he cried.

They were all in much tighter orbits than the last time, making it easier to time them. However, before he could coordinate their energies, the Tilley essence separated from the others.

"What if it's a trick?"

The move disturbed their orbits. Some slowed while others anxiously sped up. The chaos sucked away their combined energies, and he felt their pace slow.

"We need to get into sync again quickly or be lost!"

"Come back to the stream," Elissa pleaded. "We have to do this together."

The William essence tried to intertwine himself with the escaping member, but Tilley pulled even further from the stream.

"No!" she howled. "It is stronger. I know it will take me home."

As the others returned to their previous orbits, Gerry continued to focus their combined energy on the last contact point, and soon, a spot of faint light appeared in the blackness. As it grew in size and brightness, the faint outline of a tunnel appeared around it.

"Tilley! Can you see it? That is home," he cried, "You must return to us, or you will be lost to the void."

Tilley's essence turned dark gray, almost blending with the space around her. Even so, they could see she was hesitant, moving briefly toward the *Tsabbat* and then back toward them. To Gerry's surprise, the *Tsabbat* did not try to overtake them, seeming willing to wait instead for Tilley to come to it.

"It feels so strong" she cried. "What is it?"

"It is the *Tsabbat,* and *it* represents Death in one of His many forms."

"I don't want to die."

"Then you must trust me, and rejoin the stream."

While Tilley continued to vacillate, the light from the tunnel began to fade.

"Tilley! We need your energy. You must return now!"

William again tried to approach her, but stopped when Jasmina moved between them.

"Tilley," she said with a calm, even voice. "Why are you afraid of returning home?"

"I'm not afraid."

"Then why won't you come with us?"

"I don't think we can make it."

"Is that really it, or are you afraid that after all this time there won't be anyone waiting for you on the other side?" When Tilley did not respond, Jasmina sent a tendril of energy in her direction. "We'll be there for you, Tilley. You must believe that."

Tilley's essence darkened briefly then brightened again. Her attention now on Jasmina, she seemed unaware of the dark tendrils moving toward her. Knowing what Jasmina was going to do, Gerry kept his tongue and did his best to keep the others quiet as well.

"Really?" Tilley asked.

A humanoid face appeared at the end of Jasmina's stream. "I would never lie to you, Tilley. That is a human frailty, but not one of ours."

"I barely remember what it was like."

"Don't worry, my dear. In no time you will forget you were ever in this desolate place."

"Promise?"

"Cross my..." Jasmina's humanoid face looked at her stretched-out ethereal form and made a sound much like a chuckle. "I can't do that anymore, so you'll just have to take my word for it."

"The portal is almost gone," Elissa announced. "And the *Tsabbat* is coming. We must go now."

The dark tendrils began to encircle Tilley's essence as Jasmina's stream gently wrapped around her, and this time the no-longer-human girl did not resist.

"Join with us," Jasmina said soothingly as she pulled her from the tendrils. "And we will soon be safely home."

Still looking undecided, Tilley followed Jasmina back into the stream, and when she blended in with the others, the tunnel grew brighter. Gerry steered them toward the light, seeing as they went that the dark tendrils were also accelerating. To his dismay, they were much faster than his small group and quickly filled the space ahead until he could find no way around them.

"Go through them," Elissa demanded.

"We don't know what will happen," Gerry protested.

"But we do know what will happen if we don't try."

As the tendrils moved together like the enormous charcoal jaws of a grotesque mouth, Gerry changed direction so they were heading straight down. The gap ahead of them stopped shrinking as the creature adjusted to their new trajectory. When they were going as fast as he thought they could, he changed direction again, shooting straight at their destination.

"Put all your energy into this," he cried as the streaks of blackness again closed in on them, its leading edge diming the light from their objective.

"We're not going to make it," Tilley wailed.

"Oh yes we will," Gerry snarled.

Though the Interval was painfully cold, contact with the tendril was a thousand-times worse, sucking away Gerry's energy and scrambling his thoughts. They started to tumble, their formation dissolving, orbits growing erratic. It was all he could do to pull them back together and keep them going forward. The orbits of his comrades were fairly tight when they entered the tendril, but he could tell they were rapidly stretching out, weakening the whole and slowing their pace.

Closing his eyes, he pushed with all his might, fighting the urge to give up, to relax his frantic mind, to sleep. The *Tsabbat's* efforts to sedate him made him angry, and that helped him resist the overwhelming despair filling his thoughts.

"Push with all your might!" he cried as he strained against the emptiness that threatened to strip the very essence of life from him.

They pushed. They slowed. They pushed harder, fighting for every inch, every bit of consciousness they possessed and wanted to keep. Gerry could hear the groaning of his companions as they struggled against the vast emptiness. As they struggled to…

They exploded out of the tendril and found themselves nearly on top of the tunnel. It was fading, but there was still a dim outline against the blackness of the Interval.

Now free of the tendril, Gerry realized it had pushed them off course and their present trajectory would send them past the entrance. He also sensed more than saw additional streaks of blackness racing to get between his small group and the opening.

"Push harder!" he cried while changing course.

Even with Elissa prodding the others into tighter, faster orbits, Gerry felt the bitter coldness seeping into his being again. Pulling the last bit of strength from his five companions, he lunged at the opening, passing under the approaching tendrils to just slip over the lip and into the tunnel.

A flash of light temporarily blinded them, but also brought a welcoming warmth. His mind reeling, Gerry looked back to see the gaseous tendrils disintegrating. The realization that they would finally be going home filled him with unspeakable joy.

Though the tunnel initially seemed short, its far end began to move away as they raced toward it. Wondering if they were even moving, Gerry looked to the side where the tunnel walls were zipping by, but in that blur of motion he also glimpsed images. It took him a moment to realize he was seeing the past: his own group and thousands of others as they long ago ventured out through the rift. Further down the tunnel, the images moved back in time, reminding him of their departure, the long preparations they had made, and eventually their reason for leaving.

As he was taking this in, a wall of light suddenly appeared in front of them, and when they passed through it, Tilley cried, "Ohhh! It's soooo beautiful."

And the tunnel winked from existence.

Chapter 71

I was still trying to understand what was happening when Jasmina announced,

"That should do it."

Opening my eyes, I found myself back on her couch, staring at Tilley with the gun still in her hand, and my mother holding her arm down, except neither Tilley nor Mom were struggling. As a matter of fact, everyone, except Jasmina appeared stunned.

"Did it work?" Elissa asked, her eyes on Jasmina.

I felt Remmy stir, and was pleased to see color in her cheeks. She lifted her head and kissed me on the lips as Jasmina was saying,

"Like a charm."

I liked the kiss, and was moving in for another when Mom asked,

"What does it all mean? I mean, if they left with your soul, what's left?"

"They didn't take our souls, Mom," I heard myself saying, though my attention was still on Remmy. "They were piggyback souls that, like, didn't belong in our universe."

"Piggyback…what?" she asked. When she said no more, I looked up to see her giving me that what-are-you-trying-to-pull kind of look. "Oh no, no, no you don't. This is some kind of trick, isn't it?"

Dad looked at her as though she'd announced we were all space aliens. "Huh?"

Mom was now glaring at Jasmina. "Are you kidding me? Piggyback souls? I get it. You're trying to start some kind of cult and this is how you con people into joining. Well, it's not going to work with me, Sister. There is no mention of piggyback souls in the Bible."

"But Mom," I protested. "I totally had those dreams."

Looking desperate, she gave her head a sharp shake. "Probably implanted with the power of suggestion or some such wizardry. Our pastor warned us that it was easy enough to do with young people."

"Miriam? What are you talking about?" Dad asked. "We were transported out of our…"

"No you don't, Buster," she demanded, her eyes narrow slits as she stabbed a finger at him. "You're not taking the side of some…some…" She glared at Jasmina. "…whatever you are." Starting for the door, she jerked around to face me. "Bring Remmy. We're leaving!"

Without another word, she stormed out.

The room was quiet for a moment before Dad rose and held out a hand to Jasmina. "Sorry, Ma'am. This has all been…well…really weird. My wife isn't good at dealing with this kind of thing."

Shaking his hand, Jasmina mumbled something I could not hear before Dad waved for me and Remmy to follow.

After helping my girlfriend to her feet, I turned to her aunt.

"I think you just saved our lives. I totally want to thank you for that."

Nodding, she waved a hand at where Mom had gone. "Your mother going to be OK?"

I nodded as well. "She's seriously religious. It may take her a while to, like, work out what happened."

"When she calms down, tell her I wish her well."

"One more thing," I said as Remmy sagged against me. "Since we were sharing bodies with those…uh…souls, did we really have past lives, or were we just, like, remembering theirs."

Jasmina shrugged. "Do you still have the memories?"

"Totally," I answered energetically. "Like they were yesterday."

She smiled. "Then they are yours, and despite what your mother thinks, that life was once yours as well."

My response was interrupted when Remmy patted my chest.

"Take me home, Elizabeth," she said. "I'm so tired, I'll sleep for a week."

I looked down to see that though she was smiling, her eyes had the glazed look of someone very much in need of rest. An involuntary chuckle erupted from me as I kissed her forehead.

"Me too."

Epilogue

I felt more than a little nervous as I rang the doorbell and waited in front of the big white door. I hadn't been invited, nor was Remmy with me, but something I couldn't explain pulled me here.

The faint sound of footsteps sent my heart racing. I felt foolish, and wondered if this was the right thing to do. The sound of the latch clicking was like a shock to my body as I fought the urge to run.

What are you doing here? flashed in my head and I froze in place and waited until the door opened and a smiling Jasmina peered out.

"Come in Gerry," was all she said before stepping back to wave me in.

I felt both relief and shock as she led me into her living room where a steaming teapot and two cups were sitting on a small table in front of her couch.

Jasmina pointed at a chair. "Please sit."

"You were expecting me?" I asked while looking around to see if Remmy was hiding somewhere.

Jasmina shrugged. "I don't know. I had a really strong feeling that you were coming. We have a lot of unfinished business to take care of."

As we both sat, I held up both hands, palms out. "No more past lives," I protested. "That one almost killed me."

Smiling, she picked up the teapot and poured hot water into my cup. "What kind of tea do you like?"

As she rose again, I let my hands flop into my lap. "Earl Gray, if you have it."

After filling her own cup, she moved to a side table, and dug through a large bowl of tea packets.

"Yes, I do have one," she finally announced before returning to her own chair. "I'm having decaf chai. I'm too hyper today for caffeine."

"What is so different about today?"

She nodded eagerly. "Your visit."

"Me?"

She dipped her bag and played with it for a moment before looking at me again.

"You've figured it out, haven't you?"

It was my turn to fiddle with a tea bag. "What I'm thinking is totally weird, so let me ask a couple of questions first."

"Fire away."

"Yeah," I said uncertainly while releasing the tea bag's string and settling back in my chair. "What happened to Beauregard?" When she lifted an eyebrow, I added, "I mean his spirit in this life. He wasn't at the…uh, séance."

"No," she said calmly. "He wasn't."

"Then he wasn't, like, one of the spirits, if that's the correct term?"

She shrugged. "Close enough, but actually, I believe he is one of them."

I felt my heart racing. "But that means he's totally trapped here. What will happen to him?"

She lifted her tea bag, squeezed the water out of it, and sat it on the cup's saucer. After taking a sip, she shook her head.

"Maybe I should have had something with caffeine."

"Why?"

Cradling the cup in her hands, she shrugged. "I had a…visitation from your old friend. It seems he's been watching over you for a very long time."

"You're kidding."

"Nope, and that's not all."

I flinched. "Other spirits are after Elizabeth?"

After taking another sip, she shook her head. "Not Elizabeth specifically. You are a rather headstrong individual, and the strength of your spirit supports that premise. Unfortunately, you have crossed paths with someone, or some*thing* who would like to take its revenge on you."

"Another spirit?" When she nodded, I could feel my eyes bulging as I swallowed hard and shook my head. "How many are we talking about?"

"According to Beauregard, there is only one, and its manifestation in our universe is called the *Tsabbat.*"

"That's the creature Elissa and you were talking about before they took off."

She nodded. "Even though they are gone, the *Tsabbat* is still here, searching for souls to steal."

"Was this spirit responsible for getting Elizabeth sent to the gallows?"

"Probably. This is all about things that happened in the past and what the *Tsabbat* wants to do with our future."

"Our future? You mean yours and mine?"

I felt my chest tighten when her head shook. "It seems he likes creating chaos, and his plan is to wreak havoc on humanity's future. You are here to stop him."

"Me? Are you serious?"

She shook her head. "Actually, it was the spirit who once occupied your body, but now that he or she is gone, the job falls to you."

"I don't want it!"

"I'm afraid it is not that simple."

"What do you mean?"

Shrugging, she put down her cup. "Beauregard says that the *Tsabbat* and the spirit that once shared your body were enemies even before his people came here. The *Tsabbat* likes chaos, and has been trying to alter our future by interfering in ways that help evil reign."

"Sounds like some kind of comic book villain."

"Except this one is real."

"But what did my connecting with Elizabeth have to do with it?"

"She wasn't the intended victim of the *Tsabbat's* attack. It was her son."

"She didn't have any children."

Jasmina nodded. "If Phillip had not been injured in the Boer War, they would have had a son, named Phillip Robert Augustus Montgomery, who enlisted in the Foreign Service in 1913. As an undercover agent, he was able to stop the assassination of Archduke Franz Ferdinand of Austria."

"Who?"

Jasmina laughed. "This duke's assassination started the First World War."

"But you said Elizabeth's son stopped it."

"That *would* have happened if his father, Phillip Montgomery had not been seriously injured in a previous war. As a result, he was never born."

"Wait! I'm, like, totally confused now. How could this *Tsabbat* know about…oh shit!"

Auburn curls bobbed as she jerked a nod. "He can travel through time."

"And I can too?"

"Not travel, at least in the physical sense. It's more like you connect with someone living in the past, and through him or her you can disrupt his plans."

"I didn't help Elizabeth very much."

"No, but you weren't prepared for that experience. Hopefully, next time you'll get there earlier and be ready to take him on."

The sound of the refrigerator humming to life in the next room made me jerk around to look for something that wasn't there. I didn't like the idea that there really was a boogey man.

"How do we find this *Tsabbat*?"

Jasmina sighed. "That won't be a problem. Beauregard believes that when he travels back in time to disrupt history, you'll be drawn there as well. The question is, what will you do when that happens?"

"What can I do? I so don't know how to fight evil spirits."

"Your body is young, but your soul is thousands, if not millions of years old. We need to tap into the experiences of your past lives and make them work for you."

"How can I do that?"

Jasmina nodded slowly. "That's where I can help, but this is going to be different than anything I've ever done before. We'll just have to figure it out as we go."

"What about Remmy and Beauregard?"

"They'll be joining us soon, but the journey starts with you."

"Me?"

"That's right."

I lifted the cup and took a sip, feeling the liquid's warmth flowing down to my churning stomach.

"Where do we start?"

Holding out her hands, palms up, she smiled. "Put your hands in mine."

The forces controlling my life seemed so huge, I felt like a trapped hummingbird as I put down my cup and took her hands. Her skin was cool as we touched, but I quickly felt a strange energy flowing into my body.

"Take a deep breath and relax."

Filling my lungs with air, I slowly let it out, but didn't feel one bit relaxed. To make it worse, I had only one thought as Jasmina began speaking.

I'll probably never, ever relax again.

THE AUTHOR

Growing up on the Oregon coast, Cliff has enjoyed telling the stories rattling around in his head. His books are an opportunity to share his out-of-this-world adventures with a wider audience.

A fifth-generation Oregonian, Cliff has been a farmer, logger, and business owner. He now lives in the Jefferson, Oregon, working as a computer support consultant for small businesses up and down Oregon's beautiful Willamette Valley.

For more information about Cliff's books, and more, please visit:

www.scovellbooks.com

Photo by Andre Lindauer